The Life She Imagines

A GRANITE SPRINGS NOVEL

Maggie Christensen

To my wonderful husband and soulmate who
proved to me that it's never too late to fall in love.

Also by Maggie Christensen

Oregon Coast Series
The Sand Dollar
The Dreamcatcher
Madeline House

Sunshine Coast books
A Brahminy Sunrise
Champagne for Breakfast

Sydney Collection
Band of Gold
Broken Threads
Isobel's Promise
A Model Wife

Scottish Collection
The Good Sister
Isobel's Promise
A Single Woman

Granite Springs
The Life She Deserves
The Life She Chooses
The Life She Wants
The Life She Finds

Check out the last page of this book to see how to join my
mailing list and get a free download of one of my books.

Prologue

'I do.' The girl dressed in a bright pink floral-patterned sarong, a garland of pink and white frangipani crowning her long dark curls, turned towards the man beside her and beamed.

'You are now man and wife,' the celebrant intoned.

'We did it, babe!' The young tanned surfer picked her up and swung her around and around till she was dizzy, then carefully set her down again, her feet sinking into the soft white sand.

Getting married had been an impulse. Frank and Marie were on holiday on the Indonesian island of Bali. It was their first overseas trip. They'd been enjoying the sea and surf, and the respite from home and parents, when they'd seen the celebrant's sign.

'Why wait?' Frank asked. 'We don't need all the fuss of a church do back home. It would save your folks a bunch and...'

He hadn't needed to say any more. Marie knew what he meant. His dad was in poor health. The family business in Granite Springs would fall to Frank to continue the tradition, and Marie would be there beside him. This might be their last chance to be carefree.

The rest of the day and the days following passed in a blur for the young lovers. They had no doubt their love would last forever. They'd return to their small country town, settle down, have two – or maybe three – children, and The Bean Sprout Café in Granite Springs would be their life.

One

Thirty years later

'Off you go,' he said. 'I can close up. When do Dee and Lucy get here?'

'Thanks, Frank. I'm expecting them around seven.'

He was a good man. It was a pity things turned out the way they had. Their years together had been happy but somewhere along the line, they'd grown apart, the passion they'd felt had disappeared and they'd become more like brother and sister. Now Marie rattled around in the house they'd lived in together, the one they'd planned to be their family home – a home for the children who'd never eventuated. Frank seemed happy enough in the tiny flat above the café, and they were still good mates, the best of friends, just not husband and wife – though it turned out they'd never been that.

Marie thought back to the day over two years ago. She and Frank had visited their lawyer with the intention of setting in place divorce proceedings, only to discover they'd never been legally married in the first place.

'Can you believe it?' Marie asked Frank as they walked out of Col Ford's office. After living as a married couple for close to thirty years, now, when they wanted a divorce, to discover they'd never been legally married at all!

She supposed they should have known the ceremony wouldn't be official back home in Australia, but they'd been young, in love, in Bali, and a beach wedding had seemed like a wonderful idea. Until now, they'd never questioned it.

'*Would it have made any difference?*' Frank asked, running a hand through his hair. '*But to think we've been living in sin all those years.*'

'*Your parents would have had fits,*' Marie giggled. '*Mine, too.*'

They were serious for a moment, both glad their parents weren't alive to find out.

Now, they still saw each other every day in the café that had been in Frank's family for generations. The Bean Sprout hadn't changed much over the years. There were still a lot of the features Frank had grown up with, features Marie remembered from afternoons when she and her friends bunked off school. Back then it was the go-to spot for generations of Granite Springs youngsters, one of the few places that served genuine Italian coffee.

Not anymore. These days, the clientele were mostly business people, and young mothers looking for a respite from school drop-off or shopping expeditions. There had been a few tough years, years which had led to Marie offering cooking lessons and running children's parties in the back room. But they'd made it through and developed a loyal following by providing good service, good coffee and Marie's cakes, freshly baked each morning.

She sighed. The extra work was beginning to feel too much. She was seriously considering stepping back a bit, maybe even taking time away from Granite Springs. But she hadn't floated the idea with Frank yet, unsure how he'd react. Maybe she'd discuss it with Dee this weekend – get her opinion.

Marie brightened at the thought of her sister and her niece's arrival. They were going to spend two whole weeks with her, and she had lots planned. Frank had been good about her taking some days off, even though it was school holidays, and she'd agreed to be on call if the café became really busy.

'Are you sure about tomorrow?' Frank asked as she was leaving.

'Of course. You know Dee enjoys your company and Lucy loves her Uncle Frank. She'd miss it if you weren't there for our usual Good Friday barbecue.'

At fifteen, Lucy had always had a soft spot for Frank, and Marie and his separation had done nothing to destroy their closeness.

'You're sure you don't mind my taking Saturday off?' she asked.

'Go for your life! I don't expect we'll do much trade. Most of town will be at the races. You deserve the day off. You should take a few more days while the girls are here. I can manage.'

'Thanks.' Marie gave him a peck on the cheek. She was sorry they hadn't been able to make a go of it, but it was what it was, and they rubbed along pretty well these days. Marie had always been able to put a positive slant on things – that was one of her main qualities.

If only she didn't sometimes find herself wishing for something more, wishing for the sort of family life she imagined back on that beach in Bali.

*

Once home, Marie turned on a favourite playlist on her iPod and set about readying the house for her guests. First, she made up the beds in the two spare rooms, enjoying the feel of the new sheets she'd bought, glad she'd remembered to add a few drops of lavender oil to the rinse cycle. It reminded her of her mum, and she knew Dee would appreciate the familiar fragrance.

Then she headed to the kitchen. She planned to make a cheesecake for the next day. And there was a casserole in the fridge ready to be popped into the oven.

There was the sound of a car drawing up outside just as Marie emerged from the shower. She hastily pulled on a pair of cut-off jeans and a tee-shirt before running lightly downstairs and throwing open the door.

'Aunt Marie!' A tall, leggy blonde whirlwind rushed into her arms to give her a warm hug. 'We haven't seen you for ages! Mum said...'

'She's right. It's been too long,' the shorter, dark-haired woman said, following her daughter up the driveway. 'You need to take time away from that café and come visit us more often.'

'I know, I know.' Marie hugged her sister. 'I will. I promise. But look at you both. You're here for two whole weeks, and I do intend to spend some of the days with you, starting with a barbecue here tomorrow, then the picnic races on Saturday.'

'It's good to be back,' Dee said. 'I still think of Granite Springs as home and I swear, every time I drive up Main Street, I see something different. But The Bean Sprout always looks the same. You and Frank are still okay?'

'You know us. He'll be at the barbecue tomorrow.'

'Oh, good. I love Uncle Frank,' Lucy said. 'Can I put this stuff in my room?' she gestured to the rucksack which she'd dropped on the step to free her arms for Marie's hug.

'Upstairs, first on the right. And you're in the one next to it, Dee. Just like last time.'

'Don't you get lonely in this big house all on your own?' Dee asked, as Marie helped her upstairs with her case.

'Lonely?' Marie thought for a moment. 'No, I don't have time to feel lonely. And it's my home. I'm glad Frank agreed to my staying here when we…' Marie bit her lip. She'd been too ashamed to admit, even to her sister, that she and Frank hadn't been married, so hadn't needed to divorce. She'd explained away her decision to go back to her maiden name when they *divorced* as needing to establish her own identity again. But it wasn't that. Knowing she'd never had the right to call herself Beattie had given her a strange feeling, and it wasn't as if she'd changed it legally in the first place. There had been no need to. It hadn't worried Frank. But he was so easy-going. It hadn't bothered him when she went back to her maiden name either. Sometimes she wished he'd taken a stronger stance about things. But his attitude to life was one of the things that had attracted her to him in the first place, that and his dark good looks.

'Dinner's almost ready,' she said instead. 'Come back down when you're ready and we can celebrate with a glass of wine – juice for you, Luce,' she said, as she saw her niece's eyes light up, then dim again at her words. 'You'll be grown up soon enough.'

By the time Dee and Lucy reappeared, Marie had two glasses of chilled wine sitting on the kitchen benchtop along with a glass of fruit juice for Lucy, a basket of corn chips and a bowl of salsa.

'Cheers,' she said, raising her glass. 'I'm so glad to see you two. We're going to have a great time together. Now, Dee, why don't you fill me in with what's been happening in Canberra? I know we talk and skype regularly, but it's not the same.'

'Mum has…' Lucy gave her mother a sidelong glance.

Marie followed the direction of her eyes to see her sister blush. 'You've met someone!'

Dee twisted the stem of her glass. 'It's early days but, yes. I took your advice and registered on that dating site. Tony was the first guy I responded to. We've only met a few times, but…'

'He sounds fit,' Lucy interrupted. 'You should try it yourself, Aunt Marie. Maybe you could find someone, too, unless you and Uncle Frank are going to get back together?'

'No to both of those suggestions, Luce,' Marie chuckled. 'We don't all need a man in our life. But I'm really pleased for you, Dee.'

'It's been a while,' Dee said, 'but you were right, it's time. And now Lucy's getting older…'

Marie smiled at her sister's unease. When Lucy's father left Dee with a one-year-old to care for, telling her he couldn't cope with being a parent, she'd sworn off men. But Marie knew her younger sister missed the companionship a partner could bring, and for some time had been urging her to try the dating scene.

'So, tell me about him.' Marie took a sip of wine while she waited for Dee to speak.

'He's a few years older than me, widowed, no children, works in a firm of accountants in the city. Sounds boring, I know, but he's intelligent, polite…'

'I didn't ask for his resumé,' Marie chuckled. 'Anyway, if you like him that's all that matters. She saw the way Dee's eyes lit up talking about him, and her stomach turned over, hoping Dee wasn't going to be hurt again. 'Maybe I need to come over to Canberra to check him out?'

'It's far too soon for that, but all going well, maybe…' Dee said with a smile. 'Lucy still has to meet him.'

Lucy grasped her mother's hand. 'And that's going to happen as soon as we get back, isn't it, Mum?'

Dee nodded.

'Right. Dinner. I've set the table in the dining room to celebrate your arrival. But don't expect to eat there every night. I tend to make do here in the kitchen most days.'

'I love your kitchen – and this house, Aunt Marie. It's so much bigger than our Canberra place.'

'But you wouldn't swap it,' her mother said.

'No…oo, not really. Canberra's home, while this…' she threw her arms wide, '…this is special.'

'Are you sure about you and Frank?' Dee asked, when Lucy had gone to bed, unable to keep her eyes open.

The pair were enjoying a last glass of wine in Marie's family room. It was her favourite room in the house and the one in which she spent most of her time. After Frank left, she'd refurbished it to suit her needs with a plush beige velvet sofa and matching armchairs, a low coffee table and a wide-screen television flanked by a pair of bookcases. The room once designated for the children who were never born had become her personal retreat.

'Quite sure. He hasn't changed. He's still a lovely guy, but... something changed between us. I can't explain it, so I don't even try. And, as I told Lucy, I'm not like you, Dee. I don't need a man in my life. I'm content the way I am. Though...' she paused, wondering how much to confide to her sister, '...I have been thinking maybe it's time I made some changes.'

Dee raised one eyebrow.

'Oh, it's probably nothing. Just sometimes, I wonder if I'm going to spend the rest of my life here in Granite Springs, baking cakes, teaching cookery, running children's parties.'

'I thought you were happy working with Frank.'

'I am.' Marie rubbed a finger around the rim of her glass. 'Ignore me. It's probably the wine talking,' she said, dismissively, although aware this was only her third drink. 'Ready for bed?' She drained her glass, rose and held out her hand for Dee's.

'Easter tomorrow,' she reminded Dee as they headed upstairs. 'I bought Lucy an Easter egg, but I guess she's outgrown the egg hunt she used to love. And I've invited a few friends along to the barbecue besides Frank. I don't think you've met Fran and her new fellow. Owen is a fairly new addition to the town. He arrived late last year to head up a new school of Music and Drama at the uni and he and Fran got together. They live on an acreage out of town. His daughter will be here too. Pia's pregnant and due to give birth any day. Her fellow left her, and she made the decision to be a single mother. She's staying with Fran and Owen till the baby's born at least.'

'I'm looking forward to it. And to meeting your friends.' Dee stifled a yawn. 'Don't expect to see Lucy early in the morning, but I'll be available to help you get things ready.'

'Thanks, sis.'

Marie continued on to bed, but, as her eyes closed, she had the strange feeling her life was about to change.

Two

'Excited?'

'I guess. Mum hasn't said much about it. Anywhere's better than here.' Jess scuffed the toes of her shoes on the kitchen floor and pushed a strand of her thick chestnut hair out of her eyes.

Drew Hamilton had to stop himself from reprimanding her. Things hadn't been easy since Irene left, and his own move to take up the position of principal at Granite Springs High School at the beginning of the year hadn't been popular with his teenage daughter.

But he'd had to get away. Even Melbourne hadn't been big enough for him to avoid the scandal of his wife of over twenty years running off with one of the city's star football players. What he hadn't anticipated was Irene's subsequent move to the US when Jake was signed by one of the big gridiron teams over there, and Jake's refusal to be saddled with a teenage stepdaughter. It happened back in July and he immediately started looking for another position. When this one came up in the small town in New South Wales, he'd jumped at the chance.

'It'll be different from Australia, and good to see your mum again,' he said.

'I'd rather be going back to Melbourne. All my friends are there.' Jess's face took on the sullen expression that had become habitual in the last few months.

What had they done to their daughter? What had Irene done to her?

'Can't I go to Melbourne instead, Dad? I could stay with Ella. Her mum…'

'Your mum wants you to go to LA. There are lots of girls who'd give their eye teeth to spend Easter there.'

'They're welcome to it. I don't think Mum really wants me there anyway. She'll be so caught up with Jake and he...'

'That's enough!' Drew ran a hand through his thatch of white hair. If his formerly black hair hadn't already turned white, the events of the past few months would have done it. 'Sorry, Jess. Your mum wants to see you. That was part of the deal. Remember?'

Jess nodded, her eyes on the floor. 'But that's when we were in Melbourne. I didn't bargain for moving here.'

'I know. But remember the reporters, the photographers?'

She nodded again, her lips turned down in the now familiar pout.

Drew remembered. How could he forget the media storm that resulted from one of Melbourne's top Aussie Rules players defecting to the US to play gridiron? And, because he'd been married to Irene, he and Jess became part of the fallout. Unable to get access to Irene and Jake who'd already left the country, it seemed Drew and his daughter were the butt of every hack newspaper in town.

It had been a relief to arrive in Granite Springs where no one knew them. But Jess hadn't seen it that way. Drew knew she missed her friends. He had hoped his outgoing daughter would quickly make new ones. He'd been wrong.

'It's only for two weeks,' he tried again. 'It might be fun.'

'Fun?' Jess snorted. 'And then I'll have to come back here.'

'This is where we live now.' Drew was at a loss as to how to handle her. They'd come here for a new start. Granite Springs had proven to be a larger country town than he'd expected, almost a regional centre. It had a university, an art gallery, a good library, various industries and a fair selection of restaurants and cafes. The town boasted a vibrant community and was surrounded by both small and wide acres of farmland.

'That's the problem.' Jess turned on her heel and ran upstairs.

Drew heard her bedroom door slam, then the sound of music blared through the house. He sighed.

*

Next morning, the previous day's ill humour had disappeared. Jess arrived at breakfast with a smile on her face. 'I'm sorry, Dad,' she said, giving him a hug. 'I know I was a bitch last night. It's all Mum's fault, not yours. I packed last night. I'm ready to see her and make the best of it. But…' her lips turned down again, '…there's no one in this town I can relate to. They all come from happy two-parent families. They have no idea what we went through. And my dad being the school principal doesn't make it any better.'

'Sorry, sweetie. Can't be helped.'

Back in Melbourne, Jess had been enrolled in a private girls' school in a neighbouring suburb. Irene had driven her there each day. As a single dad in a new town, Drew made the decision to enrol Jess in the school in which he was principal. He'd anticipated a few issues, but predicted they'd soon disappear. As it was, he wasn't sure how many of the so-called issues were real and how many were in Jess's imagination. From his perspective, the kids in Granite Springs appeared to be a lot more communicative and friendly than those he'd worked with in the city. And he'd found the staff were dedicated to their students. He guessed it would just take time, and maybe the two weeks away would help Jess adjust better when she returned.

'Let's get some breakfast in you before we head out to the airport. I made your favourite pancakes and there are strawberries and maple syrup.'

'Thanks, Dad.' Jess slid into a chair. Leaning her elbows on the table, she took out the iPhone that was never far from her grasp and began to scroll through the messages and posts which had appeared overnight, before texting furiously. Drew knew she was catching up with the friends she'd left behind in Melbourne.

*

Drew watched as the plane rose into the sky carrying Jess off for two weeks with Irene, then turned reluctantly towards the car park. He had no idea what to do. He sat behind the wheel, contemplating his life, then roused himself. He still had one more day of school before the Easter holidays began. With a sigh, he headed out of the car park and in the direction of Granite Springs High.

He didn't expect there would be much work done today. Both staff and students were eagerly anticipating the break. Conscious of the ongoing need to keep his staff happy, Drew had organised a special lunch to be extended through the first hour of afternoon classes. A batch of student teachers from the university had been pressed into service to undertake playground duty and keep the students occupied with a series of games and other sporting activities. The day would finish with a special assembly, then they'd all be off to their respective homes and families. All except him.

When Drew and Jess made the move to Granite Springs, it had been without much thought as to what they'd find there. He'd been pleasantly surprised with the town but, like Jess, had failed to make any friends here. Correction – he hadn't taken time to make friends. So far, apart from shop assistants, the bank manager, the realtor who sold him the house, and his staff, the only person he'd spoken to was his neighbour – a man about his own age who worked at the local university and whose name he couldn't recall. How pathetic was that?

It was time to do something different. He had two weeks without Jess, two weeks in which to find out more about the town and the people in it, two weeks to make friends? It was an odd thought. Friends were people with whom you had something in common. Like Jess, his friends were all in Melbourne. But, unlike her, his friends had been one half of a couple; a couple who were friends of both him and Irene; a couple who had drifted away when Irene took up with Jake and left town.

By this time, Drew was driving through the school gates. It was time to stop musing and start the day.

The morning passed swiftly, his secretary taking care of most of the mundane items leaving him free for a couple of parent interviews – one set who were worried about their son's prospects in the Higher School Certificate later in the year and wondering if private tutoring would be of benefit; the other concerned about possible bullying of their thirteen year-old. By the time he managed to satisfy both, it was lunchtime.

'Ready for the fray?' His secretary, Mel, popped her head through his open office door. 'The troops are gathering in the staffroom. It was a good idea of yours to put this on.'

Drew waved away the compliment. It hadn't taken much organising, and it was Mel who'd made the catering arrangements. All he'd done was set it in motion. Closing his computer, he followed her to the staffroom from which came a babble of voices.

The lunch was a great success, leading to many requests that it become a standard feature of every end of term. Drew was happy to agree. It was a small thing to keep everyone happy. He enjoyed chatting to the various groups on a more informal basis than usual and was surprised how often he was asked if he'd be attending the picnic races on Easter Saturday. He'd never been much for horseracing, an annual bet on the Melbourne Cup or a ticket in a sweep being his only foray into gambling. But, here, it seemed, the picnics were regarded as more of a social event – a family day out. Maybe it was something he should consider.

It was a pity Jess wouldn't be here. She might have enjoyed the novelty, though she'd never gone through the horsey stage most girls enjoy. After a disastrous birthday trip to the Mornington Peninsula, she vowed she never wanted to get up on another horse. It was unfortunate the horse had bolted, startled by a loud sound. Jess hadn't been thrown, had managed to control the animal, but the incident had shaken her confidence.

The shorter afternoon proved a blessing, and Drew felt relieved when the final chorus of chatter finally died away and he was left alone in the deserted building. He finished off a couple of reports, then picked up a flyer someone had left on his desk. It was promoting an event to be held in one of the local churches on Easter Sunday. About to crush it and toss it into the wastepaper basket, something on it grabbed Drew's attention. He read the words. The Granite Springs Choristers were to present selected sections from the Saint Mathew Passion between two and five thirty. All were welcome and entrance would be by gold coin donation, all proceeds going to the Rural Fire Service.

Drew had heard of the choral group but, not a singer himself, hadn't given it much thought. However, he was partial to Bach. Maybe it would help pass what promised to be a lonely weekend. He folded the sheet and tucked it into his shirt pocket. It seemed Granite Springs was a hive of activity on Easter weekend. But there was still Friday to get through, a day when everything in town would be closed.

Picking up his briefcase, Drew decided to make a detour on the way home to visit the local garden centre. He'd pick up some bags of mulch and a few plants and spend the next day in the garden, something he'd been promising himself he'd do but, so far, hadn't made time for.

Back home, Drew stacked the mulch and plants in the garage, poured himself a glass of wine and, picking up the latest Garry Disher novel he'd been waiting to find time to read, settled down in his favourite armchair. But he couldn't relax and concentrate to read. The house felt wrong. It was too quiet. He'd grown used to the blare of music from Jess's room and, although he was forever telling her to turn it down, to use her headphones, he missed it. He missed her.

Three

A pair of noisy kookaburras outside her bedroom window wakened Marie on Friday morning. She stretched her arms out contemplating the day ahead. She loved this time of year in Granite Springs, the summer had gone, and the air was clear with a slight chill. Some days it was enough to encourage her to turn on the heat, others fine enough to eat outdoors. Given the temperature in the preceding week, she'd decided today it would be outdoors, even though the air might be a trifle cool.

'Morning, Marie,' Dee greeted her as she entered the kitchen to the aroma of toast and coffee. 'I woke early so thought I'd make a start. You can tell me what needs to be done while we have breakfast.'

'Oh, you're a gem,' Marie yawned. 'How do you manage to be so bright at this time in the morning? It's only…' She checked the kitchen clock. 'Gosh, it's seven already.'

'I have to get up early back home and I didn't sleep well. It's so peaceful here after the traffic noise I'm used to. Then this morning there was the dawn chorus.' She laughed.

'I'm so glad you're here.' Marie eschewed the coffee, made a mug of lemon and ginger tea and popped another two slices of bread in the toaster, before going to the fridge for the jar of her favourite lemon, lime and ginger marmalade.

'I didn't ask last night,' Dee said, as Marie was spreading marmalade on her toast. 'You may be fine without a man in your life, but what about Frank?'

'A man in his life?' Marie raised one eyebrow with a grin.

'Don't be stupid. A woman. Does Frank have anyone?'

'No.' Marie held her mug in both hands. 'Sometimes I wish he would… meet someone. He's still a good-looking man. He has a lot to offer. And it might…'

'Make you feel less guilty?'

'I don't!'

'Okay. I never knew what went wrong between you. You always say you just grew apart, but there must have been something.'

'Not really. We fell madly in love and expected it to last forever, as you do. But somewhere along the line, the passion went out of our relationship. Not just for me, for both of us. It was like living with my brother, and Frank said he felt the same way. It took us a while to actually talk about it, but once we did, we knew it was best to separate. It would give us both the chance to find someone else if… But we haven't so far.' She rose and went over to refresh her tea. Her relationship with Frank wasn't something she was comfortable talking about, not even with her sister.

'I just think it's weird, that's all – the way you're still such friends, work together, etcetera.'

'Not weird at all. The café still has to be run. It's a family business. What else would we do?' But that was something Marie had been wondering more often of late. The trouble was, she couldn't bear to let Frank down.

'Hmm.' Dee sounded doubtful. 'So, what do you need me to do?'

'Let me see.' Marie took a sip of tea to help her think more clearly. 'There are salads to be made – green with avocado and tomatoes, cauliflower with chickpeas and fetta, and that spinach and beetroot one you like with orange, goat's cheese and walnuts. Then I need to marinate the steak. It's all in the fridge. There are some cranberry sage sausages too, and potatoes to wrap in foil. They can go on the barbecue, too. I think that's all.' She yawned.

'Dessert?'

'There's a cheesecake in the fridge. I made it yesterday. And Frank said he'd bring any leftover goodies from the café.'

'You never stop, do you? Don't you ever want to slow down?'

Marie did. But it wasn't the right time to discuss it now. Last night hadn't been the right time, either. Maybe there was no right time. Maybe it was a futile yearning.

'Was that what you meant last night?' Dee asked. 'That it's time for a change?'

'Not now, Dee. I need to shower and dress and get this barbecue on the road. I have people arriving at eleven, and Frank might get here earlier. There's a lot to do before then.'

Dee agreed and helped clear up, but Marie had the feeling she wasn't off the hook. Once her sister got her teeth into something, she was like a terrier until she'd worried out the whole story.

The meat was marinating, and the two women had almost finished preparing the salads when a bleary-eyed Lucy appeared in the kitchen doorway.

'Wow! It's like a restaurant kitchen in here,' she said, grinning. 'Is there any breakfast?'

'Help yourself. There's cereal in the pantry and bread in the fridge. We had ours ages ago.'

'It's so quiet here. I'd forgotten,' Lucy said, filling a bowl with muesli and topping it with a generous amount of milk, before sitting down at the only corner of the table which was free. 'When did you get up, Mum?' she asked Dee.

'Early. You'd better get a move on. Your Aunt Marie's guests will be here soon. You don't want them to catch you still having breakfast.'

Lucy's expression didn't change and if anything, the movement of her spoon seemed to slow down. 'Who did you say were coming, Aunt Marie? Is there anyone young?'

'Probably not what you'd call young,' Marie said with a grin. 'I'm sorry I don't know any teenagers for you to hang out with. Frank, you know, and Fran and Owen are around my age. He's a musician. His daughter is younger, but she's in her twenties. Sorry.' It suddenly occurred to Marie that perhaps she should have made more of an effort to include people who were closer to Lucy's age but, while there were several teenagers who frequented The Bean Sprout, none were the children of close friends. Kay, who was in the choir with her, had two stepchildren but they were away for Easter.

But Lucy's interest had been aroused. 'A musician? Do you mean he plays in a band? Would I have heard of him?'

'I doubt it, though your mother might have. Dee, do you remember that Sydney group back when we were in our twenties? The one with the guy with the Scandinavian name?'

'Oh, yes! They were good. What was it called?'

'I can't remember, but Owen was on keyboard – Owen Larsen.'

'Hell, that was a long time ago – before you were born, Lucy.'

But Lucy had lost interest.

*

'This can't be Lucy. She's so grown up.' Frank's words brought a smile to Lucy's face and made Marie glad she'd invited him. Though there was no way she'd have excluded him. She never did.

It occurred to Marie for the first time that she and Frank still acted as if they were a couple. She didn't entertain often but when she did, Frank was always on the guest list. If she'd given it any thought at all, she'd have excused herself by saying his presence evened the numbers and he knew everyone who was coming. But was it that simple?

They still greeted each other with a peck on the cheek – just as she did with all her friends. Surely there was nothing strange about that? Though she'd been aware of Dee giving her an odd look when Frank arrived. She shrugged to herself. They'd been able to remain friends. Not every couple who split were lucky enough to be in that position.

She was saved from further reflections by the arrival of Fran and Owen along with a very pregnant Pia. In the ensuing flurry of greetings, all thoughts of her and Frank were thrust to the back of her mind.

'Hi, Dee,' Fran said when they were introduced. 'I can't believe we haven't met till now. It's been very naughty of Marie to keep you to herself when you've been here before. You should get her to bring you out to The Haven while you're here. You can help feed the goats.'

'Goats? Do you have goats?' Lucy asked, coming out of the house carrying a platter of sausages.

'We sure do. And they get up to all sorts of mischief, don't they, honey?' Owen asked Fran, throwing an arm around her shoulders.

Marie saw the look which passed between them. She remembered when Frank had looked at her like that. It had been a long time ago.

She felt a dull ache at the thought that perhaps no man would ever look at her like that again, then stifled it. She didn't need anyone in her life. The vague stirrings of dissatisfaction she'd been experiencing had nothing to do with the lack of a man.

She shook her head, as if doing so could banish her thoughts, and picked up a bottle of wine. 'Anyone for a refill?' she asked brightly.

The barbecue progressed without any upsets and with Marie promising to take Dee and Lucy out to see Owen and Fran – 'and the goats' Lucy added – on Easter Monday.

Frank stayed back to help clear up and clean the barbecue. Afterwards, he joined Marie and Dee in a cup of coffee before playing a game of Scrabble with Lucy. Much to her delight she won, to be rewarded by a high five from her uncle.

'You're more than a match for me now, young Lucy,' he said with a wry grin. 'But I should be heading off. Thanks, Marie. Good to see you again, Dee and Lucy. I hope you'll make it into The Bean Sprout while you're here. Enjoy the picnics tomorrow. Wish I could join you, but someone has to man the shop.'

'Are you sure you don't need me tomorrow?' Marie asked, as she farewelled him at the door. She was still feeling guilty about taking time off.

'Don't be stupid. I was joking. You'll have a great time with the pair of them. I'll see you back on board on Tuesday, then we'll see how it goes.'

'I'll make my usual batch of cakes and slices before we leave tomorrow and drop them in before we go,' she promised, giving him a warm hug. He was so familiar, so comfortable. For what must have been the hundredth time, Marie wished things could have been different as she watched his familiar figure swing down the driveway, giving a final wave before he slid into his car.

It wasn't till Lucy had gone to bed and the two women were enjoying a nightcap that Dee brought up Frank again. 'He's a lovely man, Marie. I think he still has feelings for you.' She tipped her head to one side. 'I saw the way he was looking at you when your attention was elsewhere.'

'Rubbish! We're good friends, that's all.'

But as Marie lay in bed trying to sleep, Dee's words came back to her. Was her sister right? And if she was, how did Marie feel about it?

Four

The day had gone well for Drew. He'd awakened to the promised text from Jess to say she'd arrived safely and would call sometime soon. He wasn't going to hold his breath but was glad the journey had gone well.

He spent most of the day in the garden as planned and was feeling very pleased with himself. He straightened up from where he'd been crouched over, trimming a small bush, put his hand to his back and gave a groan. He really needed to get more exercise. Maybe he should use these holidays to make an effort to get back in shape.

In Melbourne, he and Irene had regularly gone jogging together, until she met Jake. Then a gym in the city had been her preferred exercise venue and, loath to run on his own, Drew lost the habit.

'Hi there!' The voice came from across the fence. Drew had been vaguely aware of a car driving into the neighbouring driveway and the sound of a garage door opening but hadn't paid attention. Now he looked up.

'Hi!' He wished he could remember the guy's name.

'It's Drew, isn't it? Nick. Looks like you've been busy.'

Drew walked across, wiped the dirt off his hands on his jeans, and shook Nick's hand.

'Trying to catch up. I've neglected it. But it's not looking too bad.'

'On your own today?' Nick asked. 'You have a daughter, don't you?'

'Yes. Jess. She's spending Easter with her mother.'

'My two are with their mother, too. Have you met Kay?' he asked, as a dark-haired woman appeared behind him. 'Kay, this is Drew. We've been a tad remiss,' he said to Drew. 'We should have invited you round for a drink before now. I don't know where this year has gone to. Easter already.' He drew a hand through his thick greying hair and tugged on his beard.

'You moved in at the beginning of the year, didn't you' Kay asked. 'But if you're on your own for Easter, why not pop in for a drink tonight? Around seven?'

'That's kind of you. I don't know…'

'I won't take no for an answer,' she said with a warm smile. 'I know how quiet a house can be when its teenagers are gone.' She grinned. 'We may hate the noise and mess but miss them when they're not here.'

'Thanks.' Drew made a sudden decision. There was no reason to refuse, and he had been telling himself he needed to make friends, hadn't he? He could start with his next-door neighbours.

Seven o'clock saw Drew standing outside the house next door, a bottle of wine in one hand. He rang the bell.

'Welcome!' Nick shook Drew's hand and drew him inside, into a living room which bore all the hallmarks of a happy family home. The room boasted a comfortable sofa with matching armchairs, and a low coffee table facing a large television set. Two walls were filled with bookshelves and a couple of beanbags were lying in one corner. Kay was seated on one of the armchairs. She rose as the two men walked in.

Their glasses filled, the talk turned to work. 'I think you said you worked out at the university?' Drew said. 'Are you on the teaching staff?'

'For my sins I head up the School of Education.'

'Really? We've had a few of your students at the High this last three weeks. They've been a big help – a bright bunch.'

'Wait a minute,' Nick said. 'Drew…you're Drew Hamilton. Why didn't I make the connection? You're the new principal at Granite Springs High.'

'Guilty, I'm afraid.'

'Not surprising that you should both choose to live in this enclave,' Kay said.

Not surprising at all, Drew thought. Trust that realtor to match up two neighbours who had so much in common. Since moving here, he discovered this area was one of the most sought after in Granite Springs, located on the outskirts of town close to an old quarry, likely the one that had given the town its name.

Nick said what Drew was thinking. 'A lot of academics live up here. The town seems to think we all want to live together. I suppose the guy who sold you the house thought you'd fit right in,' he chuckled.

'I guess so.'

'I've seen your daughter going in and out,' Kay said. 'She'd be what? Sixteen, seventeen?'

'That's what she'd like you to think. She's only fifteen. I'm afraid she's taken the move hard. She hated to leave all her friends in Melbourne.'

'She wasn't able to stay with her mother? Sorry,' Nick said. 'Don't think I'm being inquisitive. It's just that my son, Ryan – he's a little older than your daughter – went up north with his mother when we split. It didn't work out, so he came back to live with me and his sister. There was no question of *her* leaving her friends. I know what teenage girls can be like.'

Drew exhaled heavily. Here was someone who did understand. 'Her mother's in the States,' he said, and took a mouthful of wine.

'Bummer.'

'How old's your daughter?' Drew didn't recall seeing her around. Maybe she and Jess could be friends.

'Too old for yours, I'm afraid.' Nick seemed to know what Drew was thinking. 'She started uni this year. Sam agreed to do her first year here, but I suspect she'll be off to Canberra next year. She's eager to spread her wings. Living here with us isn't what she has in mind.'

'Mmm.' Drew hadn't thought that far ahead, though if he'd thought about it at all, it was to consider it convenient to have a local university.

'Enough of that.' Kay passed around a platter of biscuits and cheese with slices of apple. 'Will you be going to the picnics tomorrow?'

'I don't think so.' *What was it about the inhabitants of Granite Springs – were they all racing mad?*

'Oh, but you must,' she said. 'It's one of the big social events in town.'

'The Easter picnics, the winter races, the ball, the show…' Nick gave a chuckle. 'It took me a while to understand that, too. But people do expect it of us. It's a way of showing we're prepared to integrate into the community.'

'And it's not all about the racing,' Kay added. 'We take a picnic lunch and eat it in the car park – hence the name.'

'Kay grew up here,' Nick explained. 'I'm a relative newcomer. My ex and I arrived over ten years ago and I've never regretted it.'

Drew saw a shadow cross his companion's face and guessed he still harboured some ill-feeling towards his ex. Well, he knew what that felt like. He warmed to Nick, realising they had a few things in common. But Nick seemed to have recovered enough to find a new partner. Drew couldn't imagine doing that.

'You could join our party,' Kay said, as if a sudden thought had struck her. 'We'll be meeting a couple of friends for lunch and I'm sure Jo and Col won't mind an extra bod. What do you say?'

Drew didn't say anything. He felt he was being coerced into attending. It was the last thing he wanted to do – eat lunch with a group of strangers in a car park followed by a country race meeting.

'You'd better say yes now, mate. She's not going to let you off. And Jo and Col are a nice couple. Kay and Jo have been friends forever, and I only met them when Kay and I got together. I should tell you we work together – she's my PA. I thought I was finished with women till she turned up in my office one day.' He gazed fondly at Kay and they clasped hands.

Drew looked away. He could see it would be rude to refuse the invitation. But what if this other couple were openly affectionate, too? Could he bear spending an entire afternoon with them? On the other hand, he liked what he'd seen of Nick and Kay. They were his sort of people, and it was time he tried to become part of the community.

By the time Drew said goodbye, he'd not only agreed to join Nick, Kay and their friends at the races, but had a ticket for the choral event promoted on the flyer he'd picked up. It appeared Kay belonged to the Granite Springs Choristers and was excited about their Easter performance. The conductor of the choir was also a friend who taught out at the university, too. It seemed to Drew everyone in Granite Springs was connected to each other in one way or another. It made him feel even more like an outsider.

Five

Marie was up early baking the loaves of banana bread, carrot cake, muffins and brownies for the café. As soon as they were in the oven, she set to preparing the salads for their picnic lunch. Dee appeared in the kitchen just as she was fastening the lid on the final Tupperware container.

'Something smells good,' she said, the aroma of baking filling the kitchen.

'Not for us, I'm afraid. Though I suppose I could remove a few of the brownies.'

'Oh, please do, Aunt Marie, I love your brownies.' Lucy walked into the kitchen yawning, her blonde hair a tangled mess on her shoulders.

'For you,' Marie said. 'But don't tell your Uncle Frank.'

'Promise.' Lucy put a finger to her lips.

'Breakfast?' Marie asked. 'There's plenty of muesli and fruit, or I could make porridge.'

Lucy shivered. 'No thanks. Can I have toast? And I might mash a banana on it.'

'Sure. Dee?'

'I'll take you up on the muesli, thanks. Would you like me to make coffee?'

'Would you? I need to look out my picnic basket. I forgot all about it yesterday and it's been in the garage since last time.'

'Not for me, Mum,' Lucy called from where she was dropping a slice of bread into the toaster. 'Can I have one of your herbal teas, Aunt Marie?'

'In the pantry.'

Marie headed into the garage where, sure enough, the picnic basket was gathering cobwebs. She brushed them off before returning to the kitchen, carrying the basket and dragging a fold-up table. 'We'll need this, and there are three canvas chairs in there too. I'll fetch them later.'

'When do we have to be at this race thing?' Lucy asked, taking a last bite of toast.

'Around eleven if we're to find a spot to park,' Marie said. 'Would be a good idea to shower and dress, then we can pack the car. I'll dash out to drop off the cakes to Frank while you two get ready.'

'I'll clear up here,' Dee offered. 'You do too much, Marie. This is supposed to be your day off.'

'It's my source of income, too, Dee. And I can't let Frank down.'

'He takes you for granted,' Dee said frowning. 'It might do him good to find out what The Bean Sprout would be like without your input.'

Marie stopped packing the containers and stared at her sister. 'You've changed your tune,' she said. 'Last night you were telling me how he looked at me. Make up your mind.' She slammed the final Tupperware container into the box.

'I'm just saying. It might help move things along.'

'What things? Dee, how often do I have to tell you. We're friends, good friends, and we work together. I may sometimes feel as if there should be more to my life than working in a café in Granite Springs, but it's been good to me. Frank's been good to me. I don't intend to let him down, not yet anyway.' *Despite my occasional flights of fancy.*

*

The showground was alive with cars and people when Marie drove her Toyota Rav4 into the paddock being used as a car park for the races.

'Wow!' Lucy said. 'So many people. I'd forgotten what it was like.'

They hadn't been here last year, Marie remembered. She'd gone over to see Dee and Lucy in Canberra on Good Friday and driven back to work in the café on the Saturday. There had been hardly any customers, which was why Frank encouraged her to take the day off this year.

She loved the feeling of community an event like this generated. It was a time when almost all of Granite Springs came together. It didn't matter whether they were wealthy landowners, shopkeepers, academics, or the poorest residents of the town, here at the races, there were no dividing lines. They were all here to enjoy themselves.

'Can I go off to look at the horses?' Lucy asked, as soon as they'd found a free spot, wedged between two other cars.

'Off you go, but don't get lost. And we'll be eating soon,' Dee said and with a wave, Lucy darted off. Dee shook her head. 'Sometimes she can be so headstrong, but at others, she's just my baby girl.'

'You're so lucky to have her,' Marie said, her eyes following the young girl. 'I know it wasn't easy for you bringing her up on your own, but she's a credit to you. You never hear from Robbie?'

Dee shook her head, a crease appearing between her eyes. 'The bastard wanted nothing to do with us. But, Lucy… lately she's been asking about her dad. It's tough to tell her he didn't want to be a dad, couldn't cope with it. He wasn't like Frank. He'd have made a great dad. You'd have been good parents. It's such a pity…'

'Let's get this unpacked.' Marie didn't want to spoil the day by thinking about what might have been. Sometimes life wasn't fair.

'Sorry!' Dee put a comforting hand on Marie's arm. 'I didn't mean to upset you.'

'I'm not. You didn't. But it's not something I like to dwell on. There's no point. It's not something I can change. Now, let's set up this table and chairs and we can unpack the food. I don't know about you, but I'm ready for a glass of wine.'

'Aren't those your friends over there?' Dee asked, pointing to a group seated several rows of cars away.

Marie squinted, the bright sun blurring her vision. 'Fran and Owen?' Yes, you're right. They're with other friends of theirs. Jo and Kay often come into the café. Kay's in the choir with me, but I don't know Jo well. She and her husband are Owen's neighbours and Kay and Nick work at the university. Granite Springs may have grown since you lived here but it's still a pretty small community, really. I don't know who the other man is.' She stared at the group trying to place the tall man with the thick thatch of white hair. He was wearing a beige parka, his eyes almost hidden by dark-rimmed glasses. 'He must be visiting.'

'He looks interesting. Do you want to go over to say hello?'

'No. They're in their own group. I don't want to interrupt. We saw Owen and Fran yesterday.'

'Mmm.'

Marie could see Dee wasn't convinced. As they were watching, Lucy bounded up to the group, stopped, and pointed towards them. Marie saw Fran wave. She waved back. No way was she going to go over there to be introduced.

*

Drew was enjoying himself. This picnic race lark wasn't as bad as he'd anticipated, and Nick and Kay's friends proved to be good company. In addition to Jo and Col, the couple they'd mentioned, there were two more, neighbours of Jo's who worked at the university with Nick and Kay. Owen, the neighbour, was surprising. He looked and acted as if he'd be more at home in the centre of the city and was only pretending to be a local. It appeared he was a musician so that might explain it. His partner was his complete opposite – a cool, self-contained lady. They did say opposites attract.

He was listening to Owen and Col discussing the alpacas which it seemed Col and Jo had recently added to their property, when a young girl, who looked to be about the same age as Jess, suddenly drew to a halt beside them.

'Hello,' she said to Fran, who was standing next to them. 'You're here, too. Mum and Aunt Marie are over there.' She pointed across the cars to where two women were standing by an open car boot. The men paused their conversation, and Fran waved.

Drew looked to where the girl was pointing, to see two dark-haired women – one taller than the other – returning Fran's wave.

'It's Marie from The Bean Sprout, isn't it?' Jo asked. 'Should we invite them to join us?'

'I think not,' Col said. 'They look pretty well set up over there and we've filled this space.'

Drew could see what he meant. Space was at a premium here, with cars jampacked together and every car having at least one table and several chairs set out either behind or at the side, squashed in between cars. He'd already worked out Jo was a sociable being, who wanted everyone to be friends. He had the distinct feeling she was a bit of a matchmaker too. He'd need to watch out she didn't try to find someone for him. He'd seen the gleam in her eyes when Nick introduced him as, 'The new principal at the High who's moved here with his daughter.' He was sure her motives might be good, but he had no intention of becoming the target of any matchmaking attempts, well-meaning or otherwise.

The girl moved on, back to her mother and aunt, then, seemingly oblivious, Jo explained to him, 'Marie runs one of the best cafés in town – The Bean Sprout on Main Street. Best place for coffee in the centre of town and her cakes are to die for. Have you been there?'

'Afraid not.' Drew hoped he didn't sound rude. The fact was, he'd been hardly anywhere in town apart from school and the shops. Having made the move to Granite Springs, he had every intention of checking the place out. What had happened? He guessed he'd become too caught up in the demands of a new job and the day-to-day activities of running a home and raising a teenager. But that had to change.

Coming here was a step in the right direction. Jo had said she co-owned a restaurant in town. He planned to check that out while Jess was gone, along with the art gallery which was holding an exhibition of paintings by a local artist, and there was the choral event next day. His life was suddenly becoming filled.

He'd already been recognised by several parents who'd nodded as they passed and managed to make polite conversation with the various staff members who stopped to greet him. It was a strange feeling, but Drew had the sense he was part of a community, something he'd never experienced living in the city.

'Beer, mate?'

While Drew had been musing on the differences between life in the city and here, Nick had been intent on replenishing the women's glasses of wine and was now offering to renew the men's beer.

Drew tossed his empty can into the boot of the car which was being used as a receptacle for rubbish and tugged the pull on the fresh cold can, quickly sucking up the froth that oozed out.

'I think we should eat now,' Jo said, gesturing to the large fold-up table which held several platters of meats and containers of salads.

The lunch was a leisurely one, so much so, that Drew wondered if there really was going to be a horse race. But, eventually, the food was all eaten and the remnants disposed of or packed up, and the group strolled across to the racetrack where everyone was gathering.

'Are you a betting man?' Nick asked, as they passed the line-up of bookies. Drew shook his head but, almost against his will, he found himself joining the other men to wager ten dollars on a horse called Black Knight.

Despite protesting he knew nothing about horses or betting, and feeling completely out of his element, Drew watched with interest as those around him became excited when the race started, cheering on their favourites. He had no idea which horse was which, so it was a surprise when, at the finish, he heard the result announced, and Col said, 'Black Knight was yours, Drew, wasn't it? He won!'

'Beginner's luck,' Drew claimed, as the others congratulated him. He walked over to collect his winnings, deciding to blow the unexpected windfall on a meal at the restaurant he'd heard about. But one bet was enough. He didn't intend to chance his luck and throw away his winnings. No, he'd have an early night, and tomorrow there was the choral event he'd agreed to attend. Maybe he'd manage to fill up this holiday weekend after all.

But two weeks of the Easter holiday still stretched ahead of him. Two weeks with no school. Two weeks with no Jess. Maybe he could spend it discovering more about the surrounding countryside and be able to share that with Jess when she returned, even though he held little hope of attracting any of her interest in a place she seemed determined to hate.

Six

'How big is their place?' Lucy asked, twisting from side to side as she took in the broad acres on both sides of the road. 'Do they have horses?'

'I don't think so, Lucy.' Marie grinned. She was surprised how taken her niece had been with the horses at the races. 'Have you ever ridden?'

'Mum takes me to a horse-riding trail sometimes. It's fun, and I love the soft feel of their noses. I like to talk to them.'

'Well, I think you'll have to make do with goats today. And Fran has a cat.'

'Can we get a pet when we go back to Canberra, Mum? You keep saying it's not the right time, but when will the time be right?'

Marie gave Dee a sympathetic smile. 'Your mum's like me. She's out at work all day. Pets need company.'

'But don't Fran and Owen work all day, too? And they have a cat *and* goats.'

There was no way to answer that, so Marie didn't try. 'Almost there,' she said. 'And to answer your earlier question, I think they have twenty acres. It's what's often described as a hobby farm, which means it's not large enough to make a living from. There are a few properties the same size around here. They were called soldier settlements, given to returning soldiers after the First World War.'

But Lucy had lost interest and was checking her iPhone.

'Can you hop out and open the gate, Lucy, then close it after us?' Marie had drawn up at a rusty white metal gate bearing an oval white sign with *The Haven* printed on it in large green lettering. Underneath the name, in smaller letters, it said *The Larsens*. The house was visible a little way ahead, and groups of goats were standing staring at them curiously.

'They don't bite, do they?' Now she was faced with the animals, Lucy seemed reluctant to be close to them.

Marie laughed. 'They'll likely run off as soon as we drive through. They're curious creatures but wary too, and you're a stranger to them.'

Lucy stepped out gingerly but was quick to slip back into the car as soon as she'd closed the gate. 'They look friendly,' she said, 'but that one…' She pointed to a goat which was staring balefully at her. It had a long dark coat and did look fiercer than the others.

'I'm sure Owen will be able to tell you all about them,' Marie said. 'This is the first time I've been here. It's much prettier than I imagined.'

'But I thought you were good friends with Fran,' Dee said.

'I am. She and Owen only got together last year when she returned from England. Her mother was sick, so she went there for six months, till her mother passed.'

'Oh, I'm sorry, I didn't know.'

'No reason why you should.'

'And Pia lives here, too?' Lucy asked, her confidence returning now they'd passed the goats who'd resumed grazing.

'She does.' Marie drove up to the fence around the house and parked in front of a large metal shed.

Owen and Fran came to greet them as they got out of the car, a small black cat padding behind them.

'Oh, how cute.' Lucy bent down to pick it up.

'Be careful,' Owen said, then gave a wry grin as the cat snuggled into Lucy. 'Looks like you've won a heart there. It's just me Stormy seems to have an aversion to.'

'Stormy – is that his name?' Lucy asked, scratching the little creature's ears.

'Owen found him on a fencepost after a storm. There were two other cats here at the time, so he brought this one into town for me. I don't think Stormy has ever forgiven him. But he does tolerate him – most of the time.' Fran laughed.

'Well, I think he's gorgeous,' Lucy said, carrying the cat as she followed the others inside.

*

'Lucy's disappointed there are no horses,' Marie said, when they returned from a tour of the property. Lunch had been a delicious tandoori chicken meatloaf accompanied by a roast pumpkin, zucchini, corn and red onion salad, and they'd all felt the need for some exercise.

'Aunt Marie!' Lucy exclaimed. 'I didn't…'

'Sorry, but the old lady up the lane has three retired racehorses. They're not suitable for riding, but we can walk up and talk to them, if that would satisfy you,' Owen said. 'Magda's not living there at the moment. They'll enjoy the company.'

'Yes, please!'

'Anyone else?' Owen looked at the others.

'I'll pass,' Dee said. 'I think I have one of my migraines coming on. Maybe I'll just have a quiet seat while you go.'

'Are you okay?' Marie knew Dee had suffered from migraines for years. She'd thought her sister looked a bit washed out at breakfast, but Dee assured her she was all right. Now Marie wondered if she just hadn't wanted to spoil the outing.

'I'll be fine if I can have a bit of quiet. If I could have a glass of water, Fran. I have my tablets.'

'Sure. You go on with Lucy, Owen. We can all stay here. I wouldn't mind a rest myself. How about I make us a pot of camomile tea?'

'That would be lovely,' Marie said.

Dee gave her a tired smile.

She was resting inside on the sofa and Marie and Fran were sitting on the veranda, their tea almost finished, when they saw Owen and Lucy returning. But something was wrong. When they set off, Lucy was skipping beside Owen and the pair were obviously joking around. Now they were moving much more slowly, and Owen appeared to be supporting Lucy.

Marie rose to her feet, and both she and Fran hurried across the paddock to the gate. What happened?' Marie asked, seeing Lucy's face streaked with tears as she limped along.

'My ankle,' Lucy stammered. 'I…'

'It was my fault,' Owen said. 'We'd spent some time with the horses and were on our way back, skipping and fooling about. Lucy managed to catch her foot in a pothole in the lane and twisted her ankle. I don't think it's broken, but you should get it checked out. Sorry,' he added, clearly seeing Fran's glare. 'I've done it again, acted without thinking.'

'You weren't to know this would happen,' Marie said. 'I'm sure it'll be fine, but I think we need to take you into the Base Hospital to get it checked out, Lucy.'

'I don't want to be a bother.'

'You're not. Is it painful?'

Lucy nodded. 'It hurts when I try to put my weight on it.'

'Right. We should go now. If you can help Lucy to the car, Owen, I'll go in to see how Dee is. We can drop her off home on our way.'

Dee's eyes were closed when Marie popped her head around the door to the living room. She walked in softly to touch her sister on the shoulder. Dee's eyes opened, unfocussed for a moment, then, 'What's the matter? Is it time to go already?' she asked.

'Yes, Lucy's gone over on her ankle. I'm going to take her into Emergency to be on the safe side. I can drop you off on the way.'

'Lucy? No, I need to come, too.' Dee struggled up, falling back against the cushions before finally managing to sit up. She put a hand to her head and groaned.

'Still aching?' Marie asked sympathetically. She never suffered migraines herself but had seen Dee like this before. She knew how it knocked her about.

'I'll be fine,' Dee grimaced as she rose to her feet, teetering slightly as she did so.

'Mum!' Lucy wailed, when they went outside. She was perched on one leg by the car door.

Once Lucy was settled in the back seat, a pillow under her injured ankle, Marie drove into town. She glanced worriedly at Dee as they passed the Granite Springs road sign. 'Are you sure you don't want me to drop you off? You look as if you need to lie down.'

'Mum!' Lucy wailed.

'It's okay, honey. I'm coming to the hospital. I need to be there for her, Marie. I always have been. We're a unit. It's what we do.'

Giving her sister another apprehensive glance, Marie did as she asked and headed straight to the hospital where she managed to find a wheelchair to transport Lucy into the waiting room in Emergency. Dee collapsed into a chair with a sigh.

There were only a few others waiting, so it wasn't long before Lucy's name was called and all three piled into the small examination room. The doctor was a young woman who asked a still tearful Lucy where it hurt and if she was able to stand on it.

'It hurts too much when I try to stand,' Lucy said.

'I don't think it's broken,' the doctor said, after examining the ankle and Lucy emitting a yelp of pain. 'But I'd like to have an x ray to be sure. I'll have someone take you down to radiology and your mum...' She looked from Marie to Dee and back, '...can wait outside.' 'We won't be long,' she said to them. 'Luckily, we haven't been run off our feet today.'

'Thanks,' Marie said, seeing Dee was still in pain. She should have ignored her and stopped off at home.

She watched Lucy being wheeled off, then, taking Dee's arm, led her back to the waiting room. 'I'll fetch us some water,' she said, once Dee was settled in a chair again, and headed to the water cooler which sat against one wall.

When she returned with two paper cups of water, Marie saw her sister grimace and close her eyes, dropping her head into her hands. 'How are *you*?' she asked, concerned again for Dee.

'I have the mother of all headaches. I've never had one this bad before.'

'Maybe you need to see a doctor too.' Marie was partly joking but Dee's condition was beginning to worry her.

Suddenly Dee keeled over.

'Help!' Marie called, trying to lift Dee's head. She was a dead weight. 'Something's happening to my sister!'

Almost before the words were out of her mouth, there was a flurry and a nurse came to help.

'Who's this?' she asked, while at the same time seeming to take Dee's pulse.

'Dee... my sister... she was complaining of a migraine earlier, then she said it got worse and...' Maria's voice trailed away as she saw the nurse signal to the woman in reception.

Rapidly they were surrounded by a bevy of staff who seemed to have appeared from nowhere. Marie was pushed out of the way, and Dee was carried away.

'Where…? Can I…?' Marie stood helpless, as a door closed behind Dee and her entourage.

'She'll be fine. She's in good hands. Can I get you anything?' Marie looked up to see one of the hospital volunteers looking at her, eyes full of concern.

'I… I had water.' She looked around for her cup, but it seemed to have disappeared.

'I'll get you some.'

The woman walked off to return with a cup of water which Marie gulped down. She then produced a form similar to the one Marie had already completed for Lucy. 'Can you fill this in – for our records?' she asked.

Marie complied, her hand shaking so much she could barely hold the pen. This day, which had started out so well, was turning into a nightmare.

'You came in with your… sister?' the volunteer asked.

Marie shook her head, more in an attempt to clear her thoughts than in reply. 'No, my niece. She…'

Just then, a door swung open, and Lucy appeared on a pair of crutches. She was accompanied by a nurse, who was carrying a sheaf of paper.

'Lucy's ankle isn't broken,' the nurse said. 'But it's a bad sprain, and she should keep off it for a couple of weeks. She can borrow these crutches as long as you return them when she no longer needs them. Here are some instructions for her care.' She handed over an A4 typewritten sheet. 'You can take her home now.'

'Bang goes my two weeks' holiday,' Lucy said with a grimace. 'But it could be worse. Where's Mum?' She looked around, suddenly realising Dee wasn't there.

'Her migraine is worse. She's with the doctor.' Marie couldn't explain what had happened to Dee. She didn't know herself. Her stomach was in knots. Dee had suffered from migraines for years. How bad could it be?

'I guess we can't go home yet, then? These crutches are weird. It's not as easy as it looks to walk with them. But my ankle doesn't hurt so much anymore.' She looked at the ankle brace that encased the injury and propped her foot up on a chair. 'They say I have to keep it elevated as much as possible. What a drag! Do you think Mum will be long? I can't wait to lie down.'

'I don't know.' Marie was trying hard to keep her anxiety in check. There was no sense in worrying Lucy needlessly. But the way Dee had suddenly collapsed worried her. She'd seen how the colour had left her sister's face just before she did.

Thinking like this wasn't going to help. 'We need to work out things we can do that don't entail walking,' she said to Lucy instead. 'We need to make a list.'

'Oh, good. I love your lists.'

Lucy started composing a list on her iPhone, Marie trying to make suggestions, but distracted by imagining what might be happening to Dee.

They seemed to be waiting forever, but less than an hour had passed when a young man in shirtsleeves appeared, a stethoscope hanging around his neck.

'Ms Cunningham?' he asked.

Marie nodded and rose, her stomach roiling. Was it bad news? Were they going to keep Dee in overnight?

'Will you come with me?' he gestured to one of the doors behind him, the one through which Dee had disappeared.

'Wait here,' Marie said to Lucy.

'No! I want to see Mum.' Lucy struggled upright, grasping her crutches awkwardly.

Marie helped her as the two followed the doctor into an empty room. Where was Dee?

'Take a seat.'

'Where's Mum?' Lucy asked, her eyes wildly searching the room as if Dee was going to magically appear.

The doctor clasped his hands on his knees. 'Ms Cunningham – your sister – and your mother,' he said turning towards Lucy, 'she suffered an aneurysm. I'm afraid it ruptured.'

There was silence. Marie was trying to figure out what that meant. It sounded serious. She was about to ask, when Lucy forestalled her.

'Does that mean she'll have to have an operation?'

The doctor cleared his throat. Marie began to tremble. She had a premonition about what he was going to say.

'I'm afraid we couldn't save her.'

Marie heard a loud howl. It was a few seconds before she realised it was coming from her, and that Lucy's hands were grasping hers so hard her nails were digging into the skin.

'Noooo!' It was Lucy's voice that brought her back to the present, forced her to remember. Dee! Her sister was dead! How could it happen so quickly?

'How...?' she asked, seeing the doctor watching them with a concerned expression. He'd no doubt been in this situation many times. How did he bear it? How would she bear it?

'It was sudden,' he said. 'I'm afraid she didn't regain consciousness. It was too late. There was nothing we could do.'

He continued to talk, but his words didn't register with Marie. Her eyes filled, tears streaming down her cheeks unchecked. She pulled Lucy into her arms and hugged her tight. Now, they only had each other.

Abruptly, the doctor's words forced their way through the fog. 'Is there... can I call someone for you?' he asked.

Marie started to shake her head. Then the thought of having to get into the car, to drive home without Dee, overwhelmed her. She couldn't do it.

'Is there someone I can call?' the doctor asked again.

Frank's familiar face swam into Marie's mind. Frank, who'd always been there for her. Frank, who loved Dee and Lucy too. 'Frank,' she said. 'My... Frank Beattie. He's...' She'd been about to say, 'my husband', but he hadn't been that for two years, never had been. 'I have his number in my phone,' she said instead. 'I can call him.'

Seven

Drew felt full of energy when he awakened on Easter Monday. The rendering of the Saint Matthew Passion the previous day had been beautifully executed, a credit to the choristers and their conductor. Even more so as he'd only been working with them since the beginning of the year. Drew had discovered that over dinner.

The concert over, Drew had been trying to decide whether to head home or treat himself to the dinner he'd promised, when he heard his name being called. Looking around, he saw Nick and Kay, along with their friends Jo and Col, walking towards him. Both Nick and Kay had been part of the choir and he'd noticed the other two in the audience.

To avoid seeming rude, Drew stopped to say hello and tell Nick and Kay how much he'd enjoyed the afternoon.

'We're going to The Riverside for an early dinner,' Jo said with a smile. 'Why don't you join us? It must be lonely for you with your daughter away – or are you enjoying the peace and quiet?'

'A bit of both.' Drew grinned. 'But I don't want to intrude.'

'Not at all.' Nick put a hand on Drew's shoulder. 'We see each other all the time. It's always good to have fresh blood.'

'Nick!' Kay remonstrated.

'Sorry,' Nick said. 'That may not have come out the way it was meant. But do join us. It's the best food in town.'

'So you said. And I was considering giving it a go one of these days. My winnings are burning a hole in my pocket.'

'Well, then. It's not much fun eating out on your own,' Jo said.

'And we always get preferential treatment,' Col put in.

They all laughed, and Drew remembered Nick telling him Jo owned the restaurant with her son.

'Okay, you've convinced me. Is it far?'

'We can walk from here and you can pick up your car later,' Nick said. 'It's a nice stroll at this time of day.'

Drew looked up at the sky. The sun would be down before long, and the sky was already developing a deep blue and orange hue. It would be dark and filled with stars by the time they finished eating – one of the features he liked about living here. Maybe he'd buy himself a telescope, though the view would be even better outside of town.

Dinner was excellent and the company good. At the end of the evening, Drew felt he'd made new friends, cemented the relationships begun at Nick and Kay's and the races.

*

But today, he was on his own again. He planned to drive out of town, perhaps stop somewhere for lunch, pretend to be a tourist. He wanted to call Jess, to find out what she was doing for Easter over there, but he wouldn't be able to connect with her till later. He was disappointed not to have heard anything – either from her or Irene. But what had he expected? Jess barely spoke to him when they were living in the same house. Why should he expect her to be different when they were on opposite sides of the world?

Drew enjoyed driving out into the countryside. When he passed a collection of mailboxes by a turnoff, he recognised Owen and Col's names. They must live down that dirt road. Although tempted to see where they lived, he drove on. He'd wait for the invitation which he had no doubt would eventuate. They were those sort of people – friendly, open, and unlike some of the uptight city dwellers he'd left behind in Melbourne. They hadn't all been like that, far from it. But, when Irene had moved on with her life, most had moved on too. Drew found it hard to keep up, so had buried himself in his work.

He didn't intend to make the same mistake here, though until now he hadn't made much of an effort. Maybe his own solitary attitude was part of Jess's problem.

Although keeping a lookout for a spot to have lunch, as he drove further and further from the town, Drew found himself surrounded by broad acres. While it was interesting to see sheep, cattle and the occasional horses grazing placidly in the paddocks, the sight of them and the beautiful scenery didn't assuage the hunger which was beginning to gnaw at him. Regretfully, he made a U-turn, wishing he'd thought to consult a map before leaving home. The next town with a welcoming café might be just over the hill or around the bend, but it might not. It wasn't a risk he was willing to take.

Instead, he headed back to Granite Springs where he knew he'd find something open. He seemed to recall Jo or Col mentioning a place that did good coffee, and a good strong cup would be welcome right now, along with something savoury, maybe a burger or a meat pie with mushy peas. His mouth watered at the thought.

Driving down Main Street, it appeared almost everything was closed. Damn! Easter Monday, a public holiday, he should have thought of that. He wasn't doing too well today. He was about to turn around again and head for home, when he caught sight of one place that was open for business. The Bean Sprout Café – wasn't that the one Jo was singing the praises of – the one with the great coffee? And the woman she pointed out at the picnics. But he was too hungry to worry about meeting the woman Jo identified. He parked the car, walked to the café, and pushed open the door.

Drew was immediately impressed by the friendly atmosphere. He wasn't sure how it was achieved, but there was something about the place that made him feel welcome. There were only a few tables filled, and a tall dark-haired man was working at the coffee machine behind the counter. Drew walked up to him.

'Do I order here?'

'If you would,' the man said. 'I'm on my own today, it being a holiday. Are you just after a coffee or would you like to see our menu?'

'Coffee first – black – and I'll take a menu, thanks.'

'I'm Frank. I don't think I've seen you in here before. New to town or just visiting?'

'Drew. I moved here earlier this year but haven't got out much till now.' Drew knew he sounded lame but wasn't ready to give any further explanation to a stranger.

'Glad you found your way here. I'll bring over your coffee and take your order,' he said. 'You can pay for the lot after you've eaten,' he added, as Drew began to take out his wallet.

Settled in a corner table with a view of the entire café, Drew studied the menu. Alongside the usual selection of meals, he noticed there was also a range of cakes and slices listed as *homebaked*. That figured and fitted in with the family atmosphere of the café. He decided on a burger and chips and sat back to wait for his coffee to arrive.

It wasn't long before Frank brought over a steaming cup of fragrant coffee in a large cup. Drew placed his order then, curious, asked, 'Been here for long?'

'The café or me?' Frank chuckled. 'I've lived in Granite Springs all my life, and The Bean Sprout has been in the family for a couple of generations. Marie and I took it over from my dad when he grew too frail to handle it. It's been good to us, even though the clientele has changed over the years. We do pretty well with coffees and lunches most days, and Marie does her cookery classes and kid's parties in the back room.'

Marie! That was the name of the woman at the races. But it sounded as if they were a couple. So why had Jo intimated she was single? Or had she? Had it just been Drew's inbuilt defence system switching on?

The coffee was good. Drew sighed with pleasure as the rich flavour of the beverage stimulated his taste buds and filled him with a sense of wellbeing.

Frank had dropped a copy of the local paper on the table along with his meal, and the words, 'Not sure if you've been following the local news.' Drew was browsing his way through it while he ate. He came to life with a start when he heard a phone ring loudly behind the counter followed by Frank's terse words. Looking around, Drew saw he was the only customer left. He checked his watch, wondering when the café closed. But it was still only early afternoon.

Glancing across to where Frank was standing as if turned to stone, Drew was deciding whether to order a second cup of coffee when Frank came alive and hurried over towards him. 'Sorry, mate,' he said, the colour draining from his face. 'Just had bad news. I have to close now. You can settle up another time.' He picked up Drew's empty cup and plate and went off again, clearly expecting Drew to leave.

'Sorry,' Drew said, but Frank had moved on. His mind was clearly elsewhere. Drew left, hearing the door being locked behind him. He wondered what sort of bad news had caused Frank to have to leave in such a rush he didn't even wait for Drew to pay for his meal, but it wasn't any of his business.

Eight

Marie was huddled with Lucy in two chairs in a corner of the waiting room when she saw Frank's easily recognisable figure rush through the door. He hadn't hesitated when she called, and here he was. She felt a wave of relief flow over her as he made his way toward her and pulled her into a warm hug. Marie pressed her face into his shoulder, feeling the heat of his body seep through the tee-shirt he always wore to the café, and her tears welled up again. It seemed she and Lucy should have been cried out by now. Their eyes were red and swollen from weeping and their throats scratchy from the tears.

'Oh, Frank!' she said.

'Uncle Frank!' Lucy's voice burst into her ears, forcing her to release Frank and hug her again too. The three of them stood hugging, Lucy balancing on one leg, while everything else in the room continued unnoticed around them.

'You're in shock,' Frank said. 'Let's get you both home.'

'The café?' Marie tried to think clearly. She hadn't given The Bean Sprout any consideration when she made her desperate call to Frank.

'It's closed.'

'But…'

'Let's go.'

Marie allowed herself to be led outside to where Frank had parked his car. In the back of her mind, she knew she had a car somewhere here too, but it was all too difficult. It was easier to let him take charge. Frank helped her into the front seat, and Lucy into the back, handing the crutches in after her, and passing her a box of tissues to stem the tears which were still running down her cheeks.

'I saw her,' Marie said as they drove. Frank remained silent, only shooting a quick glance towards her. Marie thought back to how Dee had been lying there so still, how cold her forehead had been when she kissed it. It didn't seem real. She expected Dee to jump up and say, 'Ha, fooled you!' just as she had when they were kids playing in the backyard. But it didn't happen this time. It was no joke. Dee was dead. She'd never jump up again.

'What'll I do?' Lucy said in a small voice barely audible over the sound of the car's engine. 'Aunt Marie, what'll I do without my mum?' She broke into heartrending sobs again.

Marie was almost glad to arrive home. At least the house was familiar. They all went into the kitchen where Frank put on the electric jug.

'I think we all need a cup of sweet tea,' he said.

Lucy was standing, balancing on her crutches. 'I'm going to lie down,' she muttered. 'I can't…'

'Let me help you.' Marie helped Lucy make her way upstairs, averting her eyes when they passed the room Dee had been using, and in which the clothes she'd discarded just that morning were still lying on the bed where she'd left them. Marie couldn't bear to look. On her way back, she closed the door.

'Will Lucy be okay?' Frank asked, when Marie returned to the kitchen.

'They gave her something at the hospital – it was for her ankle but should help her sleep. They didn't expect… Oh, hell, Frank. What are we going to do?'

'Right now, Lucy's getting some rest, and you're going to have a cup of sweet tea. You're still in shock. And maybe you should eat something.'

'I couldn't face food. I want…' But Marie didn't know what she wanted – apart from to see Dee walk in the door, for the nightmare to be over.

'You need to rest, too. Would you like me to stay? I don't think you should be on your own.'

'I'll be fine.' But would she? She'd just lost her sister, her little sister, the sister who'd been her confidante, her support, her... Out of the blue, Marie remembered she hadn't revealed her worries to Dee. She'd intended to do that tonight. She gulped down a sob. Who was there now to comfort her, advise her, listen to her woes and make her laugh? 'I'll be fine,' she repeated. Marie had always been the stronger of the two, the one who always managed to see the positive in everything. But even she could find nothing positive in this.

*

Next morning, Marie had trouble opening her eyes. She felt as if there was a heavy weight on them, on her, suffocating her. It took her only a moment to remember. Dee was gone! Pulling on her robe, Marie walked along to peer into Lucy's room. While the rumpled bedclothes looked as if the girl had suffered a restless night, she was asleep now, the crutches at the side of the bed reminding Marie of the trip to hospital and its devastating aftermath.

Closing the door gently, Marie stumbled downstairs to the kitchen where she found Frank filling the coffee machine. She was glad he'd stayed. He looked so familiar there, as if he belonged. It was as if he'd never left. But he had. She thought he was going to go home last night but had been too exhausted to care. 'You're still here?'

Frank turned at the sound of her voice, at the words which had come out more stiffly than Marie intended. She pushed back a strand of hair from her face. 'Sorry, Frank. It was good of you to stay but there was no need. Don't you have to get to the café?' Marie tried to focus on the clock, but her eyes blurred, remembering Dee again. She brushed away the tears.

'I've closed The Bean Sprout for a few days – a family bereavement, I said on the notice. I feel Dee is still part of my family. She and Lucy...'

Marie saw the tears form in his eyes and put her arms around him. He was such a kind man. They stood like that for several minutes, united in their grief.

'Now, then,' Frank carefully removed her arms from his waist, 'I think coffee will do you good. Did you manage to sleep?'

'A bit. Where did you…?'

'On the sofa.'

Marie almost had to smile at the image of Frank's large frame trying to fit onto the two and a half seater sofa. But this morning wasn't one for smiles.

'Breakfast?'

She shook her head. The very thought of food making her feel sick.

'You need to eat. You didn't have anything last night. There are things to take care of. I can help, but you need to be strong for Lucy. She'll need you now, more than ever.'

Lucy!

As if hearing her name. Lucy chose that moment to enter the kitchen, moving awkwardly on her crutches. She looked around wildly, her eyes moving from Marie to Frank and back again. 'Uncle Frank, what are you doing here? Is Mum…? Did I dream it? Aunt Marie?'

'Oh, my darling girl!' Marie moved to take Lucy in her arms. 'No, you didn't dream it. It's true. Your mum…' Marie couldn't say the word. It was too final.

Lucy collapsed into a chair, her head dropping onto her arms. She began to sob.

*

Somehow, Marie managed to gulp down the herbal tea she'd felt her stomach could handle better than coffee and swallow several bites of toast and vegemite, forcing Lucy to do the same, before they both disappeared to shower and dress. 'I can help you,' Marie said to Lucy as they left, earning the glimpse of a grateful smile.

Frank was still there when they returned. He was seated at the kitchen table making notes on a lined pad. Marie had no idea where it had come from.

'Have you thought about a funeral?' he asked.

Lucy turned her head away, but murmured quietly, 'Mum wouldn't want a fuss and she'd want to be cremated. She was an organ donor.'

'It's probably too late for that,' Frank said with a sigh. 'But we can make sure we acknowledge her wishes about everything else. Marie?'

Marie didn't want to think about it. She wanted to go back to yesterday morning, to when they were preparing for their trip to visit Fran and Owen. She wanted to change history, to bring Dee back. Dee was too young to die. She had her whole life before her and she'd met someone who… Hell, there were all her friends to contact. How could Marie do it?

She remembered Frank telling her she had to be strong for Lucy and took a deep breath. 'I'll help you, Frank. Tell me what needs to be done.

Nine

Drew gasped when he saw Jess walking across the tarmac to the terminal. He'd arrived early and was on his second cup of weak coffee when the plane landed. The coffee had been bad enough, but he almost choked when he saw his daughter coming towards him. What had she done to her hair? Her thick chestnut locks had disappeared to be replaced by a head of what looked like pink candyfloss. Involuntarily he clenched his fist, crushing the cardboard cup which still held the remains of the indifferent coffee.

'Dad!' Jess walked up to him, her expression as sullen as when she left. She made no attempt to hug him, merely dropping her bag and glaring at him as if daring him to say anything about her changed appearance.

Well, he wouldn't give her the satisfaction of making a scene here. She would keep. He picked up her bag. 'Home?'

'I guess,' she muttered, taking out her iPhone and checking the screen. Some things didn't change.

On the drive home, Drew turned on the radio to break the silence, vowing to try to find out about her trip over dinner. He'd planned to do something special to celebrate her return and had booked a table at The Riverside. Now he wondered if she'd consider it too old-fashioned, and if he really wanted to be seen with her looking like this. Then he mentally chastised himself. She was his daughter, and many teenagers dyed their hair these days, either to attract attention or as a sign of rebellion. Which was it in Jess's case?

At the back of Drew's mind was the fact he was the principal of the local high school, someone whose daughter should be a shining example of a well-adjusted, well brought up teenager. Instead she was – what? A girl who was struggling to adjust to changes which were none of her own making, to her parents' separation, to living in a new town where she hadn't been able to make friends.

Once home, Jess stomped up to her room and the music began. Although Drew had missed its continued blasting, he gritted his teeth. This couldn't go on, but what could he do? She didn't pay a blind bit of attention to his requests to turn it down – and he *had* missed it.

When Jess appeared again, Drew was enjoying a decent cup of coffee and one of the macadamia nut cookies he'd picked up at the supermarket in anticipation of his daughter's return.

She'd at least combed her hair into some semblance of neatness, but the colour looked even brighter here in the house. She'd changed too – into a pair of pink dungarees which almost matched the colour of her hair, over a black tee-shirt with a logo he couldn't identify. Jess grabbed a can of Coke from the fridge, pulled out a chair and slouched into it.

Drew pushed the packet of cookies across the table towards her. 'New clothes?' he asked, to break the silence and in an attempt to force some conversation.

'Mum bought me them.' Jess picked up a cookie and nibbled on it, before taking a slurp of Coke.

'How was it?'

'Okay. Jake was out a lot – training. And Mum has a lot of women friends. They meet for coffee and lunch almost every day.'

'Did you join them?'

'As if!' Jess snorted.

'So, what did you do with yourself when they were out?'

'Read, watched movies, and they have a pool. That was good.' She took another long gulp of her drink.

'And…' Drew hesitated, took a deep breath, then asked, 'Your hair?'

'Like it?' Jess smirked. 'Mum said it made me look like Taylor Swift.'

Drew couldn't help himself. 'But you're only fifteen. You're not a celebrity and you have to go back to school next week.' He didn't add, 'looking like that!' but Jess seemed to hear the unspoken words.

'I knew you'd be like this,' she said. 'I can't do anything to please you!' She picked up her drink, grabbed another cookie and raced back upstairs.

Drew heard the bedroom door slam. He removed his glasses, pinched the bridge of his nose then replaced them, wishing he hadn't mentioned her hair. While waiting at the airport, he'd planned what he was going to say to Jess, how he was going to try to improve the communication between them, help her adjust to life in Granite Springs. And he'd managed to blow it already.

By late afternoon Jess still hadn't reappeared. Drew knew he had to do something. He closed the book he was trying to read. It was difficult to concentrate with Jess's upset face continually coming between his eyes and the words on the page. Taking a deep breath, he headed upstairs, where Jess's music was still blaring from her room. Drew dealt with teenagers every day at work, but it was different at home. He wished he knew how to handle his own teenage daughter without sending her into meltdown. He knocked on the door.

No reply. He knocked again, louder this time. The music stopped. 'What is it?'

'Jess, I'm sorry for what I said. Can I come in?' He tried the door. It was locked. Now he regretted having agreed to put a lock on Jess's door, in response to her demand for privacy.

There was no reply, but he heard a rustling sound on the other side of the door, then it opened a crack and his daughter's face peered out. Her eyes were red and puffy. Hell! He hadn't intended to upset her so badly.

'I'm sorry, bub,' he said, using his old baby name for her. 'It was a shock to see your beautiful hair like that. Can we start again?'

'Oh, Dad!' Jess opened the door wider and flung herself into his arms. 'Mum doesn't love me anymore. She's so wrapped in Jake. It's Jake does this, Jake does that, Jake doesn't like… I don't know why she paid for me to go over there. I thought…' she gulped, '…I thought if I asked for my hair to be dyed, she'd blow a fuse, at least act as if… But she went along with it as if it was perfectly normal. I wish I hadn't done it.'

'Shhh.' Drew hugged her tightly. 'It'll be all right. It'll grow out. Maybe we can ask a hairdresser to…' But Drew had no idea what a hairdresser could do to fix things. 'We can find one tomorrow.'

Jess sniffed. 'Thanks, Dad. I know it's my own fault. I thought...' She gulped again.

'Why don't you wash your face, maybe have a shower and change into something pretty. I thought we could go out to celebrate you coming home. While you've been gone, I've been finding my way around the town. There's a pretty good restaurant by the river. I booked a table for us.'

'Really?' Jess perked up. 'It's not too fancy, not like the ones Mum goes to?'

'Not at all,' Drew said, not exactly sure what would constitute fancy to a fifteen-year-old. It was a good restaurant, but probably nothing like those Irene and Jake frequented in LA.

*

'This looks nice. Thanks, Dad,' Jess said, when they walked into The Riverside which was humming with conversation. Friday was clearly a busy night here. Drew was glad he'd booked. Jess had cheered up somewhat and was looking better. She'd scraped her hair back into some kind of bun and was wearing a short blue dress with her denim jacket. Her feet were encased in their usual ankle boots. It was a strange fashion, but probably better than the stiletto heels her mother favoured.

A man Drew recognised from his previous visit showed them to a table and handed them menus. Drew looked around the restaurant, surprised to see his neighbour sitting across the room. Tonight, he and his wife were accompanied by a teenage boy and a young woman. Nick's kids must have arrived home, too. Drew debated whether he should go over to say hello, then decided against it.

Following his gaze, Jess asked, 'Who are those people? Do you know them?'

'They're our neighbours. I got to know them when you were gone. Nick and Fran work out at the university and...'

'I've seen that boy at school.' Jess ducked her head as if she didn't want him to see her. 'I didn't know he lived next door.'

'Maybe...' But Drew stopped. It wasn't up to him to try to find friends for Jess. And he remembered what it had been like when he was that age. He had no desire to embarrass her. Instead he said, 'His name's Ryan Kerr. He'd be in Year Eleven. That'll be his sister. She's at uni.'

'As if I care,' Jess muttered, burying her face in the menu.

Now what had he said to annoy her?

He shook his head and picked up his menu. 'When I was here before, I had the steak. I think I'll try the lamb this time. What would you like, Jess?'

Jess raised her eyes from the menu. 'Can I have the mushroom risotto?'

'You can have anything you like. What do you want to drink with it?'

'Coke, please.'

When the waiter returned, Drew placed his order, adding a beer for himself.

Once their meals were served, Jess seemed to relax sufficiently to ask, 'What did you do in the holidays, Dad – besides come here and meet the neighbours?'

'You won't believe it, but I went to the races.'

Jess's eyes widened and she stopped eating, her fork halfway to her mouth. 'But you don't gamble, and you don't even like horses very much.'

'I know. But it's more of a social thing here. They're called the picnic races and people spend more time eating lunch in the car park than at the actual races – at least that's what it felt like. Nick – our neighbour – invited me, and I met some of his friends. They're nice people. You'd like them.'

'Yeah.' Jess didn't sound convinced.

'And I went to a concert on Easter Sunday. Bach. You probably wouldn't have enjoyed that.'

'No way! But at least you did things. LA was boring. I don't know why I couldn't have gone to Melbourne instead. Ella had a party. Everyone was there. And I missed it. All because Mum…' She kicked the leg of the table causing it to wobble.

Drew put a hand out to steady it. 'It's not Mum's fault. She didn't try to make your life difficult.' But, in his heart, Drew blamed Irene, too. If she hadn't left him for Jake, if she hadn't moved to LA, if she hadn't demanded Jess join her for Easter…

'It's not fair, Dad,' Jess continued. 'We're stuck here in this, this…' She stared around the restaurant as if trying to find a word horrendous enough to describe Granite Springs, then suddenly lowered her gaze and said, 'Shit!'

Drew glanced across the room to see Nick weaving his way towards them, followed by his son.

'Hi, Drew. Good to see you here again. Ryan, this is Mr Hamilton who lives next door.'

'I know who he is,' Ryan muttered, looking as if he'd rather be anywhere than here.

Drew recognised his reaction. It's what happened when you were a school principal. The kids either loved or loathed you but either way, they didn't want to meet you outside school.

Ignoring his son's comment, Nick continued, 'And this must be…?'

'Jess. Jess, this is Mr Kerr.'

Jess looked as if she'd like to join Ryan in staging a disappearing act.

While the two men carried on a conversation, Drew noticed Jess and Ryan eyeing each other surreptitiously.

'See you around,' Nick said, shaking Drew's hand and leaving.

As they walked off, Ryan half-turned. 'Like the hair,' he said to Jess.

'Dad!' Jess said, turning red. 'How could you? Ryan Kerr, he's…'

'He goes to your school and he lives next door. What's wrong with that?'

Jess just lowered her head.

Hell, she wasn't going to cry, was she? All he'd done was speak to Nick. It wasn't his fault Nick had brought his son across to… to what? Maybe so he and Jess could meet? If so, it hadn't gone too well.

'Finished?' he asked.

Jess nodded and pushed her plate away.

The evening hadn't gone the way Drew had hoped. Maybe he and Jess could do something together on the weekend, and perhaps it would be better once school started again. He heaved a sigh and called for the bill.

Ten

The past two weeks had been a nightmare. Marie didn't know what she'd have done without Frank's help. Organising the funeral had been easy compared to dealing with a devastated Lucy who couldn't understand why she wasn't able to go back to their home in Canberra and return to school and her friends. Her ankle was still bound up and she was limping but had dispensed with the crutches.

'I'm sorry, Luce,' Marie said, for what must have been the hundredth time. 'But you're stuck with me now. It's what your mum wanted and there's no way you could stay in Canberra on your own. I'm the only family you've got now – and you're all I've got, too. We have to make the best of it… together.'

'I know you said our house has to be sold. But couldn't I stay with one of my friends? I'm sure Gabi or Andrea… It's an important year for me.'

Marie sighed. They'd been over this. Many times. 'No, Luce, sweetheart. There's no way that can happen. I know it's a lot of change to accept. Losing your mum was bad enough without you having to be uprooted from your school and everything you know. But Granite Springs is a friendly place. And Granite Springs High is a good school. I'm sure you'll soon make new friends.'

But what did Marie know? She couldn't imagine how it felt to lose your mother at fifteen then to have to start afresh in a new town, in a new school, even if you had an aunt you loved and who loved you.

'We need to get you sorted with a uniform for school, then…'

Marie saw the horror in Lucy's eyes. She'd held off till now, but it had to be done. And she needed to enrol her in the local school. Frank had checked it out for her. The school secretary would be available today and the uniform shop would be open. It was all new to Marie, too.

'If I really have to,' Lucy wailed. 'But Mum…'

'If Dee was here, you'd be going back to Canberra today.' The thought of her sister's house, still waiting for them, brought tears to Marie's eyes, too. Frank had been the one to go to Canberra and put it on the market. Marie hadn't been able to handle it.

'Can I come with you? Can we go tomorrow?'

'To the school? It won't be open tomorrow.'

'No. Home. To Canberra. I know I can't stay there.' She held up her hands to prevent Marie's response. 'But I know what you and Uncle Frank have been talking about. You were planning to go there next week, once I'm in school, to…' she gulped, '…to sort out Mum's things. I want to be there. I need to be there, too.'

'Oh, Luce! Are you sure?' But of course she wanted to be there. It was her home, had been her home. She needed to say goodbye.

Lucy nodded. 'I can pick up my stuff and… there are some things…'

Marie moved to hug her niece. 'I'm sorry, Luce. We should have thought. Frank and I were trying to protect you. I see now we were wrong.'

'Thanks, Aunt Marie.' She buried her face into Marie's shoulder. 'And I'll come to the school with you today. But don't expect me to like it. You can't imagine how awful it is to be me. I feel as if my life has been taken over by forces outside my control and I'm on a roller coaster that won't stop. I just want Mum back!' She burst into sobs.

'I do, too, baby.' Marie hugged her tighter. Why did it have to happen to Dee – just when she had so much going for her? It wasn't fair!

*

The trip to the high school could have been worse. Although Lucy was determined to be unimpressed, she'd stood patiently while one of the other women helped Marie and her find a uniform to fit. She even managed to show a hint of interest when Marie told her how she and

Dee had attended this same school, saying, 'You and Mum? Yeah, it looks as if it's been here that long,'

For Marie, the visit was a trip down memory lane. She hadn't been to the school since Dee's graduation, had no reason to. Not much had changed. There was a new gymnasium, a building called a Technology Hub, and the library had been refurbished and renamed the Learning Hub, but other than that, the place looked – and smelt – much as it had during the years she and Dee had been there.

And Frank. He'd been a part of her life even then. Dear Frank. She couldn't have navigated the past weeks without him. He'd been happy to close The Bean Sprout when she needed him, despite the loss of income. Marie didn't know how she could ever make up to him for what he'd done for her.

'Are we done here?' Lucy was tapping her good foot impatiently.

They were standing in the main quadrangle, outside the all-weather shed, behind which Frank had stolen a kiss from Marie when they were around Lucy's age. Ah, the innocence of youth! Marie pulled herself back to the present. 'Yes, honey. Thanks for not making a fuss.'

Lucy rolled her eyes.

'How about we drop into the café to see what your Uncle Frank can find for our lunch?' she suggested.

Lucy brightened at once, though the shadows below her eyes underlined her ongoing grief. It would take a long time for the cheerful girl who'd arrived in Granite Springs for Easter to return. Back then, Lucy had been full of excitement and the joys of life. Now she was a mere shadow of her former self.

Almost every table in The Bean Sprout was full when Marie and Lucy walked in. Marie breathed in the familiar aromas. She'd missed this place. It was as well known to her as her own home, had been for thirty years. How could she ever have imagined leaving it? But perhaps it was too familiar – was that what had been eating at her? No, she regretted not sharing her concerns with Dee when she had the opportunity. Her sister was always able to see through Marie's worries and offer her a solution. But no longer.

'How's my favourite niece?' Frank asked, coming out from behind the counter to give Lucy a hug. Behind her back, he raised an eyebrow in Marie's direction.

She shrugged. 'We got Lucy enrolled and there are a couple of uniform dresses and a blazer in the car. That should do for now. I thought we could do the rest in a few weeks' time.' It had been difficult enough to get Lucy to stand still while she was measured for the dresses. Marie couldn't have coped with going the whole hog – winter skirts, blouses and cardigans. Time enough for those when the weather turned colder, though that wasn't far away.

'What did you think of our high school, Lucy? It's the one your mum and aunt attended, me too. It's where we met.' Marie saw a hint of what looked like regret in his eyes. Had Dee been right?

Lucy wasn't impressed. 'Aunt Marie said. It's just a school. It's not *my* school.' She pulled away from him, slumped into a chair and propped her chin on one hand, a frown forming between her eyes.

Frank raised his eyebrows at Marie again, but didn't speak.

'We came in for lunch,' Marie said. 'I'd love to have one of those smoked salmon open sandwiches. It's not often I get the chance to be on this side of the counter and I intend to make the most of it. What would you like, Lucy?'

'Anything. Nothing,' Lucy muttered.

Marie sighed. She wished she could help Lucy out of this slump she'd fallen into, but knew she had to allow her to work through her grief in her own time. 'How about a burger with chips?' she asked.

'I'm not hungry.'

'I know,' Frank said. 'I have two waffles left over from breakfast. I've been keeping them for someone special. What do you think?'

Lucy's lips turned up in the hint of a smile, which disappeared as she seemed to remember.

'I'll take that as a yes,' Frank said. 'And a smoothie. Coffee for you, Marie?'

'I'll have lemon and ginger tea. I can get it.'

'No. Time enough for that when you're back on-board next week. For now, you're another customer.'

With another sigh – of relief this time – Marie slipped into a seat opposite Lucy.

After a few attempts to talk about the town and the school, Marie gave up and she and Lucy ate without speaking. Marie could hear Frank making cheerful conversation with other customers. He was good at that and at putting his personal feelings aside for the sake of the business. She'd seen it when his father died, then his mother. It was as if he could turn cheerfulness on like a tap. She wished she had his ability, though she knew she had the reputation of being optimistic and always maintaining a positive attitude. She tried. She really did. And it usually worked. But sometimes, like now, it took an enormous effort.

When Lucy went to the ladies', Frank slid into her empty seat. 'She doesn't look good,' he said. 'It'll take a while, I expect. At least she's accepted she needs to stay here?'

'Reluctantly. But she wants me to take her over to Canberra tomorrow, Frank – to their old place. I don't know…'

Frank put a hand on top of Marie's. 'I expect she needs to go, to get closure. It'll be hard for her – hard for you, too.'

'I'd intended to go over one day next week… to sort out Dee's things. I can't do that with Lucy there.'

'Let her do what she needs to. It's been a shock – for all of us – and she needs to deal with it in her own way. Going there may be her way of coping with Dee's death.'

'I've been wondering…' Marie withdrew her hand from under Frank's and twisted her fingers together. 'Do you think she needs a counsellor? I feel so responsible. I never expected… Dee was such a great mother. I know nothing about taking care of a teenager.'

'You'll do just fine.' Frank patted her arm, just as a large group entered the café. 'I have to go now. I'll be in touch. Be thinking of you, tomorrow.'

On the spur of the moment, Marie said, 'Come for dinner. I'll probably need some company.'

'No need to cook. I'll bring something.' Frank gave Marie's shoulder a squeeze as he left.

Marie felt comforted, less alone in the new and unfamiliar role that had been thrust upon her. If she and Frank had been able to have children, they'd have been older than Lucy by now. They'd have successfully – or unsuccessfully – made their way through the various childhood and teenage stages and be at university or working with them in the café. Maybe she and Frank would be grandparents. That was a thought!

Instead, she'd fallen heir to her sister's daughter and had to try to help her make sense of what had happened to her, while learning how to be a parent herself.

She'd imagined her life as a parent so often, but never like this.

Eleven

The first week of term had been hectic. At school, there were more than the usual number of challenges – a broken window in the Learning Hub, staff disagreements to settle over timetabling, teenagers to discipline, and a new member of staff who was having difficulty fitting in. At home, things hadn't been much better. Jess still had the habitual sullen expression she'd worn since they arrived in Granite Springs, and Drew hadn't succeeded in improving their communication.

So it was a surprise when, over dinner on Friday, she paused, stared across at him with an expression that dared him to refuse and said, 'I'm seeing a friend tomorrow.'

'That's nice.' Drew held his breath waiting for more information.

It wasn't forthcoming. Jess continued eating as if nothing had happened.

'Does this friend have a name?' he asked, trying to sound nonchalant, as if this wasn't the news he'd been hoping for all year.

'Lucy. She doesn't have a mother either.'

Drew felt something stir in his gut. He knew who she meant. He was aware of the new girl who'd started this term, heard the staff talking about her, about how sad it was for her to lose her mother at such a young age. But Jess's mother hadn't died. She'd just spent two weeks with her.

'But your mother's not dead,' he said, shocked.

'She might as well be,' Jess muttered, dropping her cutlery onto the plate with a clatter, pushing her chair back, and leaving.

Drew gazed at her retreating back. He sighed. While he was glad Jess had finally made a friend, found someone in Granite Springs she could relate to, this wasn't what he'd hoped for. He'd anticipated her being drawn into a group of teenagers who would help her integrate into the community. To make friends with another girl who was an outsider, who was grieving for the loss of her mother, how could that help?

As he was clearing away the dishes – Jess's plate still half-full of uneaten spaghetti – Drew remembered he'd been meaning to contact his neighbours to return their hospitality. He'd waited till Jess was home in the hope she could perhaps make friends with Nick's son. It might be a forlorn hope, but he decided it was worth a try. He'd all but forgotten what it was like to be a teenager himself, but was surrounded by them every day, and, despite the advent of the internet and social media, young people hadn't changed that much.

Once the dishwasher was filled and turned on, he left the kitchen to seek the comfort of his study. There, he picked up his phone, holding it for a few moments before finally keying in Nick Kerr's number. It seemed crazy to be calling someone who only lived next door.

He heard the number ring several times, then Nick's voice, 'Hello. Nick Kerr.'

*

'We're having guests tonight,' Drew told Jess over breakfast on Saturday morning.

'Guests? I didn't think you had any friends here.' Jess spooned up the last morsels of her cereal and drained her glass of orange juice.

'I made a few while you were with your mum. I told you.' But Jess probably hadn't listened, considering anything he said would be boring.

'Oh, yeah?'

Drew tried not to show his exasperation at Jess's attitude. 'Our neighbours. You met them at The Riverside when you came back from LA last week. Nick Kerr, his wife, and their two children. At least, I expect their children to come too.' For the first time it occurred to him Nick's two might be just as resistant as Jess to this idea.

To his surprise, his daughter turned bright red. 'Well, I may not be here,' she said, pushing her chair back with such force it almost fell, and stomping out.

Drew dragged a hand through his hair. What had he done now?

He was checking the shopping list he'd hurriedly put together the night before when Jess reappeared. She was dressed in an outfit he hadn't seen before – a pair of purple jeans which were so ripped at the knees they looked as if they belonged in the garbage, and a loose grey long-sleeved tee-shirt tied at the waist. Her feet were encased in her usual ankle boots.

'Another new outfit?' he asked.

'Mum gave me money for clothes,' Jess said with a smirk. 'That was one good thing about the trip.' Her face brightened for a moment, before settling back into its customary sullen expression. 'Can I have…?' In a sudden about face, she gave him a wheedling look.

Drew sighed and reached into his pocket. He'd given Jess her pocket money this week already and they had a deal she had to do chores for any extra. But she'd found a friend. He was glad about that. 'Will you be back for lunch?'

'Probably not. Thanks, Dad.' She accepted the proffered note and tucked it into the bag slung over her shoulder.

'Make sure you're back in time to change for dinner,' he said, as she turned to leave.

Jess didn't reply. She merely rolled her eyes.

Drew could imagine what she was thinking. He heard the front door slam behind her, the house echoing with the sound.

*

The meat was marinating, the barbecue was fired up, and Drew was unpacking the pre-mixed salads he'd bought that afternoon, when Jess came downstairs. A very different Jess from the one who'd gone out that morning. This time, she was wearing a pair of leggings topped with a tight red top – no doubt another outfit from the States – which made her look older than her years. As she neared him, Drew could see she had taken time to apply eye makeup and lipstick. This was a first. He wasn't aware she even owned makeup. Doubtless another result of her visit with her mother. Drew wondered what Irene had been thinking – or had Jess been left to her own devices?

The plan to change Jess's hair had fallen by the wayside with her deciding she liked the colour after all. Drew wondered if Ryan Kerr's remark had anything to do with her change of mind.

Before he could make any comment, the doorbell sounded. 'That'll be them,' Drew said, seeing Jess take a step backwards.

On the doorstep, Nick and Kay stood side by side, the two children a step behind. The girl, who Nick introduced as Sam, was dressed in much the same way as Jess, while Nick's son Ryan's face held the same expression it had when they met in the restaurant. Drew wasn't quite sure how to react. He wasn't accustomed to meeting his students socially and felt as awkward as Ryan looked.

The choice of a barbecue turned out to have been a good one. This was lucky as Drew's cooking skills were limited. The steaks and sausages soon disappeared, and the cheesecake Kay brought along suffered a similar fate.

The food finished, Drew was returning to the barbecue area with another bottle of wine when he saw Sam whispering to her dad, and Jess and Ryan looking secretive. The three had been huddled together when Drew left.

Nick chuckled, glanced at Kay and said to Drew, 'It seems we've become boring. Sam's suggested the three youngsters…' His words brought a glare from his daughter. 'The three younger members of the group,' he corrected himself, 'go next door to watch a movie. We have Netflix and it seems you don't?'

'No, we don't.' It was a bone of contention between Drew and Jess, especially since she'd returned from visiting her mother. She might have disliked a lot about the trip, but there were things which she claimed to miss. The availability of streamed movies was one of those. Though she was able to watch on her iPad, Drew placed a strict curfew on its use and, as she was quick to remind him, it was nothing like a wide-screen television.

'Are you okay with that?' Nick asked. 'Sam and Ryan know what they're allowed to watch.'

'Dad!' Sam said, clearly considering she was too old to be told what to do.

Drew looked at Jess who had a pleading expression on her face, and at Ryan who was studiously avoiding all the adults' eyes. 'Okay by me,' he said.

The three were off in the blink of an eye, even closing the door quietly behind them. Drew filled the others' glasses and leant back in his chair.

'How old did you say Jess is?' Kay asked, after they'd spent a few moments enjoying the silence.

'Fifteen going on twenty-one,' Drew said with a sigh. 'Any advice will be gratefully received.'

'Not from me,' Kay said with a chuckle. 'I'm pretty new to parenting – step-parenting, I should say.'

'You're doing a great job,' Nick said, covering her hand with his. 'But I know exactly how you feel, Drew. I was in your place not so long ago. Both of mine chose me over their mother and it hasn't been easy. But, although they do visit her and her new husband during school holidays, they love Granite Springs.'

'I wish I could say the same for Jess. She still thinks of Melbourne as home. And she spends half her time texting the friends she left back there.'

'She hasn't made friends here? You came when?' Kay asked.

'The beginning of the year and no, till now she hasn't. But I think that may have changed. She spent the day with a girl who's new to town.' He frowned.

'That's good, isn't it?'

'Yes, though it's a girl who recently lost her mother. I'm not sure she's the best companion for Jess right now – or Jess for her.' He took a gulp of wine, embarrassed at having shared so much with people he hardly knew. But he and Nick did have a lot in common and he felt comfortable with the couple.

As the conversation moved on to the current state of the education system, Kay rose and collected their now empty glasses.

'There's no need,' Drew began, only to have her wave away his objections.

'You and Nick have a lot to talk about,' she said. 'It was a lovely meal, but I can see this discussion going on all night.' She chuckled and leaned over to give Nick a peck on the cheek. 'I'll check on the kids and send yours back, Drew, shall I?' she asked.

Drew nodded.

'She's a good woman,' Nick said, after she'd gone. 'I didn't think I'd marry again, was prepared to spend the rest of my life alone. Then Kay walked into my office and… It makes a difference, you know, having someone to talk to at the end of a hard day, to share things with, not to mention other advantages.'

'Your children seem to have accepted her.'

'Yes.' Nick gave a heartfelt sigh. 'She was a breath of fresh air after the way their mother and her new fellow treated them – particularly Ryan. They still see them of course, but this is their home.'

Jess returned soon afterwards, in a better mood than Drew had seen her in for some time. This dinner had been a good idea. Maybe Jess would come around to the idea of living here after all.

After Nick left and Jess was holed up in her room, Drew made himself a coffee and went into his study to finish some paperwork. But he found it difficult to concentrate. Nick's words kept coming back to him. He thought of how comfortable Nick and Kay were together, their small gestures of affection. It was a long time since he and Irene looked at each other, touched each other that way – long before Jake came on the scene. Maybe there had always been something flawed in their relationship.

Drew sighed. It was tough being a single parent – and lonely. But he didn't want Nick's solution. He wasn't going to risk being hurt again. And he was sure Jess wouldn't take kindly to the advent of another woman in his life, even if he was so inclined.

Twelve

'How are you coping?' Fran asked Marie.

The two women were seated in Marie's kitchen enjoying cups of herbal tea.

'I'm not sure, to be honest,' Marie said, clasping her cup in both hands. 'I feel I'm taking one step forward and two steps back. I never expected to have to do this. I have no experience as a parent. I've always been fun Aunt Marie, now it seems I'm cast as the equivalent of the wicked stepmother. I'm finding it hard to cope with a reluctant teenager while struggling with my own grief.'

'You're back at work?'

'This week. Yes. Now Lucy's at school. But Frank let me have today off. He said I needed a day to pull myself together. A day? I need a month at least. But the routine of the café helped me get through the week. Lucy seems to have settled in at school better than I hoped – she was so determined to hate it and everyone there.'

'Where is she today?'

'She's made a friend. I can't tell you how relieved I am. I know nothing about the girl, but Lucy seems to think they have things in common. She's gone to meet her today.' Marie's forehead creased.

'That's good, surely?'

'I guess so. It just seems so sudden. One minute she was full of resentment about her new school, the next she tells me she's found someone who understands her. I find it a bit odd, that's all. I don't even know the girl's name.'

'I'm sure it's nothing to worry about. Can't you remember when you were her age?'

Marie grimaced. 'That was a long time ago, Fran. I think that's the trouble. I'm completely out of practice in dealing with the day to day stuff Dee coped with.' Her eyes misted over as they always did when she thought of her sister. 'I knew the holiday Lucy, the one on her best behaviour. Now I'm dealing with a girl who has not only lost her mother, but her home, her friends, her entire way of life.'

'How did it go last Saturday. Didn't you say you were both going over to Canberra?'

Marie closed her eyes, remembering. 'It was awful. I felt Dee everywhere. The place smelt like her – her perfume intermingling with her makeup. It must have been worse for Lucy. She just wandered around picking up things and putting them down again. It felt wrong to pack up Dee's clothes. She had such nice things.'

'You wouldn't…'

'No! Apart from the fact we've always been different sizes and had different tastes, I couldn't bear to wear anything of hers. There is a scarf I did bring back after checking with Lucy. And she picked out a few of her mother's things as keepsakes. We packed all of her jewellery, of course, and her books and personal items. Lucy may not want them now, but in years to come… It was so difficult, Fran. You can't imagine.' She paused, remembering Fran's own story. 'Oh, maybe you can.'

'No, Marie. My experience of loss was completely different from yours. But I do understand how it feels to lose someone you love. It's difficult to believe at first, then the awfulness hits without warning at the most unexpected times. I can only say it gets easier with time, but that's of no help to you right now.'

'And I have to be there for Lucy, too. I'll be glad when the house in Canberra is sold. Despite the mortgage, there should be quite a bit left over for Lucy. We can put it into a term deposit for when she's older.'

'How is Lucy? She's made a friend, you say?'

'Yes, but…' Marie bit her lip. 'It sounds as if the girl is another loner. I'd rather Lucy had found herself in a group of friends – something to help her become part of the school community, not…' She shook her head. 'Oh, listen to me! I should be glad she's found someone she can relate to, talk to, wants to spend time with. It's just… she's only fifteen, Fran. It's a lot for her to have to cope with.'

'Mmm.'

'How about you? All is well with you and Owen?'

'Great! I never imagined I could feel this way again, and with Owen of all people.' Fran shook her head in disbelief. 'But here we are, and we're about to be grandparents. Pia's such a lovely girl. We've become friends. I'd never try to replace her mother. You're lucky that way, I guess. You already have a connection with Lucy. She loves you.'

'As her aunt – not as a mother substitute. But you're right. I've known Lucy all her life. We've both been thrown into this situation without any warning and we have to make the best of it. Frank's been wonderful, the way he's helped out. And Lucy loves her Uncle Frank. I sometimes think she's fonder of him than she is of me.'

Marie saw a speculative look appear in Fran's eyes. 'You and Frank – there's no possibility of your getting back together? I've always been amazed how the two of you have managed to maintain a friendship, work together, still act like family.' She tipped her head on one side.

'No. That part of our relationship is over. As you said – friends.' But even as she spoke, Marie remembered how Frank had dropped everything to be with her; how comforting his arms had been around her; how Dee had believed he still cared for her. 'No,' she said again, wondering if she was trying to convince herself, rather than Fran.

*

'Did you have a nice time?' Marie asked Lucy as she strolled into the house in the late afternoon, carrying several bags. 'Did you have something to eat?'

'We ate at the new McDonald's on Main Street. And, yes, it was good. Jess's been here since January and she thinks Granite Springs sucks.'

So, her name was Jess. That was a start.

'I was about to make tea and there's carrot cake leftover from earlier. Fran came around this morning.'

But Lucy didn't show any interest in Marie's day. She started out the door without replying.

'Looks like you did some shopping. Buy anything nice?' Marie tried again, determined not to let Lucy off with being rude. This wasn't the girl she knew.

Lucy stopped in her tracks and turned reluctantly, dropping her bags on the table. 'I bought a couple of tops. Jess has been to the States and knows what's trending there. She's pretty chill. Then we went to the library and I joined, since it seems I'm going to be staying here. Jess is into this author I haven't read. I've borrowed the first in her series. It sounds lit. I need to check if Ella has read them.'

Marie tried to keep a straight face, to avoid showing her surprise at this flow of information. She fixed two cups of the lemon and ginger tea she was making and cut two thick slices of carrot cake, pushing one of each towards Lucy in the hope she'd take the hint. It worked.

Lucy pulled out a chair and sat down, clearly forgetting her rush to go upstairs to her room. She greedily took a bite of the cake. 'Oh, Aunt Marie, this is yummy. I wish you could show Mum how to make it like this.' Then she stopped, a hand to her mouth, realising what she'd said.

Marie almost broke down but reached across the table to take Lucy's hand in hers. 'It's okay to forget what happened, and it's okay to talk about your mum. Dee was never much of a cook. I seem to have inherited all the baking genes, though working in the café certainly helped me hone my skills. Needs must, I suppose.'

'Could you… teach me?'

'To bake? I'd love to. It's really quite easy and I find it relaxing.' Delighted at this change in Lucy, Marie decided to tread carefully. 'I do run classes at the café – or I could teach you here.'

'Here, please! When can we start?' Lucy gulped down her tea and took a last bite of cake.

'Anytime.' Surprised how quickly Lucy's mood changed, Marie decided to take advantage of it. 'How about tomorrow morning? We could begin with brownies. I need to make a batch to take to the café on Monday. I usually do some of the baking here and some there.'

'Okay.' Seemingly having forgotten her earlier distress, Lucy collected her bags and headed for the door again, but this time there was a suggestion of the old Lucy in her manner.

Marie exhaled loudly and put a hand to her heart. Maybe things were about to change. But there was one more hurdle to cross. She hadn't been able to contact the man Dee had been seeing from the dating site – Tony she said his name was; none of the women friends she'd spoken to knew who he was. Damn her sister for being so secretive! It had been over two weeks; the poor man must be wondering what on earth had happened. Marie was going to have to take a step she was hoping to avoid. She was going to have to check her sister's phone.

Thirteen

The school term was barely three weeks old, and already Drew was close to tearing out his hair. He'd been approached by more than one of his staff with claims more students than usual were disappearing behind the sports sheds at break time and that the smoke rising from there was not from tobacco. Of course, the smokes were quickly extinguished as soon as an adult loomed into sight, and the groups of students dispersed just as quickly. Drew had seen this happen before. But that had been in a school in inner-city Melbourne. It wasn't something he expected to come across in Granite Springs.

He sighed as he prepared once again to harangue the students at today's assembly. It was his least favourite task. He much preferred to leave discipline matters to his deputy. Alison Griffith was as fierce as her name implied – he'd been amused to discover Griffith stood for *fighting chief* in Welsh – a fact Alison informed him of when he first arrived and proudly boasted to all and sundry. As a result, he'd been wary of crossing her.

'Ready, Drew?' Alison popped her head through his open office door. 'I can do it if you'd rather.'

'Thanks Alison. I appreciate the offer. But this is one I should do myself.' He hoisted himself to his feet and joined her to make their way to the school hall which was already heaving with the noisy presence of just over a thousand teenagers. When the staff filed onto the stage, followed by Alison, Drew coming up in the rear, the noise reduced to a muttering which finally ceased completely.

Alison walked forward to recite the welcome to country, the recorded music for the school song began, and the thousand voices joined together in the uplifting words which students of Granite High had been singing for generations. When they fell silent again, there was the usual murmuring and rustling as they all sat down.

Drew walked up to the podium, his eyes searching the throng for the pink hair which identified Jess, and which stood out from the other less distinctive heads in the room. He spotted her, sitting with the rest of her year, leaning towards another girl whose blonde hair fell to her shoulders. He wondered if his daughter knew how easily he could recognise her even from this distance.

He cleared his throat and began. But as he spoke, he could see the glazed eyes in the front row and hear the subdued whispers from around the room. They'd heard it all before. Why did he bother? He did it in the hope that if he repeated the message often enough, it might sink in. If he could save even one of them from a life of addiction it would be worth it. Drew knew the stats for those who progressed from marijuana to harder drugs and didn't want that fate for any of his students – not if he could help it.

'Glad that's over.' Drew exhaled as the students filed noisily out of the auditorium, and the staff went off to meet their first class of the day. He was left on an empty stage with Alison and the school caretaker who was packing away the sound equipment.

'Do you have a minute, Drew?' Alison asked, as they walked together back to the administration block.

'Something else the matter?' he asked. Surely one problem at a time was enough?

She waited till they were back in his office. 'May I take a seat?'

Drew gestured to a chair and settled himself behind his desk to put a barrier between them. He leant his elbows on the desk and steepled his fingers. 'Well?'

Alison fidgeted awkwardly in her seat. Unusually for her, she seemed to be having trouble in starting to speak.

Drew looked impatiently towards his computer. He had a lot to do this morning. How long was this going to take?

'It's about Jess,' she began hesitatingly.

Drew sighed. What now?

'Her appearance… It's… It's not what we expect from our girls at Granite Springs. I wondered if you'd like me to have a word with her. I'd be happy to step in. I know it can't be easy for you, with her mother…' Alison's voice trailed away as she obviously interpreted Drew's icy glare. 'I'm sorry if you think…'

Drew almost laughed at the expression on his deputy's face. He'd never seen her so discomfited. But, then, she'd never before tried to interfere in his personal life. 'Is her work suffering?'

'No. Her grades are still up there. She – and the new girl, Lucy Cunningham – they're both bright girls. I just thought perhaps I could…'

Drew glared at her again. 'I think you've said enough, Alison.'

'I'm sorry if I spoke out of turn, Drew. I was only trying to help.' She sniffed, as if by pretending to be upset, she could gain his sympathy. 'I'll leave you to think about it. As I said, I'm always happy to help.' She gave a small smile and left.

Drew removed his glasses and gazed into space. What had all that been about? There was more here than Jess's pink hair and short skirt. The hair would grow out and her uniform wasn't any shorter – or tighter – than most of the other senior girls. Was it Alison's misguided attempt to gain some sort of intimacy with him? Surely not? When he took up this position, he was warned he'd be fair game for designing women. But Alison? No, he couldn't believe it of her. But that smile before she left – she almost simpered. Drew sighed as he replaced his glasses, fired up his computer and tried to forget the incident. But the idea his deputy, a woman he had to work with every day, might imagine there could be any more between them than a professional relationship, kept interrupting his thoughts.

*

Jess walked into Drew's study, twisting a strand of hair around one finger. She picked up a piece of paper from his desk, gave it a fleeting glance then dropped it again. 'That was pretty rough at assembly this morning,' she said. 'Marijuana isn't like ice or other stuff. The guys thought you went overboard with your warnings. It's not like they're addicted or anything. And they're not dealing the stuff.'

Drew sighed and put down the book he'd been trying to read. He took off his glasses. 'That's the whole point, Jess. And if it's around, then someone is dealing. If not in the school, then in the town. And that's when the police will get involved. So, if you know anything…'

'How would I? I should have known you'd take this line. Can't you ever forget you're the school principal?'

'Jess, let's…'

'I hate you!' She flounced out, leaving Drew gazing after her in dismay.

He'd done it again, managed to alienate Jess without even trying. He picked up his book but couldn't concentrate. Perhaps Alison was right. Maybe he did need help in dealing with Jess. But not from her. He'd put Jess's belligerent attitude and sullen behaviour down to the difficulty she was having dealing with him and Irene separating and the move to Granite Springs, telling himself she'd soon settle down. And it seemed she was doing that. She'd found a friend – one friend, but it was a start – and even Alison admitted her grades were good. His mind ranged around his acquaintances trying to think who he could discuss Jess with. He still hadn't come to a conclusion when his phone rang.

Pleased to be interrupted, Drew picked it up to see his neighbour's number. Of course. Nick Kerr. He had teenagers too. He'd understand. Though Drew didn't imagine Nick had experienced such difficult behaviour as Jess was exhibiting right now.

'Nick, good to hear from you.' Drew heard Nick chuckle.

'I hope you'll still think so when you hear why I've called. I need a favour.'

'Yes?'

There was a pause, then Nick spoke again. 'Kay and I are going away this coming weekend and we wondered if you'd mind keeping an eye on things here. Not childminding you understand – Sam and Ryan would have a fit if they thought we didn't trust them. But it would set our minds at rest to know you're there in case anything goes wrong.'

'Of course. No worries.' Drew couldn't imagine the Kerrs' two getting up to anything. From what he'd seen of them, they had their heads screwed on, unlike Jess. He took a deep breath. 'Can I ask for one in return? I know I spoke about Jess with you before, but I really need some advice.'

'Sure. Look, why don't we have a drink together. Can you leave her on her own?'

'No problem about that for an hour or so.' Drew thought Jess probably wouldn't even realise he was gone if he didn't let her know. 'When did you have in mind?'

'No time like the present. In half an hour? We can take my car. Meet you in our driveway.'

Telling Jess he was going out for a bit meant going upstairs and into her bedroom. She ignored his knock on the door, only glancing up briefly with a frown when he put his head around it. She merely nodded absently, moving to the sound on her iPod and refocussing on her iPhone. Drew stood in the doorway for a few moments, till Jess raised her eyes again.

'Anything else?' she asked, in a tone bordering on rudeness.

'Maybe you could tidy this place up sometime?' he suggested, seeing the piles of discarded garments, the scattered sweet papers and the dirty mugs. No wonder she normally refused to let him in.

'Yeah, yeah.' She looked back down at her phone as it pinged with a message.

Drew closed the door and went back downstairs.

By the time he reached the next-door driveway, Nick was already in his car. Drew hopped in and they set off. Apart from a desultory conversation about the weather, the men barely spoke till they reached the club.

Once inside, the noise hit them like a blow. Thursday was clearly a popular night.

'Pizza night,' Nick said by way of explanation. 'I should have remembered. I used to come here with my ex. They have a special woodfired pizza. It's pretty good. But I expect you've eaten.'

Drew nodded. But the pizza sounded better than the tuna bake he'd tried to master. He was learning to cook, but it was a slow process plagued with many failures and burnt offerings, much to Jess's disgust.

They pushed their way through to the bar to order two beers, then back again to claim a free table by the window overlooking the eighteenth green.

'Now, how can I help?' Nick asked, when both had taken a first swig of beer.

Drew toyed with a beer mat, standing it on its end then spinning it around, before beginning, but when he did, it all poured out – the drug problem at school, Jess's rudeness, her apparent disregard for him, even his loneliness.

Nick was such a good listener, Drew found himself opening up to him as he never had to anyone else. 'Sorry,' he said at last, 'I didn't mean to unload on you like this. I don't know how you can help, but I'm at my wits' end with Jess. I don't seem to be able to get through to her. And her mother's no use. Even if she wasn't at the opposite side of the world, Irene was always more interested in her own life than in me or Jess. Sorry,' he said again, dragging a hand through his hair.

'Let's take your drug issue first.' Nick frowned. 'It's not unique to Granite Springs High. We're having the same problem at uni. It's harder to police there. They're all adults, and Sam tells me both marijuana and some harder drugs are readily available. So, it's no surprise it's percolated down into the schools.'

'What's to be done?'

'Not a lot we can do on our own. Your assembly sounds like a good start. I've talked with the local police about it and they put a guy on campus for a while.'

'And?'

'It appeared to die down while he was there, but I think it only went underground and has bubbled up again recently. They can't seem to discover how it's coming into town and who the dealers are. Not much help, I know.' He pulled on his beard. 'You say Jess defended her peers. That's to be expected at her age. Ryan would no doubt do the same if asked. Their friends are more important to them than we are – until they get into trouble.'

'I can't imagine your two getting into trouble.'

'You'd be surprised. They've not always been as squeaky clean as you saw. Sam gave me more than a few sleepless nights.'

'What changed? She seems like a responsible young woman now.'

'She is – I think. We can never be sure what goes on in their minds. But Kay was what made the difference in my case.'

'Kay?' Drew slumped back in his chair, feeling defeated. He didn't have a Kay to provide him with a solution. 'What did she do?' he asked without much hope.

'She tried to make me see things from Sam's point of view; to remember what it was like to be a teenager; to try to develop empathy.' He gave a laugh. 'Empathy for a seventeen-year-old – can you imagine?'

'But it worked?'

'Seemed to. She's turned out all right so far. Though I don't know how I'll cope if she heads off to Canberra next year and is out of sight. I guess Kay will calm me then, too.' He paused. 'And wait till your Jess discovers boys.'

Drew blanched.

'Unless she already has. Some start early. She's fifteen?'

Drew nodded. Boys! He hadn't considered that prospect. Hell, bringing up a girl wasn't easy; the path was fraught with all sorts of obstacles. He thought of what Nick said about remembering what it was like to be a teenager. He remembered what he and his mates were like – the sly comments, the dirty jokes, the snide asides. Was Jess fair game for all of those with her pink hair and the outfits she chose?

Nick seemed to know what he was thinking. 'The boys aren't all bad. I don't think Ryan is, but then as parents we're the last to know.' He took a long draught from his glass. 'Getting back to your daughter, is there anyone you could ask, talk to – a woman friend?'

Drew shook his head. The image of Alison Griffith appeared in his mind's eye only to be dismissed immediately. She was the last person whose advice he'd seek. Since coming to Granite Springs, he'd studiously avoided any women he came across, determined not to become involved in a relationship ever again. 'What about Kay?' he asked.

'My Kay?' Nick appeared surprised. 'I don't know how she'd feel, but I can ask her. She can certainly speak from experience. In addition to taking on Sam, she has a daughter of her own. That's where we're going this weekend – to Brisbane to visit her daughter and grandson. Little Noah's a great kid, only six, so no problems as yet.'

For a moment, Drew envied Nick, envied his contentment, his certainty about his life, the new family which seemed to have blended so seamlessly with his.

'Thanks,' he said. 'Maybe when you get back.'

When they drew up outside Nick's house again, the door opened and, in the glow from the hallway, Drew could see Kay waiting for

Nick, a welcoming smile on her face. 'You're lucky,' he said with a heartfelt sigh.

Nick turned towards him with a smile. 'Sometimes we have to make our own luck. I was in your position once.'

Nick's words rang in Drew's ears as he made his way into his own home. But Nick's solution had been to get involved in another relationship. That wasn't for him.

Fourteen

In the event, it hadn't been too difficult. A check on Dee's phone revealed a series of missed calls and a flurry of texts. But now Marie had the information, she was at a loss how to use it. One didn't suddenly call or text someone to tell them their loved one had died – supposing their relationship had gone that far. Marie chewed the inside of her cheek as she tried to decide what to do. How she wished Dee had been more forthcoming about the guy she was seeing. She only said he was called Tony – no surname. And he was worried. His texts indicated there was more to the relationship than casual friendship. And Lucy was right, he did sound like a good guy.

'Something on your mind?' Frank's eyes were filled with concern, and Marie realised she'd been talking to herself. It was a bad habit, one she must try to overcome.

She turned from the cakes she was arranging in their glass cabinet and wrinkled her brow. 'I checked Dee's phone last night.'

'Oh!' Frank made a move to take her in his arms.

Marie looked around warily and moved out of his reach. 'Not here.' Only a few tables were filled, and their occupants were busily chatting, but Marie didn't want to be seen hugging her ex.

Unfazed, Frank asked, 'What did you discover?'

'I found messages and missed calls from the guy she was seeing, but not much else. I suppose I could have asked Lucy, but she's been so upset I didn't want to make her worse by reminding her of what might have been. Dee was going to introduce them when they returned to

Canberra. I don't know how to handle this, Frank. I can't tell him about Dee by a text or phone call, but I have no other way of getting in touch.'

'Hell! If I'd known, I'd have invited him to the funeral.'

'Sorry, I was so spaced out. I should have mentioned him.'

'What would you like to do now?'

'I need to talk with him, tell him face to face.'

'Well then.' Frank folded his arms and put on what Marie used to call his thinking expression.

She waited.

Finally, he said, 'Could you perhaps let him know something has happened, be unspecific and arrange to meet him?'

'Go to Canberra? I could do that. But what if he thinks…'

'What? He can't imagine anything worse than the truth.'

'No,' Marie sighed. 'You're right.'

'Text him now. Tell him you'll be in Canberra tomorrow and arrange to meet for coffee.'

'Coffee?' Could Marie tell this Tony about her sister's death over coffee?

'What else? It might be difficult to invite yourself round to his place… or there's Dee's.'

Dee's house, the house that still smelt of Dee, where Dee's presence still seemed to lurk in every room, every corner; the house Marie had hoped never to have to enter again. Although she knew she'd have to go there once it sold to arrange to get rid of the furniture, she'd put that task to the back of her mind.

'No, I guess I should meet him somewhere neutral. But if I go tomorrow, it means I'll miss another Saturday. I'll be letting you down.'

'You could never do that.' Frank's eyes crinkled in a familiar way.

'I suppose I could meet him then. I'll have to tell Lucy.' The thought of telling Lucy was a problem. It was difficult to gauge the girl's moods.

'Do you want me to…?'

'No!' Marie shook her head to emphasise the point. Frank had been wonderful, but she needed to stand on her own two feet. At the back of her mind was Dee's comment about Frank – that he still had feelings for Marie – feelings of more than the friendship she felt for him. It was stupid, of course. They had an agreement. But Dee had always been more perceptive than she had, and Marie couldn't dismiss the niggle of worry that her sister might be right.

'Do it now,' Frank suggested.

Slowly, Marie went to where she'd stashed her bag and took out Dee's phone. For a few moments she held it, thinking of her sister, then she opened it up to the last of Tony's texts. Taking her own phone out, she entered his number into the address book and, her fingers fumbling on the keypad, typed a brief message.

*

'I have to go to Canberra tomorrow, Luce.' Marie held her breath waiting for her niece's response.

'To our house?'

'No. I've managed to contact your mother's friend – Tony. I need to meet him, to speak to him…'

'Oh! Of course. He doesn't know?'

'It seems not. He's been trying to contact your mum and I feel I need to see him, to tell him.'

'Do you want me to come? I'd like to meet him.'

'I think not.' It was going to be a difficult enough conversation without Lucy's presence. 'Maybe you can see your friend, or help your Uncle Frank in the café?' This last was a suggestion Frank made and one Marie wasn't sure she agreed with.

Lucy's eyes brightened. 'Can I invite Jess here?'

'Of course. What will you do?'

Lucy looked at Marie as if she thought she was mad. 'Hang out, watch a movie, I don't know.'

Marie tried to remember what it had been like to be fifteen. She'd enjoyed just spending time with her friends. They'd talk for hours – mostly about boys – play music and, she remembered with regret, close the bedroom door on Dee who always wanted to join in on whatever the older girls were doing. 'Okay. We can make brownies before I leave and…'

'I know how to bake them now, Aunt Marie. Can Jess and I make them while you're gone?'

'I suppose so.' Did Marie really want to let two teenagers loose in her kitchen? Probably not, but it would be churlish to refuse and what harm could they do? Visions of returning to a kitchen strewn with dirty dishes, spilt chocolate and more flashed before her eyes, only to be dismissed. Surely Lucy had more sense than to make the sort of mess she was imagining?

'Good.' Lucy began to text furiously, leaving Marie to wonder if she'd been manipulated.

*

Drew was trying to write a report when Jess wandered into his study, clasping her iPhone.

'I'm spending the day with Lucy tomorrow,' she said. 'I may even stay overnight.'

Drew looked up, startled. 'You barely know her. Have you met her parents?'

'Duh! She doesn't have any. She lives with her aunt.'

How could he have been so stupid? Of course, Drew knew Lucy Cunningham – he recalled that was her name – had lost her mother. If she'd moved to Granite Springs to live with her aunt, it followed there was no father on the scene. 'Her aunt, then?'

'Not yet. Lucy says her aunt's going to Canberra today, so we'll have the house to ourselves.' She didn't add, 'with no boring adults to bother us.' She didn't have to. Drew could read her expression.

Assuming the aunt would be there when Jess arrived, he said, 'Okay, but let me have the phone number.'

'Dad! Don't you trust me? I'm not a little kid you need to check up on. I'm only going to spend the day with a friend. Isn't that what you've been wanting me to do – make friends?'

Feeling suitably rebuked, Drew nodded and drew a reluctant Jess into a hug. 'I love you, sweetheart. I'm only concerned for your safety.'

Jess stayed in his grasp for a moment, then pulled away. 'What harm can I come to in this sleepy town, Dad? It's not like Melbourne.'

She was right. Perhaps he shouldn't be concerned. But, since Irene left, Drew had felt the weight of the responsibility of being a sole parent. He'd never quite appreciated it before. Now he had a better understanding of the parents he had to deal with, many of whom were in a similar situation.

Drew went back to his report, trying to forget his inadequacies as a parent. He knew Irene would be no better, and that Jess was better off with him than with her mother and her new fellow in LA. But he wished he had more understanding of the teenage mind – *her* teenage mind. The conversation with Nick Kerr still bothered him.

What was Jess keeping from him? Was she really planning to spend the day with Lucy or had she some other agenda in mind? If she was going to be gone for the day and perhaps overnight, should he contact this girl's aunt to check? His hand reached for the phone and stopped mid-air. What was it Jess said about trust? She was right. She wasn't a child. Difficult though it might be, he had to trust her.

Fifteen

On the drive to Canberra next morning, Marie tried to work out what she was going to say, but nothing she thought of seemed appropriate. Finally deciding to play it by ear, she turned on the radio in an attempt to distract her from the meeting ahead.

She'd chosen to meet Tony in the café in the National Gallery. It might seem a strange place to choose, she thought, but it had been a favourite of Dee's. And Marie knew its location, overlooking the sculpture garden, would provide an atmosphere to help calm her shattered nerves.

The first to arrive, Marie ordered camomile tea to help her relax and had just taken her first sip when a tall, dark-haired man wearing grey pants and a sports jacket walked up to her, his face red with annoyance.

Without giving her time to greet him, he launched into an attack. 'I'm Tony Clarke, I suppose you must be Dee's sister. What's happened? I don't know what you and Dee are playing at. If she doesn't want to see me again, why can't she tell me to my face? Why does she have to send you to do her dirty work?'

Stunned, Marie took a deep breath. There was no good way to handle this. 'I think you'd better sit down. What can I get you? Coffee?'

Tony Clarke seemed to suddenly realise all was not well. 'A short black,' he said, sliding into the seat opposite, a crease forming between his eyes.

Marie felt his eyes on her as she placed his order. When she returned to the table, he appeared to have calmed down. 'Has something happened to Dee?' he asked. 'I need to see her.'

Marie looked down at her clenched hands, then raised her eyes to meet his. 'I'm sorry,' she said, her eyes filling with tears. 'Dee, she…' Her voice broke.

'Dee?' His voice rose. 'She's not…? She can't be…' He gazed wildly around, then focussed on Marie who was trying to stem her tears. 'What happened?' he asked, his voice slurred, his shoulders sagging. 'Was she in an accident?'

'It was so sudden.' Speaking about it, Marie relived those moments in the hospital, the doctor's words, Dee's lifeless body. 'An aneurysm.' She wasn't able to say any more.

They sat in silence for what seemed like forever. Then Tony roused himself. 'I loved her,' he said. 'We hadn't known each other long, but we knew we had something special. I can't believe…' He tried to pick up his cup, but his hand was shaking too much. 'I'm sorry.' He drew a hand across his eyes, and Marie saw he was trying not to cry, too.

Her heart went out to him. Dee had been right. He was special. How Marie wished they could have met under different circumstances, that Dee was with them. Dee with her quick smile, a sparkle in her eyes, showing off her new man to her big sister.

'Her daughter?' he asked. 'We never met, but Dee talked about her so much I feel I know her.'

'Lucy's with me.'

'Right. Well.'

There didn't seem to be any more to say. It wasn't an occasion for small talk. They stood up together. Marie had to look up to meet his eyes. Tony was tall. He'd have been taller than Dee, too.

'I'd like… Could I have something of hers – a memento?' he asked, haltingly.

'Of course.'

'Thanks for coming all the way here to tell me.'

'It was the least I could do. I'm sorry it took me so long to contact you. We only had a private funeral for Lucy's sake.' Marie shifted uncomfortably at the memory of that dreadful day which had passed almost in a blur.

'It must be hard for you, too.'

'Yes.' He could have no idea. No one could. Except perhaps Frank, who knew both of them, had done for years. Suddenly Marie longed for his comforting presence.

Before parting, they exchanged addresses, and Marie promised to send him a small keepsake. She'd discuss what that would be with Lucy.

Now it was over, Marie was restless. The conversation – the entire meeting – had exhausted her. Leaving the café, Marie decided to wander around the gallery, her feet taking her to a painting she knew Dee loved. *Hot Wind*, painted by James Condon in 1889, was a soulful image evoking the bright light of an Australian summer, the female form on an Australian beach said to reflect the artist's sense of mortality. It seemed fitting to visit it today.

Finally, Marie turned away and blinked. Time was passing. She should get back before Lucy began to wonder where she was.

*

Back home, Marie pushed open the door to be greeted by the delicious aroma of chocolate brownies. After the afternoon she'd had, it was comforting to return to normal. 'Lucy!' she called. But there was no reply. Going into the kitchen, Marie found a tray of brownies on the table, the gaps showing Lucy and her friend had already made inroads into them. The mixing bowl was sitting on the draining board along with dirty plates and glasses and there was a pool of chocolate on the top of the stove.

Marie sighed, but it could have been worse. 'Lucy!' she called again, making her way upstairs to where Lucy's bedroom door stood wide open. There was no sign of the two girls. It was almost seven o'clock. She'd spent longer in the gallery than she intended. It was dark outside, had been for some time. Where could they have gone?

Marie went back to the kitchen deciding, against her better judgement, to clear up the mess. She knew she should wait till Lucy returned and make her do it, but it was easier to do it herself. She'd talk about responsibility to Lucy later. It seemed as if she was always having to act the disciplinarian with the girl. Had it been as difficult for Dee? Lucy always seemed well-behaved on their visits, even offering to help on occasions. Was Marie doing something wrong?

The dishes were washed and put away, and Marie was starting to prepare dinner, when it occurred to her to check her phone. When she did, she cursed herself for not doing so sooner. She should have known Lucy would use a text to communicate. There it was, sent while Marie was on her way home from Canberra.

Hi Aunt M, Me and Jess are going to a party. One of the guys from school. Won't be late. Lx

As Marie read the message, contradictory emotions flashed through her. On the one hand, she was pleased Lucy had been invited to a party – it showed she was beginning to be accepted by the other girls. On the other, there was a niggle of worry. A party? Where? Who was holding it? She checked her phone again to make sure she hadn't missed vital information. But the message was as brief as before.

Marie hesitated. Should she reply, ask the questions buzzing around in her head? Or would doing so alienate Lucy further?

By ten o'clock, Marie was almost at her wits' end. How could she have let Dee down like this? She should have agreed to Frank's suggestion, should never have left Lucy with a girl Marie had never met. It wasn't late by most standards, but later than Marie was comfortable with. They were only fifteen. Her mind was going around in circles as she tried to avoid thinking of all the things which might have happened – an accident, an assault, the list went on.

Sixteen

When Marie's phone rang, she grabbed it gratefully, disappointed it wasn't Lucy yet relieved to hear Frank's voice.

'I was thinking about you all afternoon, thought you might have called to let me know how it went.'

Marie's mind went blank. Then she remembered. Her trip to Canberra. With her worry about Lucy, she had almost forgotten the meeting with Tony Clarke. Now it came into sharp focus again. 'Oh,' she said. 'It went as well as could be expected. After he got over his initial annoyance it was me not Dee meeting him, he calmed down. He seems nice. He would have made a good match for Dee if things had been different.'

'What's wrong?'

Marie should have known Frank would detect the worry in her voice, worry that had nothing to do with Tony Clarke. They hadn't lived together for all those years without being able to gauge each other's state of mind. 'Lucy,' she said, glad to be able to get it off her chest to someone who'd understand. Why hadn't she called Frank earlier? Because she was too independent and pig headed – she answered her own question.

'What's my favourite niece done now?'

'She's gone to a party.' As she said it, Marie realised how ridiculous she sounded, a sentiment echoed by Frank's response.

'That's good, isn't it? You were worried about her not fitting in, missing her old friends.'

'Ye…es.'

'But?'

'It's ten o'clock on a Saturday night, and I don't know where she is. What would Dee think?'

Frank chuckled. 'Are you more worried about Lucy or your sister's opinion of you?'

'I…' Marie didn't know. She tried to think how Dee would react and failed. What was wrong with her? She, who always saw the glass half full, who helped others find a silver lining, was worried sick about her niece going to a party.

'Would you like me to come over?'

Marie sighed. There was nothing she'd like more, but she was aware of relying too much on Frank's good nature since Dee died. It was high time she took hold of herself and got back to normal. 'No. It'll be fine. You're right. It's only a party. I expect she'll be home soon. Thanks for listening, Frank, and for helping me see sense.'

But despite her best intentions, Marie couldn't settle to concentrate on anything and found herself switching channels on the TV to find something to attract her interest. She was deciding between an episode of a new Nordic noir thriller and the rerun of an old comedy program when the phone rang again. She grasped it, relieved when she saw Lucy's face on the screen.

'Luce! At last!'

'Aunt Marie.' Lucy's voice was subdued. She sounded as if she'd been crying. Marie's stomach clenched. She knew something had happened. Frank was wrong.

'Where are you?' Marie switched off the television and rose, ready to go to pick her up. She could find out what had occurred later.

'I'm… at the police station.'

That was the last thing Marie had expected to hear. Of all the possibilities swirling through her head, Lucy being arrested wasn't one of them. She felt the blood drain from her face and took a deep breath.

'Can you come? They said I need an adult here before I can leave.'

'I'm coming right away.' As she spoke, Marie was slipping on her shoes and grabbing her bag and keys. 'I love you, Luce,' she said, as she rushed out of the house.

The drive to the police station passed in a blur. Marie couldn't believe her niece had been arrested. She was only fifteen. What could she possibly have done? By the time she drew up outside the redbrick building with its large blue sign, she'd almost convinced herself it was a mistake.

But when she walked in, to be led into a small interview room where Lucy and another girl – this one with bright pink hair – were seated together holding hands, their faces blotched, their eyes red and puffy from crying, Marie knew it was all too real.

'Ms Cunningham?' The policewoman who was seated at right-angles to the girls rose to greet her.

Marie nodded and gazed towards Lucy who met her eyes for a brief moment before looking down again.

'I'm WPC Penny Carstairs. Please take a seat.' She gestured to two chairs opposite Lucy and her friend.

Mesmerised, Marie did as she was told.

'I understand Jess's father is on his way. With your agreement I'll wait till he arrives before we discuss this incident.'

Incident? There had been an incident? Had someone assaulted the two girls? Was that why they were here? Were they innocent victims?

'What…?'

The door opened again, and a tall man strode in, his thick head of white hair ruffled as if he'd been repeatedly thrusting his hands through it. He was wearing dark-rimmed glasses and had a tense expression, his lips tightly pressed together.

Marie saw Lucy give him a scared look.

'Take a seat, Mr Hamilton,' the police officer said.

With barely a glance at Marie he took the seat next to her. 'What's all this about?' he asked, ignoring Marie and glaring at the two girls.

'I'm afraid Lucy and Jess were discovered to be in possession of several grams of marijuana and showing signs of being under the influence of alcohol. Since they are both underage, we immediately contacted – or had them make contact – with their parent in your case, Mr Hamilton, and guardian in yours, Ms Cunningham. Can you confirm that is correct?' She paused, looking at both of them.

The man nodded and for the first time made eye contact with Marie.

She almost gasped to see the hostility in his expression. Then she digested what the policewoman had said. Drugs and alcohol. 'Luce, is this true?' But she didn't need to ask. Lucy's hangdog expression said it all.

The man – he was called Mr Hamilton, Marie remembered – spoke again, this time his words were angry and directed at Marie. 'What on earth were you doing, letting two fifteen-year-olds make free with drugs and alcohol? Have you no sense of responsibility, no sense at all? I can't believe you'd allow them access to illegal substances. What were you thinking? Where were you when they were indulging in all this?'

'How dare you!' Marie felt a flood of anger flow through her. 'Your daughter…' Marie began, looking at the girl whose pink hair was hanging in stringy strands, sticking to her tearstained cheeks.

'My daughter went for a sleepover with your niece.'

'Sleepover? I don't know anything about any sleepover. I was out all afternoon and when I returned the two of them had gone. I got a text about a party.'

'If I can intervene?' It was WPC Penny Carstairs' calm voice. 'The girls were arrested at a party along with several other, older, teenagers. Since it's a first offence for both of them, we mean to release them with a stern warning.' She turned her gaze on the girls whose eyes showed their relief at being let off so lightly.

'They can go?' Marie asked, unable to believe her ears.

'Yes. But they should count themselves lucky,' the police officer said, rising.

The four left the police station, the door swinging shut behind them. Once outside, Mr Hamilton turned to face Marie. 'I hope this is the last we hear of this. In future I don't believe Jess can remain friends with Lucy. I know they'll see each other in school, but it must stop there.'

'Dad!' Jess seemed to find her voice. 'It wasn't Lucy's fault.'

'Enough!' Her father took her by the shoulder and led her off.

'I'm sorry, Aunt Marie. We didn't know there would be drugs at the party.' Lucy tried to apologise as they drove home.

'So alcohol would be okay, would it?' Marie couldn't keep the sharpness out of her voice. 'I can't imagine what your mum would say.' She pressed her lips, together shocked by her automatic reference to Dee. Seeing the tears stream down Lucy's cheeks, she immediately felt guilty. She knew how Dee would react – she'd react with sadness,

sadness she'd failed as a mother. But it was Marie who'd failed her sister's daughter. She'd failed to vet her new friendship with this girl who looked and dressed like a tramp. Well, she'd do better from now on.

Then Marie remembered the girl's father, his accusations. Who did he think he was, blaming her like that? She might have failed Lucy, but it was *his* daughter who must be at fault.

'I… we…' Lucy began.

'I don't want to hear the whys and wherefores, thank you very much. Count yourself lucky you got off with a warning. It could have been much worse.' So much worse, Marie thought, recalling visions of juvenile detention centres she'd seen on television. 'I just hope you've learnt your lesson and choose your friends more wisely in future.'

'But, Aunt Marie…'

But Marie didn't want to hear any more. She'd made up her mind. Dee would agree. She hoped her dead sister knew nothing about what had gone down this evening. She'd never forgive Marie for allowing this to happen. Marie should have insisted on meeting Lucy's new friend; she should never have left the two of them alone; she should have set stricter boundaries. But, Marie wondered as the lights of her house came into view, would any of that have made a difference?

Seventeen

The last customer had just left, and Marie was wiping down the tables when she heard the café door open behind her. She started to say, 'We're closed,' and turned slightly, realising she'd forgotten to put up the CLOSED sign, when a familiar voice said, 'I'm sorry. We need to talk.' It was the belligerent man from Saturday night – Jess's father.

'I don't think we have anything to say to each other. And I'd like you to leave,' she said, scrubbing the table with more force than was necessary. There was no sound except the humming of the large refrigerator holding the soft drinks. When she looked up again, he was still there.

Marie glared at him.

He held up his hands defensively. 'I came to apologise.'

Apologise? Marie felt her anger drain away at the same time as Frank emerged from the back of the café.

'Hello again. I'm sorry. We're closed.' Frank wiped his hands on his apron, ready to shake the newcomer's hand. He gave Marie an enquiring look.

'This is Jess's dad,' she said. 'Mr...?' She realised she'd forgotten his name.

'Hamilton, isn't it?' Frank asked, smiling. 'He's been in several times, but I don't think you were here, Marie. He's the principal at the High. What's up?'

'There was a bit of a fracas on Saturday night – my daughter was involved and your niece?' The man looked towards Frank, as if expecting a reaction.

'Marie?' Frank appeared perplexed.

Marie bit the inside of her cheek. She hadn't told Frank about the episode at the police station. She'd been too embarrassed to admit Lucy's deceitful behaviour, her own failure. When he'd asked about Saturday, she'd just said Lucy was safe.

Lucy herself had been tight-lipped about the events leading up to their arrest and had spent most of yesterday in her room, leaving Marie to speculate as to what had actually happened. She believed Lucy's impassioned plea of innocence on the drive home, which meant it had all been the Hamilton girl's fault.

'Can we at least talk about this?' the man asked, gesturing towards the table Marie had been cleaning so assiduously.

Frank motioned to Marie to take a seat. 'I'll get us coffee,' he said, disappearing behind the counter again.

'Drew,' the man said, holding out his hand.

'Marie,' she said, ignoring the outstretched hand and, for the first time really looking at him. At any other time – if they'd met under any other circumstances – Marie would have considered him good-looking. Today, the angry expression was gone, and he looked almost human. What had Frank said? He was the high school principal? How could he allow his daughter to behave so recklessly as to take Lucy to a place where there were drugs and alcohol? Though the alcohol wasn't such a surprise. Marie remembered her own first foray into experimenting with cider and her mother's cooking sherry when she wasn't much older than Lucy.

'You and Frank are Lucy's guardians?'

'I am. Frank and I aren't together.'

'Sorry, I assumed.' Drew seemed surprised, but quickly recovered. 'I have sole care of Jess too. I know it's not easy.' He pushed a hand through his hair, giving him a rakish appearance.

Marie felt herself soften to him, then stiffened again. It was his daughter who'd led Lucy astray, his poor parenting. She conveniently forgot her self-reproach about her own attempt at parenting.

'How could you permit her to lead Lucy – an innocent child – into a drug den?'

'Hey, steady on. I said I came to apologise, but you need to hear the whole story.'

At that moment, Frank appeared with three large mugs of coffee. 'I think we'll all feel better with a caffeine hit,' he said, joining them at the table. 'Now what's this all about? Will someone fill me in? I know the two girls went to a party on Saturday and that you…' he nodded to Marie, '…were worried when she was out late. But you told me she was safe? What don't I know?'

Marie looked down into her cup. She knew she should have been honest with Frank. Lucy was his niece too.

It was Drew who spoke first. 'I managed to have a long talk with Jess yesterday. It wasn't easy, but I did make her sit down and explain what happened. I feel it's partly my fault.' He looked contrite. 'Since we moved here at the beginning of the year, I've been disappointed Jess didn't make friends. She didn't want to move from Melbourne away from all her friends, but we couldn't stay there. I won't bore you with my history.'

Marie nodded. This explained why the two girls gravitated together – two loners missing their friends.

'I was delighted when she made friends with Lucy,' he nodded in Marie's direction. 'and then I introduced Jess to my neighbours. Nick Kerr is a professor at the university and he has a son a year older than Jess and Lucy.' He raked a hand through his hair again. 'I suppose I thought they could be friends too. It turns out Jess has had a crush on Ryan – that's the boy's name – ever since she arrived but was too shy to speak to him. Anyway, it seems he told Jess about this party his mates were having on Saturday. When Lucy contacted Jess, the girls saw it as the perfect opportunity to spread their wings and mix with the older students.'

'Oh!' Marie sat back, deflated. She knew who Ryan Kerr was – he was Kay Kerr's stepson. 'And this boy – Ryan. Did he get arrested too?'

'Arrested?' Frank's eyes widened.

'That's the rub. He didn't go to the party after all. His parents were out of town and he and a couple of mates decided to raid their alcohol supply at home. I was asked to keep an eye on the place – and them – but they did it very quietly.' He took off his glasses and pinched the bridge of his nose, before replacing them.

Marie notice how vulnerable he seemed without the dark frames and she almost sympathised with him.

'I spoke with Ryan yesterday, after I talked with Jess. He said he was sorry, that he didn't know about the drugs. We've had a spate of this at school. I've been trying to get to the bottom of it. But now the police are involved, it's out of my hands.'

'They were all schoolkids? Seniors?' Frank asked.

'That's not clear. Ryan didn't know. The boy whose house the party was at is in Year Twelve. He's a bit of a rough diamond, though I wouldn't have thought… But Jess had a fright so hopefully it's the last time she'll do anything so stupid.'

'It was just a party. How could she know?' Frank asked.

'Frank!' Marie almost yelled. 'Are you condoning what they did?'

'No, but you have to admit, Marie, neither of the girls knew what they were getting into. If what Drew's saying is correct.' He put up his hand as Drew opened his mouth to speak. 'And I have no reason to doubt him – nor should you. I know you're worried about Lucy and who she associates with. But it sounds as if they're just two impressionable girls who got caught up in something beyond their control. I bet if you ask Lucy, she'll tell you the same.'

'But…' Marie couldn't believe Frank was taking this attitude. She expected him to support her, not to…

'I don't think you should ban the girls from remaining friends, do you?' Frank looked from Marie to Drew and back again and waited.

'Well said,' Drew agreed, while Marie still felt doubtful. 'I know what I said on Saturday but that was in the heat of the moment. Since then, I've had time to reflect, get more information. I've come to the conclusion there would be no advantage in trying to keep Jess and Lucy apart. They'll see each other at school anyway and…'

'So what do you propose?' Marie asked. 'That they get off scot-free?'

'Marie,' Frank said, gently putting a hand on her arm. 'From what I've heard, I think they've both had punishment enough being taken to the police station and having to face your and Drew's anger. It may be time for a more moderate approach.'

Marie was gearing herself up for a response when Drew spoke again. 'I agree there should be some form of punishment, some community service. I've had an idea.'

Marie looked at him as if he'd developed horns. 'Community service?'

'Of a sort. I've been struggling to get my garden into some sort of order. I've all but mastered the front part, but so far, the back garden has beaten me. What I suggest is this. They spend time – starting this coming Saturday – helping get it into some semblance of order – weeding, trimming, planting.'

'For how long?'

'Until we're satisfied. I wouldn't expect you to take my word for it. Of course, you'd be welcome to come along to help supervise. What do you say? At least they'd be too tired after a day's gardening to do any socialising.'

'I wouldn't count on it,' Frank said, chuckling, 'But it's a good idea. Don't you think so, Marie?'

'I normally work here on a Saturday,' she said. 'Last week was an exception.'

'You could go to Drew's when you finish here,' Frank suggested.

Marie glared at him. *Whose side was he on?* But the idea did have merit. 'Who'll tell them?' she asked.

'I'll tell Jess, and perhaps you could break the news to Lucy? We could all have dinner together afterwards. Maybe get to know each other better?' He stood and held out his hand again. This time, Marie took it.

As their hands met, she felt a jolt of electricity run through her – a sizzle as they made contact. She almost jumped back in alarm. Had he felt it too?

Eighteen

What had possessed him? 'Get to know each other better.' What was he thinking? Drew regretted the words as soon as they left his mouth. But it had been something about the way Marie Cunningham looked at him, the sudden flash of something he couldn't name that had had passed between them when their hands touched. She was a good-looking woman, especially when she was angry; when her dark spiky curls seemed to match her words.

It surprised him when she said she and Frank weren't together. The man certainly acted as if they were. But maybe it was only the café that held them together. He tried to remember what Jo Ford had said about her at the race meeting. He didn't recall any mention of Frank. But each time he'd visited prior to today, it had been Frank manning the decks with no sign of Marie.

He wondered about her name. Marie sounded Italian and she looked Italian with her dark hair and eyes and tanned skin. Were she and Frank brother and sister? That might explain things. What had Frank said about her? That he and Marie had taken over the café when his father became too frail – or had he said *their* father? Drew shook his head in frustration. He couldn't remember. It hadn't seemed important at the time. It still wasn't. What was he doing racking his brains over a woman he'd just met, a woman he had no intention of getting to know better apart from joint supervision of their respective teenagers?

But there was something about her that intrigued him, made him want to know more about her – and he had invited her to dinner.

*

'We need to talk again, Jess,' Drew said, walking into Jess's bedroom. His eyes flitted around the room seeing again the untidy bundle of clothes on the bed, the unwashed mugs and plates lying on the floor, and knew there was more to discuss than the idea of community service. But one thing at a time.

'What now? I explained what happened. And you've banned me from seeing the only friend I have in the world. What else do you have to say?' Jess asked from her perch on the window seat where she was claiming to be doing homework.

Drew almost laughed at the indignant expression on Jess's face. She looked so like her mother when she chose to put on this act. It had never worked for Irene and didn't work for Jess now. 'That's just it,' he said, pushing aside some clothing and taking a seat on the bed to face Jess. 'I may have overreacted.' He adjusted his glasses.

Drew saw a gleam of interest appear in Jess's eyes. She laid down the book she'd been pretending to study.

'I went to The Bean Sprout Café after school today. That's where Lucy's aunt works.'

'I know that. It belongs to her aunt and uncle.'

So, he might have been right – brother and sister. Drew wasn't sure why, but the news made him feel better.

'Right. Well, I explained what you told me and…'

'We can be friends again?'

'Yes, but we agreed you both need to be punished.'

'Punished?' Jess's voice rose. 'The policewoman only gave us a warning.'

'I know that, but I'm – we're – not sure the pair of you realise the seriousness of what you were involved in. You could so easily have gone to jail.'

'But we didn't.' Jess turned back to her book.

Drew reached over to put a hand on it. 'Hear me out. We decided – Lucy's aunt and I – that a stint of community service would be a good idea.' He forbore to mention it had all been his idea, and Marie had only agreed under sufferance and with Frank's encouragement.

'Community service?' Jess almost spat out the words. 'What's that?'

'It can be many things but in this case it's to be gardening.'

'Gardening? I don't know anything about gardening.' She pouted.

'You'll soon learn. As you know, I've been working on the patch out front, but the back yard is still a mess. Starting Saturday, I'll…'

'What about Lucy?'

'She'll be joining you here. Her aunt will come over after the café closes and they'll both stay to dinner.'

'So, Lucy and me – we'll be doing this together?'

'That's the plan.'

'Hmm.' Jess turned her attention back to her book.

With a last glance around, Drew shook his head and left, closing the door behind him. He wasn't sure how to gauge Jess's reaction but at least she hadn't refused to cooperate.

*

Across town, Marie was having a similar conversation with Lucy. As she explained the idea, she wondered again why she'd agreed to it. The shock of Drew's touch was still jangling her nerves. 'I'll be there once we close the café,' she finished.

'Mum and I used to garden together,' Lucy said with a faraway look. 'It won't be hard. And it'll be good to be with Jess. How was Mr Hamilton? He was really angry at the police station.'

'He'd calmed down. It seems Jess explained what happened, about their next-door neighbour. You didn't tell me.'

'Didn't think you'd listen.' Lucy gazed down at her feet.

'Oh, Lucy!' Marie felt guilty. Had she been such an ogre, Lucy was afraid to confide in her? 'I'm sorry you felt that way. I was angry and upset. I guess I felt partly to blame for leaving the two of you here alone.'

'Why? We're not kids!'

But you are, Marie thought, *big kids with no understanding of the evils that can befall you. And this has been a hard lesson.*

'He's invited us for dinner,' she said, trying to put a positive spin on things.

Lucy didn't respond, then, after a pause, asked, 'How did you go in Canberra with Mum's friend?'

Tony Clarke! It all seemed so long ago. 'It was okay. He was devastated. He was really fond of your mum. I think if she hadn't… They'd have made a good couple. You'd like him. He'd like to have a memento,' Marie remembered. 'I thought we could decide on one together. Maybe a photo?'

Lucy seemed to consider this. 'Perhaps that one you took at the races – the one where she's grinning at the camera with a wine glass in her hand and her hair all over the place? She looks so happy. It was almost the last time…' Her eyes filled.

Marie gave her a hug. Why hadn't *she* thought of that? Dee had been fooling around during lunch while Marie played with her phone, and the shot Lucy was referring to had been a lucky attempt. It showed a Dee who was full of the joys of life, who had no idea her life was soon to be cut short. 'Good idea, Luce. I'll organise it and mail it to him – or would you like to meet Tony?'

Lucy seemed to consider for a moment before shaking her head. 'I don't think so. It's not as if… but…' She bit her lip and gave Marie a timid glance, before asking, 'Aunt Marie, do you know where my dad is? Mum would never talk about him. But now I've been wondering…'

Marie felt a ringing in her ears. This was the last thing she'd expected. Dee would be devastated. But if Dee was alive, this might never have come up. Robbie had left when Lucy was a baby, unable or unwilling to accept the responsibility of being a father. As far as Marie knew, there had been no contact between him and Dee over the years. She had no idea where he was, but… a tiny voice in her head said, she did know where his parents had lived – if they were still alive. They'd shunned Dee too, seeming to believe whatever tall tale he'd spun them about the break-up.

Dee had told Marie at the time how she'd attempted to contact them, to keep in touch for Lucy's sake, only to have her calls remain unanswered, her letters returned unopened. 'I don't think…' she began.

'He's my dad!' Lucy said. 'I want to meet him.'

Nineteen

'I'm off now,' Marie called out to the back of the café where Frank was checking the day's takings.

He came through as she was about to open the door. 'Take care, and make sure you keep your temper,' he said.

'Temper? Me?'

'Yes, you. I know how you can get fired up and I'm not sure you've completely forgiven Drew Hamilton. I saw how easily he managed to rile you.'

'It's been a tough week.' Marie hoped Frank hadn't noticed the effect Drew Hamilton had on her aroused more than her anger. Her relationship with Frank might be over but he might have a strange aversion to seeing her interested in another man. Was she? Was she interested in Drew Hamilton as anything other than the father of Lucy's friend?

But Frank had other things on his mind too. 'Is Lucy still determined to look for her dad?'

Marie sighed. 'She's been trying to find him online. Luckily, he doesn't appear to have a social media presence, but it's probably only a matter of time. I dread to think how he'll react if she does manage to run him to ground.'

'You haven't mentioned his parents – her grandparents – to her?'

'No, and she hasn't asked about them.'

'Not yet. Maybe you should bring them up before she does.'

'Maybe. Let me get over tonight first and I'll think about it.'

*

There was no answer when Marie rang the bell at the house in what was often called the mortgage belt of Granite Springs. She hadn't visited this part for a long time, and it seemed to have grown exponentially with the opening of the university. From even a cursory glance, she could see the front garden had been carefully trimmed and planted, just as Drew said. She rang again and when she still received no answer, tentatively made her way around the side of the house. As she pushed open the side gate, Marie heard sounds of laughter. Not such a punishment after all!

The back garden bore no resemblance to the neat beds out front. Here, there was a mass of weeds – some of which were now forming a large pile in one corner. A rundown shed sat at the edge of what had once been a lawn but was now overgrown. The only habitable part was a paved courtyard next to the house, on which sat a large wooden table and where a state-of-the-art barbecue held pride of place.

Lucy and Jess were engaged in attempting to remove a large plant and were giggling as they tugged at it without falling over. Drew was watching with a smile, hands on his hips. It was a happy picture, one which Marie didn't want to interrupt.

'Aunt Marie!' Lucy caught sight of her and dropped the part of the plant she was holding triggering Jess's collapse onto the ground in a fit of giggles.

It wasn't what Marie expected. 'Punishment?' she asked Drew with a raised eyebrow. 'Looks to me like they're having fun.'

'It's been a blast,' he agreed. 'But they're getting the work done. I think they've surprised themselves how much they're enjoying it. Gardening can be therapeutic, you know. Maybe you should try it sometime.' He grinned again to take away the barb.

What was he trying to tell her? Did she seem to him to be always on the defensive, ready for an argument? Frank had suggested that, too. But she wasn't like that, not usually. People had told Marie she was the most even-tempered person they knew; that she always made them feel better. What had changed her, transformed her from the bluebird of happiness to this new creature who gave the impression she was ready for a fight?

As Lucy moved to help her friend to her feet, Drew said, 'They're about finished for the day. Why don't we leave them to it and have a glass of wine? We can supervise from a distance. They're not going to get up to any mischief here.'

With a glance to where the two girls were again busy trying to free the stubborn weed, Marie agreed and took a seat at the stained wooden table, surprised to find a soft cushion providing protection from the hard seat.

'Courtesy of the sales staff.' Drew chuckled at her astonishment. 'The cushions came with the table setting. Hope you like chardonnay,' he said, holding up a chilled bottle.

'Lovely.' Exactly what she needed to dull her feelings of… Marie wasn't sure how to describe them. She took a grateful sip, feeling the cool liquid course through her. 'It seems to be going well.'

'Better than I hoped. They were slow to start with. I had to demonstrate the basics. But once they got the hang of it, they set to with gusto. I was considering paying a gardener to come in. Maybe I should pay those two instead.'

Marie shook her head slowly.

'Well, maybe not. How was your day? Busy?'

On more comfortable ground, Marie took another sip before replying, 'Yes, it was. The good weather seemed to bring people out. Normally weekdays are our busiest but today we were run off our feet.' *Gosh, how boring I sound*, she thought.

But it seemed Drew didn't think so. 'I've always wondered what it would be like to own a café,' he said, leaning back in his seat and gazing at Marie with an indefinable expression. 'Frank told me it's been in your family for generations.'

'Frank's, not mine. And I don't own it. I guess I'm what you might call a non-contributing partner.'

Drew appeared surprised. 'But I thought… aren't you brother and sister?'

Marie laughed. She and Frank had often been taken for siblings by strangers. Perhaps because they were both dark-haired, brown-eyed with olive complexions. 'No, only partners. We…' She looked down into her glass, uncertain how much to tell him, then her gaze moved across the yard to where Lucy and Jess seemed to be engaged in a tussle over the wheelbarrow. If she didn't reveal her relationship with Frank, Lucy no doubt would.

'We were a couple,' she said carefully. 'For years, but brother and sister is almost right. Frank and I got together in school and as time went on our relationship changed, evolved, deteriorated – whatever you might call it – into a friendship, more like brother and sister.'

'But you still manage to work together?'

'Oh, yes. Nothing's changed there. And Frank's my go-to person when things go wrong. He's been wonderful since my sister died. You do know about that?' She assumed he would. News spread fast in Granite Springs. He was the high school principal and Jess's Dad.

'Yes. I'm sorry. I should have said before now.'

Marie nodded and clasped both hands around her glass as if it could protect her from the sadness which welled up when she thought of Dee.

'It must be hard for you. You and Frank… you have no children of your own?'

Marie shook her head. 'Now I have to learn how to be a parent to a teenager. But Frank's been good there, too. Lucy's always loved her Uncle Frank.'

Marie could see him thinking, *But you didn't tell him about the incident with the police.*

'I didn't see the need to worry him about Lucy being arrested. There was nothing he could do and…' she bit her lip, '…I can't keep running to him when I get into trouble. I have to work out how to do this on my own.' Her last words were muttered more quietly, as if she was telling them to herself.

'What about you?' she asked, eager to change the subject. 'You're on your own with Jess, too?'

'I am.' Drew rubbed the back of his neck. 'My wife found someone she liked better and headed off to LA with him. He's a well-known footballer so things became too hot for us in Melbourne, hence the move to Granite Springs. Jess hasn't taken kindly to the move. I can't blame her. She misses her friends, her school, her whole way of life. I sometimes wonder if I was wrong to uproot her, if I should have stuck it out. But it's too late now, and she and Lucy seem to have found something in common.'

'They were both lonely and resentful,' Marie agreed, finding she had more in common with Drew than she anticipated. They were both trying to bring up recalcitrant teenagers on their own, in a place the young people didn't want to be, isolated from all they knew and loved.

'Here's trouble,' he said, gesturing to where the two girls were making their way across the expanse of grass. 'Okay, girls,' he called. 'You can wash up in the downstairs loo and help yourselves to a cold drink. Dinner will be on soon. I hope steak and salad's okay with you,' he said to Marie. 'I'm not much of a cook, I'm afraid, but I barbecue a mean steak.'

Marie smiled. She wasn't used to a man who didn't know his way around the kitchen. Frank had learned to cook as soon as he was able to reach the stove, earlier probably, she thought, remembering his mother's high kitchen stools. 'That'll be fine,' she said. 'Is there anything I can do?'

'Just sit there and talk to me while I cook the meat,' Drew said, with a smile that made her stomach flutter.

She stifled an impulse to touch him – *where had that come from?* – and crossed her legs, taking another sip of wine to calm herself. Drew was a pleasure to watch as he fired up the barbecue, then fetched a platter of steak and sausages.

She sat in silence listening to the sizzle as the meat hit the hot grill, the only other sounds the shrill call of the cockatoos flying overhead and the distant chattering of Jess and Lucy from inside the house. It was pleasant, and Marie gradually felt herself begin to relax, something she hadn't been able to do for days, weeks, even.

'You're very quiet. Everything all right?'

'Yes. I'm just enjoying the evening. Since Dee… things have been hectic. The only time I've had to myself was that night Lucy went to the party and I was beside myself with worry. It's good to be able to unwind.' She stretched out her arms and legs to prove her point. 'I don't think I'm cut out for this parenting gig,' she said, recrossing her legs and picking up her glass again.

'None of us is.' Drew deftly turned the meat as he spoke, throwing a glance over his shoulder to where Marie was sitting. 'But we learn all the same and adjust. You'd have felt inadequate even if you'd given birth to Lucy. But I agree, it's hard to go it alone. That's what I'm finding now Irene's not here to back me up or take up some of the slack. I know I'm making mistakes. It's only natural. But there's no need to beat yourself up about it.'

How did he know?

'But you deal with teenagers at the high school every day. You must know what to do.'

'Don't you believe it! Your own child is a whole different ball game as I'm finding to my dismay. Maybe it would be easier with a boy. At least I'd have my own experience to draw on.'

'I don't find it helps.' Marie fell into silence again, trying to absorb what Drew had said.

'Are you completely on your own with Lucy? What happened to her dad?'

Marie hesitated. It was a reasonable question, but a contentious one right now. 'He left Dee when Lucy was little,' she said, running her finger around the rim of her glass which was still damp with condensation. 'He didn't take time to adjust to parenthood, didn't want a bar of it. Dee was left with a toddler. She's been on her own with Lucy ever since. She'd finally met someone when…' Marie took a gulp from her glass as she felt her eyes moisten again. *When would she ever be able to think of her sister without crying?*

'That's rough. And there's no one else?'

'There's Frank.' She could almost feel Frank's comforting presence as she spoke. She quickly continued. 'Lucy's dad's parents didn't want to know once he left and my own have been dead for years.'

'So, looks like we're in the same boat. My folks are gone, and Irene's spend their time on cruises. I think they're somewhere in the Pacific right now. These look ready.'

Drew carried over the platter and headed into the house leaving Marie to wonder why she'd felt able to unburden herself to him. But she hadn't told him everything. Lucy was still determined to search for her dad and Marie didn't know how she could dissuade her.

Any further soul-searching was avoided by the arrival of the two girls and the flurry of getting settled at the table and serving of the meal. There was no chance for any private discussion, each girl vying with the other to fill any gaps in the conversation.

At the door, Marie thanked Drew for what had been for her, a pleasant evening – much better than she'd anticipated.

'I enjoyed it too,' he said, a tinge of surprise in his voice. 'But the community service isn't over. There's still a lot to be done in the garden. Shall we repeat the performance next Saturday?'

Shaken, Marie agreed.

On the drive home, Lucy was more cheerful than Marie had seen her since Dee died. She chatted on about Jess and their attempts at gardening, then said seriously, 'Jess's dad's nice. Not what I expected. He's different from what he is at school. It must be weird having a dad who's the school principal. I don't think Jess likes it much. But she does have a dad.' Lucy fell into an awkward silence again.

Marie glanced at her out of the corner of her eye, trying to work out what her niece was thinking. Was she thinking of her own dad, imagining what he would be like? Marie wished Lucy would forget all about him. But she did agree with her niece about one thing. Drew Hamilton had turned out to be much better than she'd expected.

Twenty

Drew watched the car reverse out of the driveway and turned back into the house. Jess had already disappeared into her room and the familiar sound of music was blaring from upstairs. But tonight, it didn't disturb him as much as usual. His head was filled with thoughts of the woman who'd just left.

Marie Cunningham wasn't what he expected, though he had no idea what his expectations had been. She'd proven to be vulnerable, beset with self-doubt – and, like himself, been thrust into responsibility for a teenage girl without warning. Though in his case that wasn't entirely true. He'd been Jess's dad before Irene left, and her leaving wasn't entirely unexpected. They'd been drifting apart for years. He suspected Irene only stayed as long as she did for Jess's sake. But when push came to shove, and Jake was offered the US contract, her daughter's needs came a poor second. Drew's needs didn't come into the equation at all.

But it had been different for Marie. She was the girl's aunt. Not only had she been suddenly thrust into being the sole guardian of a teenager, she'd also lost her sister. He couldn't imagine what she was going through. It was no wonder she had been so angry with him the other night. She had every right to be angry – angry with him, angry with everyone, angry with life.

But he had the impression negativity wasn't her normal frame of mind. In the midst of her telling her story, he'd caught a glimpse of what he thought was the real Marie. And that woman was someone he'd like to know better.

He went through to the kitchen and loaded the dishwasher, vowing to encourage Jess to take more of a role in household chores. Since Irene left, everything had fallen to him. It made him appreciate how much of the load Irene had shouldered when they were a couple. If he ever married again, he'd be more understanding of what was involved in running a household.

Woah! Where had that come from? Married again? That was the last thing he wanted. Had one dinner with an attractive woman turned his mind?

Marie Cunningham was attractive. He was in no doubt about that. But it didn't mean he was going to do anything about it. The two girls were friends, so it would be impossible to avoid her. But if he was to seek anything more than friendship, there would no doubt be challenges. There were always challenges. And he hadn't successfully avoided women since Irene's departure only to be swayed by the first pretty face who sat opposite him at dinner.

He poured himself another glass of wine and headed into his study, putting all thoughts of Marie Cunningham to the back of his mind and focussing instead on Jess. Nick and Kay had been back for a week and he hadn't been in touch yet. Drew promised himself he'd drop over next day to check if Kay was willing to provide him with any tips on how to handle his daughter. Though Jess had been more biddable in the past week, he feared once the shock of being arrested subsided, it would be situation normal.

*

'Can I come too, Dad? Ryan said he'd help me with my maths.' Jess hopped on one foot, iPhone clutched in her hand.

Ryan? Maths? What had he missed? When Drew said he was popping next door for a bit, he'd assumed Jess would be happy to be left alone.

'Dad?'

'Sure. I didn't know you and Ryan…'

Jess turned bright red. 'It's not like that. He always comes top in maths, and when I said I was having trouble with an assignment, he offered to help.'

'Hmm.' Drew hadn't been aware Jess was having difficulty with maths, but what did he know? He was only her dad. Though he did wonder when the two had spoken. 'Are you ready to come now?'

'Yeah!' Jess flourished the laptop she was holding. 'All set. We won't disturb your adult conversation.'

Drew hoped not, since the conversation was to be about Jess. When he'd called round that morning, Kay had been about to go out and had suggested she'd be happy to help over an early evening glass of wine.

'Welcome,' Nick greeted them at the door. 'You'll find Ryan in the family room, Jess.' He'd barely finished speaking when Ryan appeared behind him, and he and Jess disappeared together.

'Maths?' Nick asked, pulling on his beard. 'That's not what we called it in my day.'

'You don't think?' Drew asked, stunned. 'Jess is only fifteen. She's…' He was about to say, 'She's too young to be interested in boys.'. Then he remembered the makeup and outfit she'd worn when the Kerr family came to dinner, and that it was Ryan who'd been the attraction at the infamous party – the one he hadn't attended himself.

'I think that son of mine has a lot to answer for,' Nick said, when the adults were settled in the living room with wine and nibbles. 'From what I can gather, he was the one who instigated the party where your daughter and her friend were caught up in a drug bust. He assures me he knew nothing about the drugs, but he did stay away himself. He says – and I believe him – he had no idea the girls would go.'

'It was wrong of him to tell them about it,' Kay said. 'He should have figured out they'd make every effort to be there – if Jess does like him and thought he'd be there, too. I remember being Jess's age and wanting a boy to notice me. I'd have gone to any lengths. But you didn't come here to talk about Ryan leading Jess astray, Drew. Or did you?' she chuckled. 'She could do worse.'

'Kay!'

'Sorry, Nick.' Kay picked up her wine and tucked her legs under her. 'Nick said you'd like my advice on how to deal with her, Drew. I'm not sure I can be a lot of help, but I do have some experience of teenage daughters. Though, believe me, they don't necessarily get any better as they get older.' She grimaced. 'My Zoe is doing well now and we're good friends, but she has her moments.' She took a sip of wine. 'Now, what's the problem?'

Drew took a gulp from his glass before replying, then listed all of what he saw as Jess's shortcomings and his own failings as a father. 'You must think me a fool,' he said as he finished. 'I can run a school full of teenagers but can't handle my own daughter.'

'Not at all. Nick was the same.' She threw her husband a loving glance. 'I can appreciate it's hard for a man to understand the workings of a teenage girl's mind. But they're really not too complicated. The main thing to realise is they think the world revolves around them and everything is a major challenge or achievement. There's no middle ground.'

'That's it?' Drew had expected more.

'Not entirely. I bet you and she don't talk much, apart from you finding fault or making demands, and what seems like rudeness on her part.'

'You're right there.' This was more like it. 'How can that change if she's not willing to...'

'Have you tried talking with her – really talking? Explaining how you feel about your wife leaving, about moving here, about her?'

Drew winced.

'She hits home, doesn't she?' Nick asked. 'Refill?'

Drew held out his glass. 'So...?' he asked.

'Is there anything you like to do together?'

Drew was about to say 'no' when he remembered the previous day spent in the garden. 'Perhaps. Yesterday I had Jess and her friend work on the back garden with me. It was intended as a punishment for the scare they gave us but turned out they enjoyed it. It was a fun afternoon and...' Drew smiled as he remembered how much he'd enjoyed Marie's company, too.

'Sounds like a good start. Have you any plans to do it again?'

'Next Saturday.'

'Maybe between now and then, you could try to have some meaningful conversations about your feelings. I don't know if you've ever studied the principles of conflict resolution, but it can often resolve differences if you take the "you" out of the equation. Instead of saying "when you..." say, "when this happens, I feel..." It can open up a whole new discussion, one which is focussed on feelings not a person's actions. Oh, I know how difficult it can be for you men to talk about feelings. But it's worth it. Ask Nick.'

Drew looked across the room to where Nick was nodding sagely with a grin on his face.

'Listen to the expert, Drew. It's good advice.'

'Mmm. I'll try.' He wasn't so sure, but it couldn't hurt, though he'd feel a fool unburdening himself to Jess.

'We're done, Dad. Can we watch a movie?' Ryan popped his head around the door, Jess's smiling face peeking out from behind him.

Drew was delighted to see her looking happier than usual. The only other time she'd looked like this had been with Lucy. Maybe that had been the problem all along – Jess's lack of company of her own age. If it was that simple, maybe he could dispense with Kay's advice. But he caught sight of her expression and knew she'd read his mind. 'Thanks, Kay,' he said.

*

'Maths all good, now?'

'What? Oh, yes, Dad. Ryan was a big help.' Jess smirked.

I'll bet.

'How about a hot chocolate with your old dad before we turn in?' Drew decided there was no time like the present; if he was going to have this discussion with Jess, he didn't want it hanging over him all week.

'Okay – with marshmallows?'

'If we have any.' Drew tried to prepare himself as he heated the milk and spooned the hot chocolate into two mugs. He found a bag of marshmallows he didn't remember buying in the back of the pantry and chose three for Jess and two for himself. A little bit of sweetness wouldn't go astray.

'This is nice,' he said, one hand clasping his ankle on his knee, the other holding the mug of hot chocolate. 'I probably haven't spent as much time as I should with you, Jess. I'm sorry if I always disappear into my study. It's my way of coping, I'm afraid. I'll try to change.'

Jess raised an eyebrow.

Drew ploughed on. 'I know it was hard on you when Mum left. It was hard on me, too. And I tried to hide it by losing myself in my work. I wasn't fair to you. I should have realised you were hurting. I should have talked with you then, but it was too painful. I forgot you must be hurting, too.' He paused.

'When Mum left…' Jess twirled a strand of hair with one finger. 'I thought… I thought maybe I'd done something to push her away. But it was all about Jake, wasn't it? She loved him more than she loved us.' Jess took a gulp of her drink, then tried to fish out a melting marshmallow.

'You're right. It was nothing to do with you. I'm sorry if you thought that for even a minute. If I'd known…' Drew pushed a hand through his hair.

'But leaving Melbourne to come here? Why did we have to do that?' There was a hint of the old whining in Jess's voice. 'That made it even harder, Dad.'

'I know, sweetheart. I hated doing that to you. We were both happy there. We had a home, friends. I had a good job. But… it all became too much. Remember the journalists, the photographers? We couldn't go out without being harassed. It was no life for you. Then this position came up, and I thought we could make a fresh start. Was I wrong?'

'Maybe… if we'd stayed, they might have stopped, and life would have gone back to normal, except…'

'Mum would still have been gone. Life would still be different.'

'Yeah, but…'

'Can we try to get on better, to make the best of living here in Granite Springs? And can we agree to share our feelings with each other instead of bottling them up?'

They sat in silence for a few moments, then, 'Is that it? Can I go to my room now?' Jess rose and left.

Drew watched her go. He'd tried but had the impression he'd made a hash of it. Maybe Kay was wrong. Maybe he should have left things as they were. Instead, he'd laid himself bare to a daughter who didn't seem to care. Had he got through to her? It was impossible to know.

Marie Cunningham seemed to be able to cope better than he did. He wondered what she was doing tonight.

Twenty-one

'Sounds as if you like him,' Fran said to Marie as they made their second round of the oval. They'd started this exercise regime only the week before in an attempt – in Marie's case at least – to bring some sense of routine to a life which seemed chaotic. Marie would drive out to the campus when the café closed on Tuesdays and Thursdays to meet Fran. They'd spend up to an hour alternately walking and running around the sports oval before Fran joined Owen to drive home, and Marie went to meet her niece.

To Marie's surprise and delight, after the debacle of the party, Lucy and Jess had decided to join the chess club which met after school on those days. She hadn't enquired too closely into the reasons for their choice, suspecting it had something to do with boys. Marie remembered how, at Lucy's age, she'd been enamoured with a boy who belonged to a strict religious sect and she and her friend had attended lunchtime prayer meetings to see more of him. Of course, that hadn't lasted for long, replaced by after-school coffee at The Bean Sprout where she and Frank had got together.

'Drew Hamilton?'

'Who else? He's the one you've been talking about.'

'Only to tell you what Lucy's been doing with his daughter. But, yes, he's different to what I expected.'

'Different how?'

'Oh, I don't know. He's the principal at the high school. I guess I was thinking about old Baldy Wilson who was principal when I was there.' She laughed. 'It was unkind, but what all the kids called him. He was a tall skinny man who seemed as old as the hills and, yes, he was bald, bald as a coot. He used to sweep through the corridors in a long black gown. We were terrified of him.'

Fran laughed. 'Drew's nothing like that.'

'Have you met him?'

Fran nodded. 'He joined us at the picnic races. Kay and Nick live next door to him and his daughter.'

'Oh!'

'So, what *is* he like?'

'Well, he's not bald for a start.' Marie chuckled. 'He has a good head of hair. It's white, but he's not a lot older than us. He must have gone white early.' She thought of her own hair slowly turning grey, and requiring the frequent assistance of her hairdresser. 'He's tall, but not too tall, has deep brown eyes, wears…'

'I didn't mean his looks.' Fran grinned. 'But you have noticed him, haven't you?'

'Not like that. But he's not the sort of boring, staid guy I'd have expected. He says… he seems to have similar issues with being a single parent as I'm finding with Lucy. He…' Marie hesitated. She wasn't sure how to describe the bond that appeared to forge between them. 'I found him very… amiable,' she said at last.

'Ha!' Fran grinned again. 'That's how it starts.'

'Oh, you! Just because you and Owen decided to make a match of it doesn't mean I'm going to follow in your footsteps. It's Lucy and Jess who are friends. Drew's just not what I expected, that's all. I'm not looking for a relationship, and neither is he.'

Running out of breath, Marie halted and bent over, hands on her knees.

'I didn't mention a relationship,' Fran said, running on the spot. 'Methinks you protest too much. When are you seeing him again?'

'Next Saturday,' Marie said without thinking, then quickly added, 'With the girls. They have more gardening to do, though it's not turned out to be the punishment it was intended to be.'

'Uh oh!'

Marie began to run again in the hope she could tire her friend out and prevent her from asking anything more. But as they came to a halt outside the building which housed the School of Music and Drama, she saw Drew Hamilton walking towards them.

'Isn't that…?' Fran nudged Marie who could feel herself blush.

Embarrassed to meet Drew dressed in her running gear, her face red from exertion, and her hair damp with perspiration, Marie tried to appear calm.

'Are you going to speak to him?' Fran asked.

Realising there was no way she could avoid the meeting, Marie decided to put on a brave face. With a smile, she pushed back a stray curl. 'Afternoon, Drew. What are you doing up here?'

'Hi, Marie. I don't need to ask you the same. You've clearly been taking the exercise I so sorely need.'

Marie felt his eyes rake her up and down, suddenly conscious of the leggings and snug-fitting top which showed off her figure. She wished she could disappear in a puff of smoke.

'I've come to have a chat with Owen Larsen,' Drew said. 'To ask for some help.'

Fran stepped forward. 'You've come to the right place. Hi, Drew. We met at the races. Remember?' she chuckled. 'And, as you've no doubt guessed, I'm Marie's friend, too. You'll find Owen's office at the top of the stairs.'

'Thanks, ladies. Good to see you, Marie – and you, too, Fran.'

As soon as Drew disappeared through the door, Marie turned on her friend. 'You knew, didn't you? You knew Drew was coming to see Owen this afternoon. How could you?'

'I knew he had an appointment with Owen, but how could I know he'd arrive just as we walked up? He is rather dishy – as you said.'

'I said nothing of the sort!' But Marie's initial embarrassment and exasperation with her friend was disappearing. 'Asking for Owen's help? What's that about?'

'I have no idea. I'm not privy to all Owen's business.'

'I find that difficult to believe. You and he are joined at the hip. And don't you keep his diary? I recall you saying he wouldn't remember to blow his nose if you didn't schedule it for him.'

'I may have exaggerated,' Fran laughed. 'But I admit he is a tad disorganised. How's Lucy's ankle, by the way?'

'Back to normal, thank goodness. I have enough to worry about without her injury. I may have taken on more than I anticipated, Fran.'

'So you keep saying, but I think you're doing a great job. What's happened to the old Marie who counselled me last year? You're usually so on top of things, so able to see the silver lining. I know Dee's death hit you hard, but it's time to bounce back – for Lucy's sake, and your own.'

'It's not so easy. But I suppose you're right. Frank says so, too. It's not doing either of us any good for me to be in this slump I seem to have fallen into. I need something to pull me out of it.'

'Or someone?' Fran asked with a wicked glint in her eye.

'Don't go there!' Marie checked her watch. 'I should be going. Lucy will be home soon, and I don't like to leave her on her own for too long.'

'She's fifteen. You need to trust her.'

Marie bit back the retort that came to her lips. Fran wasn't a parent – you couldn't count Owen's grown-up daughter. How could she possibly understand? But it would have been cruel to say so. Marie knew how Fran's hopes of motherhood had been dashed all those years ago when she first arrived in Granite Springs. Instead she said, 'You may be right. Frank thinks so, too.'

'See? Frank knows a thing or two. Maybe you should listen to him. You and he have stayed close.'

Marie gave Fran a quick glance to see what she meant, but her friend's expression gave nothing away. 'I'll be off, then. See you on Thursday.'

'You're not ready to come back to the choir? It's tonight.'

Marie hesitated. Dee had been so effusive in her praise of the choristers' Easter performance, then... After what happened, Marie had found it too difficult to go back to choir practice, using Lucy as her excuse. 'Not yet. Lucy needs me to be home.'

'Why don't you bring Lucy out to see Pia and the baby? It might help her to see the miracle of a new life – you too.'

'Oh, Fran! I'm sorry. I've been so remiss. I've been so caught up in my own affairs, I haven't asked about Pia and the baby. It's a boy, isn't it?'

'Tor Larsen. Pia decided to keep with the Scandinavian influence in naming him. He's a dear little man, almost two months old now, and Owen's besotted. He has visions of teaching him guitar as soon as he's big enough to hold one, and as for keyboard…'

'You're right. I'm sure Lucy would love to see him – and Pia. Maybe Sunday, if that suits you?'

'Sounds good. Come for lunch, and I promise Owen won't take Lucy on any more escapades.'

'It wasn't Owen's fault.'

Marie hugged Fran and went to her car. Driving home she thought about the miracle of life. Dee's had ended, and almost at the same time, Fran's tiny step-grandchild had come into the world.

Twenty-two

Drew was surprised to see Marie Cunningham on the university campus. As the two figures drew closer, he felt his stomach lurch as he saw one of them was the woman he'd been thinking about since Saturday.

She'd clearly been exercising, reminding him yet again of his own deficiency in that department. He took in her dishevelled appearance, the way her sports gear clung to her body, and felt his temperature rise. She was surprised to see him, too. He could tell the sudden redness in her cheeks wasn't due to her recent exercise. And Fran Larsen, too. He'd all but forgotten meeting her at the races. He was becoming confused with the various people he'd met here since Easter.

Following Fran's directions, Drew pushed open the door and headed upstairs, drawn by the sound of a keyboard playing an unfamiliar melody. He knocked on the open door.

The man at the keyboard swung round, his dull blond hair falling over his face on which there was a wide grin. Unlike Drew, who was dressed in his customary business suit, Owen Larsen wore a pair of threadbare jeans and a loose, grey, long-sleeved tee-shirt. 'Good to see you again, Drew,' he said, rising and extending his hand.

'What were you playing?' Drew asked when he was seated. 'It was beautiful – haunting – but I didn't recognise it.'

'Oh,' Owen replied, waving a hand in the air as if to dismiss Drew's question. 'Just a little something I'm working on. It may come to nothing, but… However, you didn't come here to talk about me. Your secretary said something about you needing my help.'

'Not exactly. I've been asked by our parent group to source a venue for a fundraising event they're planning. I wouldn't normally get involved myself,' he said, seeing Owen's look of surprise, 'but given the stature of the university and your good self…'

Owen burst out laughing. 'Stature… me? That's a joke. Anyone who knows me would tell you that.'

Drew rubbed the back of his neck. This wasn't what he expected. Why had he allowed himself to be put in this position?

'Sorry, mate. I tend to forget I'm a *professor* now and should develop suitable gravitas. But it's not me. So, tell me about this fundraiser you've been roped into helping arrange.'

'I'm not exactly helping arrange it *per se*,' Drew said, feeling more comfortable. 'It's to be a mock race meeting. I don't know what it is about this place – Granite Springs – with the focus on racing. No offence intended,' he added, running a finger around the inside of his collar.

'No offence taken, Drew. I'm new to Granite Springs, too. You and me both. Arrived here last year from Sydney and I know what you mean. But that picnic thing where we met was a hoot, wasn't it? I love it here, wouldn't move back to the city for quids. Fran and I have an acreage on the outskirts of town with a herd of goats. It's not for everyone but it's my idea of heaven. But, enough of me. What is it you need help with? I'm no horseracing aficionado.'

'Nothing like that. I've only been asked to source the venue. I'm told you have a large open hall in your new school.' Drew gazed around, unsure where in this seat of learning, such a space could be located.

Owen laughed. 'Not here, Drew. But the auditorium next door has several different sized spaces. One of those might suit your needs. I'm sure the school can come to some arrangement with the powers that be on campus. It's for a good cause. But, tell me,' he leant back in his chair, crossed his legs at the ankles revealing a tired pair of trainers worn without socks, and clasped his hands behind his head, 'what on earth is a mock race meeting?'

'You might well ask. It threw me at first. But it seems people pay for a dinner; there's what they call a Calcutta – I'd never heard of that one before – then a mock race call, and some sort of race with toy horses or some such. I can't quite imagine it.' He spread his hands.

'Sounds a lark. Put me and Fran down for a couple of tickets, and I bet Jo and Col will be up for it, too. Hey, we can maybe make up a table. One thing I've discovered here in Granite Springs is the social life is tremendous. I thought when I left Sydney, I was going to hibernate here in the country. Far from it. Especially in the cooler months. Just when you think everyone will be hunkering down in front of their fires with a good book, there's race meetings, balls, dinner parties, the annual show and, weirdest of all to my way of thinking, progressive dinners. You name it, you'll find it here. You haven't discovered that yet?'

'Afraid not. I seem to have been living in my own little world – until now.' Drew reflected how, ever since he'd been alone at Easter, his life seemed to be changing. Maybe it was a good thing. Maybe he should be more sociable, try to fit into the community. Wasn't that what he wanted Jess to do? Why should he be any different?

'When is this scheduled to happen?'

'July or August. At this stage they're flexible with their dates. So, I can tell them you agree?'

'Why don't you have the relevant person get in touch with Fran? She can tee it up this end. It might be best to choose July when the students are on a break. There'll be no chance of the hall being used then.'

'Great, thanks. I'll pass it on.' He rose to leave.

'Before you go.' Owen leapt to his feet so suddenly he startled Drew. 'Why don't you come out to see us at The Haven one of these days? Here's my address and number.' He tore the corner from a sheet of paper, scribbled on it and handed it to Drew. 'No need to stand on ceremony. Just drop in when you feel like a trip out of town. Maybe your daughter would enjoy seeing the animals, and we have a new baby, too. My daughter's,' he added, clearly seeing Drew's look of surprise. 'That's a story for another day.'

'Thanks.' Drew tucked the scrap of paper into his pocket and shook Owen's hand before leaving. As he walked out of the building, he glanced around hoping to catch another glimpse of Marie Cunningham but, of course, she was nowhere to be seen. She'd have left while he was busy with Owen Larsen. He was an odd sort of guy, but Drew felt drawn to him. He had the impression he'd be interesting to get to know better. He tapped the pocket where he'd put the address and phone number. Maybe he'd take him up on the invitation, despite how weirdly it had been worded; maybe he'd enjoy getting out into the countryside; maybe Jess would too.

Twenty-three

Marie place the closed sign on the door and turned towards where Frank was cashing up. 'I'll be off now.'

'Already? Why don't you hang on? Maybe we can have a bite of dinner together, Lucy too. I'd love to see more of her. I thought…' He pulled on one ear. 'Hell, I don't know what I thought, but you and me – we're all she has left.'

Marie sat down with a thump in the nearest chair. 'I told you she wants to meet her dad. She hasn't given up.'

'But she won't be able to find him, will she? Does she even know who he is?'

'His name's on her birth certificate. Robert Drake,' she said, as if the name was a dirty word, which for her it was.

'Well, let's cross that bridge when we come to it.'

Sometimes Frank's easy acceptance of things exasperated Marie, but there was some comfort in knowing she wouldn't be coping with this on her own. Frank would always be there for her.

'About tonight?'

'Sorry, I have to pick Lucy up. She's doing another stint of community service, and…' Marie gave Frank an apologetic look, 'I said we'd stay to dinner.'

'Dinner with the high school principal, huh? Guess I can't compete with that.'

'Oh, Frank!' Marie didn't know how to explain. It wasn't as if she and Frank were still a couple. But, she realised, they'd never quite made a total break from each other. Until now, it had never been an issue. Neither of them had wanted to see anyone else. So, what was different? Drew Hamilton was the father of Lucy's new friend. That was all. 'I'm doing this for Lucy,' she said, knowing it wasn't her only reason. There was something about Drew Hamilton that made her skin tingle.

On an impulse, Marie stopped in at home on the way to Drew's. Despite telling herself this was all about Lucy, she didn't want to go to dinner wearing the same outfit she'd been wearing in the café all day. As she stood in the shower, the anticipation of having dinner with Drew Hamilton again filled her with an excitement she hadn't experienced for years. By the time she'd dressed in a pair of smart blue pants topped with a white angora sweater, she had to stop, take several deep breaths, and remind herself this man had no interest in her as a woman.

The drive over to Drew's helped calm her, and by the time she arrived, Marie was feeling a lot better and wondering what had got into her back home.

*

This time, Marie knew to go along the side of the house to where she found Lucy, Jess and Drew. They were seated by the table, the girls with cans of soft drink, and Drew holding a glass of beer.

'We thought you'd changed your mind,' Lucy said. 'You're late. Look what we did today.' She pointed to the now tidy stretch of garden, the neat pile of weeds, and the freshly mown lawn. 'Jess's dad cut the grass, but we did the rest. Doesn't it look great?'

'It certainly does. You've been busy, all of you,' she added, catching Drew's amused gaze.

'Welcome,' he said with a grin. 'I expect you'd like a glass of wine.'

'Thanks.' Flustered, but not knowing why, Marie took a seat next to Lucy while Drew disappeared inside the house and quickly reappeared with a bottle of sauvignon blanc and two glasses. 'I'll join you when I finish this.' He held up his beer. 'I thought we'd have pizza tonight. The girls will enjoy it and we can have it delivered. Okay with you?'

'Fine.' Marie was unable to say any more, her tongue sticking to the roof of her mouth. This was crazy. She took a gulp of wine.

'A busy day?' Drew asked as he had before, his grin giving Marie the impression he was aware of her discomfort and amused by it.

'Yes. The usual Saturday. Now the weather's turning cold, we get a lot of shoppers coming in for a hot drink and, of course, the usual crowd when kiddies' sports finish.' *Shit, he must think I'm a moron, talking about the weather. Last time, we had an adult conversation.*

'Jess, why don't you and Lucy pop inside and call in our order. You can choose what you want. You'll need to order three large ones.'

'Okay.'

The girls jumped up and went inside.

'Is something the matter?' Drew asked when they were alone. 'You seem to be… I don't know, different.'

'No, it's nothing. Just a busy day,' Marie replied, feeling a fool.

'That's all right then.' Drew drained his beer and leant back seeming satisfied. 'We've had a productive day. The girls are good workers and they seem to be enjoying doing this together. They were telling me about the chess club, too. They're pretty keen, though I imagine it won't last. A bit like my attempts at exercise,' he said ruefully. 'You seem to have that under control.' There was a wicked gleam in his eyes which made Marie want to curl up into a ball.

'I… Fran and I run around the oval at uni a couple of times a week. It helps get things in perspective.' Not sure what she meant by that, Marie added, 'You caught me at a bad time. You must have thought…' Her voice trailed away. What must he have thought of her hot, sweaty appearance?

'It reminded me of my own slackness in that department,' he said. 'In fact, seeing you looking so energetic forced me to get out and run myself. I've done a circuit of the school oval twice this week already.' Drew looked so pleased with himself, Marie couldn't suppress a grin.

'Congratulations,' she said.

'And you're right, it does help put things in perspective. It's difficult to worry about the proliferation of drugs in the school or Jess's poor attitude, when I'm gasping for breath and wondering how I'm going to make the next corner.' Drew laughed, and Marie joined him, suddenly feeling more relaxed.

'All sorted,' Jess said, as she and Lucy returned carrying a bowl of dip and a basket of corn chips. 'They should be here in the next half hour. Okay to have these, Dad? Lucy and I are hungry.'

'Of course, as long as Marie and I can share them.'

'Sounds good,' Marie said, liking the sound of her name on his lips more than the idea of corn chips.

When he smiled his eyes crinkled up sending a tremor through Marie and forcing her to look away.

Marie and Drew sat quietly drinking wine and nibbling on the chips and dip, while the two girls shared videos on their iPhones. Once again it was peaceful sitting here. Marie felt no need to make conversation. It was as if she and Drew were in their own private bubble, the hum of chatter from the teenagers only serving to provide a background to the relaxed atmosphere. She felt she could stay here like this forever.

The loud ringing of the doorbell echoing through the house jolted her out of her reverie, bringing her back to earth with a bump.

'Pizza!' yelled Jess. 'I'll get them.' She dashed off, followed by Lucy.

Saying, 'Someone will need to pay for them,' Drew went after them more slowly, leaving Marie to reflect on the peaceful moment which had just been shattered.

She stood up and, remembering where they were kept, fetched four plates and napkins and set them out on the table in the dining room. It was getting dark and was a trifle too cool to remain outside. Strange how things could change in a week, not only the weather. She was beginning to feel at home in this house. Drew's presence definitely had an effect on her.

The pizzas finished, Jess and Lucy disappeared again, leaving Drew and Marie alone, just like the previous Saturday. *Like an old married couple.* Marie stifled the thought. *Where had that come from?*

'Coffee?'

'Yes, please.' If Marie was having thoughts like the one that had just passed through her head, she'd drunk enough wine. 'I'll take these through.' She gathered up the empty plates while Drew picked up the discarded pizza boxes.'

In the kitchen, it seemed only natural to perch on one of the high stools at the bench as Drew fired up the coffee maker, the aroma of the beans soon tantalising her senses.

As she cupped the coffee in both hands, Marie marvelled how comfortable she felt with Drew. The only other man she felt so at ease with was Frank – and she'd known him almost all her life.

'Penny for them?'

Marie blushed. She took a sip of the hot liquid. 'I was just thinking what a lovely home you have,' she lied. *Had she told him that before?* She couldn't remember.

'I like it. It was the first one I looked at when I arrived in town and it fits the bill. My neighbour, Nick Kerr, thinks the realtor sized me up and decided this was where a high school principal should live. He could be right.'

'Of course he was. We need to keep all you academic types in one place,' she joked.

'What about you?' Drew studied Marie so intently she was in danger of blushing again.

What did he see? A short, middle-aged woman with wild hair who was trying too hard?

'I'd lay a bet you live in the centre of town, within walking distance of the café, though you probably drive there half the time.' He narrowed his eyes. 'Am I right?'

'Pretty much. When Frank and I got... together, we bought this old place – big enough for the family we intended to have. It didn't happen. When we separated, he was happy to move out into the flat above the café and leave me in the house. I thought of selling it, but...' she shrugged, '...it's home.'

Drew nodded as if he understood.

After that, it was easy. They chatted comfortably about their marriages – with Marie keeping quiet about the fact she and Frank had never been legally married. She felt sorry for Drew as he described how he and Irene had grown apart, staying together for Jess's sake until Irene finally left and chose to go overseas.

'It must have been a difficult decision to leave Melbourne,' Marie said, unable to imagine moving away from everything she knew and loved. She was glad she and Frank had an amicable arrangement.

'It seemed like the only solution at the time. This position came up, and I leapt at the chance to make a fresh start.' He rubbed his chin. 'I like it here. I think it was the right decision, but Jess is finding it hard to adjust.'

'Lucy, too.'

The pair fell silent, then they both spoke at once.

'Jess says Lucy…'

'Jess has helped Lucy…'

They laughed.

'You first,' Drew said.

'I was about to say that Jess has helped Lucy a lot. She misses her mum so much, and to have to relocate here, away from all her friends. She didn't find it easy either. I think she feels she's found a kindred spirit in your daughter. What were you going to say?'

'Much the same. They've become joined at the hip. I'm sure they'll both make other friends in time, but at the moment…' He sighed.

'You're right. But girls do tend to have one special friend.' Marie thought of Christine, the girl who'd been her own constant companion throughout her teenage years. Then they'd drifted apart. Chrissie had gone off to university in Sydney, while Marie had chosen to remain in Granite Springs and marry Frank. Her friend was now married with a family while Marie… Maybe that was why she and Fran had become friends when Fran arrived in town. It was soon after Marie heard of Chrissie's marriage and realised she'd never return to her home town. Now they communicated at Christmas and birthdays, though not always at the latter in recent years. Life got in the way of even the best of friendships.

'I'm not sure if boys are the same,' she said.

'I don't think so. Not if they're like me. I ran with a group of mates all through high school, then formed another group at uni.'

'Are you still in touch?'

'Sadly, no. Life got in the way,' he said, putting Marie's thoughts into words. 'We all married, changed. I don't even know where most of them are these days. I guess that's life.'

'Hmm.'

Marie glanced at her watch, surprised to discover how much time had passed. 'I should collect Lucy and get us home.' She rose and looked around for her bag.

Drew rose, too. 'I've enjoyed your company,' he said awkwardly, then paused as if about to say more.

'Can I stay overnight?' Lucy asked, as she and Jess burst into the living room like a whirlwind. She gave Marie a pleading look.

'Oh, I don't think…'

'I don't have a problem, if you don't,' Drew said.

'Thanks, Drew. But not tonight, Luce. We have plans for tomorrow. Remember? Some other time?' She looked at Drew.

'I'll fix it with Luce, Dad,' Jess said, hugging her friend.

As they drove away from Drew's home, Lucy chatted about Jess and their plans for a sleepover. It was good to have the old Lucy back, at least for the time being. But Marie felt a sense of disappointment. There had been no mention of her seeing Drew again. She wondered what he'd been about to say when Lucy and Jess burst in.

Twenty-four

'Why don't we do something together?' Drew asked next morning at breakfast. He'd been mulling over Kay's advice for the past week without doing anything about it. The gardening had proven successful, but that was due to Lucy's presence, nothing to do with him.

'What d'you mean?' Jess's voice had lost its sullenness and there was an edge of something like interest in her tone.

'I don't know. You choose.' Drew took a sip of coffee and waited.

'You mean anything?' Jess sounded dubious.

Drew nodded, stifling the urge to say, 'within reason'.

'Well…' Jess gave him a wary glance, '…there's this place Lucy talked about. It's in Canberra where she used to live,' she added, as if Canberra was the end of the earth.

'That's okay. It's only a couple of hours' drive away.'

'It's called Question or something like that. It's this place where they have all sorts of science stuff and I thought…'

'Questacon? The National Science and Technology Centre. I've heard a lot about it, but I've never been there either. Let's clear up here and we can make a day of it.'

'Thanks, Dad.' Jess picked up her plate, got up and came over to give him a hug.

Drew watched as she took the empty plate across to the sink. If he'd known it was going to be so easy, he'd have tried this tack weeks ago. But he was aware it wasn't only him. Jess's friendship with Lucy had gone a long way to changing his daughter's attitude to life in general and Granite Springs in particular. It was some time since he'd heard her rubbish their move or whine about wanting to go back to Melbourne.

Thinking about Lucy brought her aunt to his mind. The image of the pint-sized woman who pressed all his buttons made him smile. He'd been about to suggest another meeting – one without kids next time – when Jess and Lucy appeared and interrupted them. Now he'd need to figure out a different way to contact her. He knew he could go into the café to see her, but had detected a proprietary attitude from Frank which made him hesitant to approach her there.

Marie said the relationship was over; they were friends and workmates, nothing more. But Drew wondered if Frank saw it that way. He'd heard Lucy talking to Jess about her Uncle Frank as if he was still very much part of the family. No, he'd have to think of something else – maybe ask Jess where she lived or get Lucy's phone number?

Once in the car, Jess was bubbling with excitement. 'What's Canberra like, Dad? It's the capital so it must be big. Is it like Melbourne?'

'Not as big as Melbourne. Canberra is a planned city. It was built at the time of Federation in the early part of the twentieth century– remember your history lessons? Melbourne is the largest city in Australia. Canberra would be about a third its size.'

'Why do you always have to sound like a school teacher?'

'I guess because I am.' Drew glanced at Jess who had taken out her iPhone and was swiping at the screen. *Mistake number one*, he thought. But he was surprised by Jess's next comment.

'I've just googled Questacon. There's all sorts of chill stuff. You can check out your heartrate, there's a thermal camera, and a wild-sounding freefall thing. Can we do that?'

Drew nodded, delighted to see Jess so enthusiastic. 'We can spend as long there as you want. I think there's a café where we can have lunch.'

Jess went back to her phone, then raised her eyes. 'There is! Thanks for this, Dad. Lucy will be so envious.'

As they drove on, past Lake George which had almost dried out, Jess was busy on her iPhone again. But, this time, Drew didn't feel excluded.

'I'm texting Lucy,' she said. 'She wishes she was coming with us.'

Drew's pleasure in the day took a nosedive. Of course, Jess would have preferred to have her friend with her. Her boring dad was a poor substitute. Should he have invited her along – perhaps her aunt, too? His stomach gave a now familiar lurch at the thought of spending a whole day with Marie.

'She's okay with it,' Jess reported after what seemed to be a series of texts. 'She says she's been there lots of times. She's going with her aunt to visit some people who live on an acreage. They have goats, and there's a new baby.'

Drew breathed a sigh of relief. There were to be no recriminations about his failure to include Lucy in the excursion.

Seemingly satisfied, Jess turned on the radio, fiddling with the controls till she found a programme which belted out the type of music she enjoyed. They spent the remainder of the trip with her bopping around to her favourite tunes, and Drew trying to block out the noise.

The morning passed in a haze of activities as Jess pulled Drew from one exhibit to another, culminating in the Freefall activity she'd seen on the Questacon website. It turned out to be an enormous metal slide around six metres high with a tall stairway leading to a narrow entryway at the top. After insisting Drew joined her, they both passed the necessary medical and physical checks before donning the requisite Questacon blue overalls and climbing up the stairs, a cacophony of voices echoing around them in the large hall.

The idea was to sit on the edge of a vertical drop, hold on to the bar above your head in front of you, and push yourself off. Apparently, the vertical drop gave you a feeling of weightlessness, if only for a second, before the drop curved out and friction brought you to a stop.

'My heart's beating so fast,' Jess said, as she as she sat down near the edge and inched herself forward.

Drew knew exactly what she meant. His heart was pounding and his brow sweaty. What the hell had he agreed to?

'Here goes,' Jess said, gripping the bar in front of her.

She pushed herself forward and was gone from Drew's sight in an instant, her scream drowning out the chattering in the hall.

Looking down the slide, Drew regretted his decision, but he knew he couldn't back out. He sat himself down, edged forward, and there was Jess waving at him.

'Come on, Dad!' she yelled, 'You can do it!'

Yes, he could do it. Just seeing the smile on Jess's face, he *had* to do it.

He took a calming breath, reached up for the metal bar, pulled himself forward, and had to close his eyes before he could ease himself off the edge, hanging only momentarily before he dropped.

After a flash of fear, a strange sensation of weightlessness took over. For one petrified second, it was as if he was falling through space, before the slide curved and he was slowed to a standstill by the friction of the overalls.

'Well done, Dad,' Jess said as he got to his feet. 'That was amazing, can we do it again?' Her eyes brimmed with excitement. This was clearly the highlight of the visit.

Once was enough for Drew, though his daughter's smile made it all worthwhile – and her praise.

'You have another go,' he said, 'I think I need a rest.'

'Of course,' she said, touching his arm. 'One more go, then we'll get something to eat.'

Watching her go up those steps, waving at him from her seat on the ledge. Drew was glad they'd made this trip. He felt quite proud of his daughter, not to mention pleased with himself.

*

After healthy servings of smashed avocado, hummus, soy linseed sourdough, greens, grains and dukkah, which both deemed delicious, washed down with a banana smoothie for Jess and mug of coffee for Drew, he was ready to go a second round. But Jess surprised him.

'I think we've done it, Dad. What else is there to do in Canberra?'

'Where do you want me to start? We could visit the mint, the art gallery, the war museum, parliament house…'

Jess's lips turned down. 'Sounds too much like a school excursion. Let's call it a day and I'll ask Lucy's advice before we come again.'

'Suits me.' A trifle irked his suggestions were dismissed so speedily, Drew nevertheless felt a tinge of relief they could go back home. Then he remembered what Jess had said about Lucy's plans for the day – an acreage with goats and a new baby. Drew knew a place fitting that description and he had a standing invitation. 'I think I know where Lucy and her aunt are today. I know the people, too. How about we drop in on our way home?'

Twenty-five

The sun was shining in a clear blue sky as Marie and an excited Lucy drove out to visit Fran and Owen.

'I promise I won't do anything stupid this time,' Lucy said, then her eyes clouded over as they both remembered their last visit when Dee was with them.

'It's okay, Luce.' Marie put a hand on her knee. 'She wouldn't want us to be sad all the time.'

'I know. It's just… I can be feeling good then it suddenly hits me and…' she sniffed.

'Take a deep breath and look out the window. Think how much your mum would enjoy seeing all this again. You're her eyes now. Remember how happy she was; how she loved the Australian countryside? She'd want you to enjoy it, too.'

'I guess. Do you think she knows, Aunt Marie? Is she somewhere watching over us? Did she see me getting into trouble?' Lucy's eyes widened at the thought of her mother looking down on her every action – good and bad.

'I don't know, honey. But wouldn't it be wonderful if she were. And it might be a good idea to behave as if she *can* see you. Would that change anything?'

'I'd hate her to know about the drugs and the police station. She'd be so angry – even angrier than you were.' She slid her eyes towards Marie.

Marie squeezed Lucy's knee. 'I know. Your mum could be a terror when she was roused. I remember when we were growing up, how she always wanted to do everything I did, even when she was too young. She could throw such a tantrum.' Marie smiled in reminiscence. 'What you need to do, Luce, is remember the happy times.' *And that's what I must do, too.*

'I'll try.'

When they arrived at the property, Lucy hopped out of the car to open the gate without needing to be asked, then closed it again, before jumping back into the car. As before, the goats stood watching them while they chewed on the short grass or reached up to the lower branches of the scattered trees.

Fran's cat was sunning himself on the veranda when Lucy approached the house. She immediately picked the creature up and hugged him to her.

'Look, Aunt Marie, Stormy remembers me!' Lucy exclaimed, as the cat snuggled against her and began kneading her with his paws.

'You found Stormy already?' Fran came out of the house to greet them. 'I'm afraid he's been banished outside a lot these days. Pia's worried about the baby. I thought it was an old wife's tale about cats smothering babies, but she doesn't want to take any chances.'

'Oh, the baby! Where is he?' Lucy gently put the cat down and looked toward the open door. Meantime, Stormy scampered off, only to stop several metres away to begin grooming himself.

Fran and Marie hugged, then Fran led the way into the house where Pia was sitting in a bentwood rocking chair nursing a small baby.

Although eager to see him, Lucy held back.

'On you go.' Fran gave her a gentle push towards Pia who looked up with a welcoming smile.

'Come and meet Tor,' she said.

'He's so tiny!' Lucy gazed down at the little face, the blond hair so like his mother's. 'Oh, he's beautiful. I've never seen such a tiny baby before.' She held her breath as if he'd blow away.

'You've caught him at a good time,' Pia said. 'He's just been fed and will be falling asleep soon.'

Marie watched the interplay, feeling the familiar ache for the children she'd never had. 'You're okay with this?' she asked Fran, knowing Fran suffered a similar longing.

Fran nodded, a smile etched on her lips. 'Pia and Tor are my family now – and Owen, of course – just as Lucy is yours.' She clasped Marie's hand tightly, and the two women stood united in the emotion of the moment.

'Come to pay homage to my grandson?' a voice said, breaking into their thoughts.

'Owen, Marie and Lucy just got here. I was about to make tea for us. Coffee for you?'

'I'll do it. You women seem too engrossed with young Tor. Isn't he a charmer? I think he looks like me.' Owen headed off to the kitchen humming to himself.

'No horses today, Lucy?' Owen asked, when Tor had been put down for his nap, and they were all seated around the large kitchen table.

Lucy turned red. 'I don't think so.'

Fran threw him a warning look.

'Sorry!' He raised his hands defensively. 'I always manage to put my foot in it. Fran keeps me on the straight and narrow. I sometimes wonder how she puts up with me,' he chuckled.

But, seeing the loving glance that passed between them, Marie had no doubt. It was lovely to see her friend so happy, so in love. Life had thrown her a few challenges, but now she was settled in a good relationship. She and Frank had been like that once.

Lucy sat quietly while the adults chatted, then, in a lull in the conversation, she asked, 'Does the baby have a dad?'

There was a stunned silence. All eyes turned to Pia.

Lucy squirmed and looked embarrassed. 'I mean… I know the facts of life. I'm not stupid. But some women decide to have that invitro thing and do it themselves. I just asked…'

Marie felt for her niece.

'Her birth dad didn't want to know about her,' Pia said. 'So, I came home to *my* dad and he's been wonderful.' She took Owen's outstretched hand. 'Fran, too. I couldn't have asked for a better place for Tor to start his life.'

Lucy's eyes clouded over. She didn't say any more.

But Marie could see she was trying to come to terms with Pia's words. She sighed inwardly, knowing she hadn't heard the last of Lucy's search for her own dad.

The conversation became more general again, then Owen took them for an inspection of the vegetable garden. It had been large when he bought the property, he explained, but he'd managed to extend it, adding a tubular steel greenhouse with a transparent covering to protect the plants in cold weather.

It was fun to see him so enthusiastic and, to Marie's surprise Lucy expressed interest, asking sensible questions.

'I must tell Jess's Dad about this,' she said. 'He has lots of room, and it would be fun for Jess and me.'

'Jess?'

'Lucy's friend. Jess Hamilton,' Marie said.

'Hamilton? Not Drew Hamilton's daughter? I met with him recently about a fundraiser the school P&C are arranging. I'm planning to organise a table. You must join us, Marie.'

'Oh, I don't know…'

'Can you fix it up with Marie, Fran?' Owen asked, ignoring Marie's attempt to object.

'It's best to go along with him, Marie,' Fran advised. 'He's like a runaway train when he gets going on an idea. You'll do it in the end anyway, so it's easier to agree right away.'

Lunch was a cheerful affair with Owen's exuberance and Lucy's new interest in life. For the first time since Dee's death Marie felt a renewal of the old relationship she and Lucy always enjoyed.

After lunch, they took their tea and coffee outside to a sheltered spot on the north-facing veranda. Lucy was playing with the cat, Owen strumming on his guitar, and Marie and Fran chatting quietly when they saw a car driving up the lane towards them.

Twenty-six

'Is this it?' Jess asked, as the car turned at the large white mailbox in the shape of a milk churn and swung onto a dirt road. 'It's a long way from everything.'

'By everything, I guess you mean town? And it's not too far. Lots of people prefer to live on an acreage. They enjoy the peace and the privacy.'

Jess didn't look convinced, then, 'Oh, look, there are the goats!' she yelled, twisting in her seat.

This was paradise, thought Drew. He had driven past this way at Easter. He recalled working out the friends he met at the races must live here but hadn't fully appreciated the beauty of their chosen location. He slowed to a stop as they approached a rusty white metal gate. The lettering of *The Haven* and *The Larsens* on the sign attached to the gate indicated he'd come to the right place. For a moment, Drew hesitated, wondering if he should have taken Owen at his word, or called ahead. But Jess had already leapt out of the car and was swinging open the gate.

He drove through.

As the car approached the house, Drew could see the four adults sitting on the veranda and Lucy crouched close by. Owen rose to meet the car as Jess let out a whoop of joy.

'There's Lucy. You were right, Dad.' She jiggled around in her seat and unfastened her seatbelt.

'Wait till we stop,' Drew insisted, but he was pleased this had been a good idea, at least as far as Jess was concerned. He was already having misgivings on his own behalf. What if Marie thought he was stalking her?

Jess jumped out as soon as the car stopped, and Owen and Lucy came through the gate in the fence surrounding the house.

'Jess, what are you doing here?' Lucy yelled, running across to hug her.

Owen walked over at a more sedate pace. 'Glad you decided to drop by.'

'We're on our way back from Canberra, and I decided to take you up on your offer.' Now he was here, Drew felt awkward. Lucy had already disappeared with Jess in the direction of the house.

'We're having coffee. As you see, Lucy Cunningham is here along with her aunt. You know Marie, don't you?'

'Yes.' Drew followed Owen to the veranda where the three women were seated.

'Look who it is. I think you all know Drew,' Owen said.

Drew saw Marie's expression change from one of surprise to – he hoped it was pleasure.

'Hello,' she said.

'I'll make more coffee,' Owen said.

Muttering something about something to eat and drinks for the girls, Fran rose to follow him. There was the sound of a baby crying from somewhere inside the house, and the younger woman left too.

Alone with Marie, Drew ran a finger around the inside of his collar. He cleared his throat.

'I didn't realise you were going to be here, too,' Marie said, as Drew was trying to work out what to say.

'I wasn't. That is, I wasn't invited for today. It was an open invitation from Owen to drop in. We were on our way back from Canberra,' he repeated.

'Canberra? What were you doing there?'

'Jess wanted to see Questacon. She heard about it from Lucy. It was a chance to do something together, just the two of us.'

'Did it work?'

'If you mean did Jess have a good time; did we manage to communicate? Then, yes, I believe it did.' Drew grinned, feeling more at ease. 'In fact, she suggested we go another time, but she didn't like my ideas. I thought perhaps…' he felt his face and ears turn hot, '…we might go together – all four of us.' There, he'd said it.

What was it about this dainty woman that made him so tongue-tied?

After a startled glance as if to make sure he wasn't joking, Marie replied, 'Lucy would like that. She misses Canberra and has a lot of favourite spots. I'm sure she'd love to share them with Jess.'

Not exactly the response Drew was hoping for, but positive, all the same. 'Good, Let's do that, then.' He hesitated, then gained the courage to say, 'It's not just by chance we dropped in to see Owen today. Jess told me you and Lucy would be here. I thought…' He coughed. 'I wanted to see you again. I was about to suggest it yesterday when Jess and Lucy burst in.'

Marie's eyes twinkled with… amusement?

'Here we are.' Owen and Fran reappeared with a tray holding four mugs and a plate of some yummy looking home cooking.

'Fig and banana bread.' Fran said. 'I know it's not long since we had lunch, Marie,' she said apologetically, 'but I thought Drew and Jess might be hungry.'

Realising he was hungry again, Drew took a slice. 'Thanks, Fran. This looks good.'

'I'm nowhere near as good a baker as Marie,' Fran said. 'Have you tasted her brownies? They're to die for.'

'I haven't.' Drew gave Marie an admiring glance. He remembered what Jo said at the picnics about the homemade cooking at The Bean Sprout, and being impressed by the display the first time he visited the café. 'I'd love to try them sometime.'

'Come by the café any day,' Marie said, helping herself to a slice of Fran's loaf, too. 'We always have them – until we sell out,' she laughed. 'But you sell yourself short, Fran. I love this loaf of yours.' She took a bite as if to confirm her words.

Suddenly, a small streak of black which revealed itself to be a cat came darting round the corner of the house, followed by two laughing teenagers. They stopped when they caught sight of the plate of food.

'Bet you two are hungry,' Owen said. 'How about a Coke to go with it?'

'Yes, please,' Lucy said, a shyer Jess following her to take a seat on the bench under the window.

'I didn't mean to interrupt your afternoon,' Drew said to Fran, when Owen had gone back inside, knowing full well that had been his intention.

'No worries. It's good to see you again, and Jess and Lucy seem to be great buddies.' She gestured to where the two were now giggling over something they were looking at on Jess's phone.

Later, when Marie rose to leave, Drew did the same. As they were about to get into their cars, Jess asked, 'Dad, can we stop at Lucy's on the way home? I want to borrow a book she's been telling me about.'

'Can't it wait? You'll see each other at school tomorrow.' But even as he spoke, Drew hoped Jess would insist. He was interested to see where Marie lived. A person's home said a lot about them, and he was eager to learn more about Marie. Drew wondered what his home said about him. Probably not very much. The furnishings he'd brought up from Melbourne still bore the imprint of Irene's taste. Maybe he should have tossed them and started afresh. But they were what Jess was familiar with. She was finding it hard enough to adjust without having to get used to a whole new set of furniture. And he'd have no idea where to start. He'd always left that sort of thing to Irene.

He wasn't disappointed.

'Da...ad!' Jess's petulant look was back.

Marie seemed to catch sight of it. 'Why not?' she said. 'And why don't you both stay to dinner? You've cooked for me twice now. It must be my turn.'

This was more than Drew could have hoped for. 'If you're sure it won't be too much trouble.'

'I'm sure. And it'll be good for the girls to have more time together. You can follow me or... Jess knows where we live.'

Twenty-seven

Marie noticed Lucy was very quiet on the drive home, her earlier liveliness had dimmed and she was lost in thought. Aside from glancing at her a few times, Marie let her be, figuring out Lucy would tell her what was wrong in her own good time.

They were on the outskirts of Granite Springs when Lucy turned to face Marie. 'Aunt Marie, why didn't Tor's dad want him? Didn't my dad want me either? Was there something about me he didn't like?'

Marie chewed on the inside of her cheek. She'd wondered when Lucy would ask this. Her question to Pia about Tor's dad had been an innocent one. It was natural to want to know where the baby's dad was, but it opened up the can of worms that had been simmering away ever since Lucy decided she wanted to find hers. She wished Lucy had chosen a better time.

'No, sweetheart. There was nothing wrong with you. You were perfect – still are, most of the time,' she added with a forced laugh. 'But some men aren't ready for the responsibility of being a parent. It's hard work.'

'But Tor's only a baby.'

'Yes. In Pia's case, the man who is Tor's dad didn't want to be a parent at all. It didn't fit into his plan. Luckily, Pia's dad had recently moved here, and she had somewhere to go. I don't know if she'll stay now Tor is born. She may want to go back to the city. But I know both Owen and Fran hope she'll decide to make her home in Granite Springs. It's a good place for a child to grow up.' Marie was more comfortable talking about Pia than about Dee.

Lucy was silent for a few moments then, 'But my dad didn't leave Mum before I was born, did he?'

'No, he stuck around for just over a year before deciding he'd had enough.' Marie's voice hardened as she suffered a recurrence of the long-forgotten rush of anger she'd experienced when Dee had called in tears.

'Robbie's gone, Marie. He's left me and Lucy. He says he can't handle being a dad anymore. He's tired of the endless nappies, the broken nights, the mess. What am I going to do?'

Marie tried to comfort her, went to Canberra and spent several weeks trying to help Dee come to terms with her situation. But she couldn't stay forever. Frank needed her. The Bean Sprout needed her. Marie's life was here in Granite Springs. She'd even suggested Dee move back. Frank said she could stay with them while she worked things out. But Dee was adamant. Canberra was her home now, and she was determined to make a go of it; to bring up Lucy as best she could.

'Why?'

'I don't know, honey. But being a parent is hard.' *As I'm finding out.* 'And some people aren't strong enough to cope.'

'Wasn't my dad strong enough?'

'I guess not. But you had a great mum, didn't you?'

'Yeah.' Lucy fell quiet again. 'Do you really not know where he is?'

'No, sweetie. I'm sorry, but I don't.'

'Where did Mum and he meet?'

Fortunately for Marie, they arrived home before she could frame a reply, and Lucy shot out of the car to catch up with Jess as Drew's car stopped behind them. Marie breathed a sigh of relief, though she knew it wasn't over. Lucy would come back to the topic another time. But it gave Marie breathing space and time to prepare her response.

When Marie got out of the car and closed the garage door, Drew was standing, legs apart, staring at the house. She walked over to join him.

'This is lovely.' He gestured to the red brick federation-style home with its typical elaborate gables, timber features, dominant roofline, and leadlight windows.

'Yes.' Marie tilted her head to one side as she studied the house she'd called home for so many years. 'It's a perfect example of the period. They don't build them like this anymore.'

'Makes my place look as if it just came off the assembly line,' Drew said ruefully.

'Not at all. There's a place for more modern houses, and yours fits in perfectly with its neighbours. Come and see the inside.'

'Wow!' Drew walked into the hallway with its high ceiling, wooden picture rail and skirting board. The floors had been sanded and stained to give a warm appearance. 'Was it like this when you bought it?'

'Not exactly. Though we were lucky. The previous owners had made a good start to restoring it. Frank did the rest. The only room I had input on was the kitchen, though Frank had his own ideas about that, too.' Marie chuckled, remembering the friendly arguments before she always gave in. Frank knew about kitchens.

'He did well.' There was a catch in Drew's voice which made Marie glance at him quickly. But his expression remained unchanged.

They walked into the kitchen where Lucy was already pouring out glasses of juice for Jess and her.

'We're going to my room till dinner's ready,' Lucy said. 'Okay?'

Marie nodded.

Drew rolled his eyes. 'What is it about teenagers and their rooms? Jess seems to spend half her life in hers, leaving me to rattle around in the rest of the house.'

'It's only natural for them to want a place of their own – somewhere private where they can hide from the world. But I know what you mean. It's something I've had to come to accept since Lucy moved in. When she and Dee came to visit, Lucy was always with us, wanting to share what we were doing. That all changed after Dee's death.' Marie paused, her breath catching. This was the first time she'd actually said the word. She ploughed on. 'It took me a while to understand… I thought she was hiding from me, but Frank…' she hesitated, realising she'd mentioned Frank again, then continued, '…Frank counselled patience, and now I know Lucy needs to have her space and that she'll be with me when she's ready. Right now, she wants to be with Jess, and our company would be a bore.'

'You may be right. How did you get to be so wise?'

'Oh, believe me, I still have a lot to learn. Most days will see me tearing my hair out. But I think I'm getting there.' Surprisingly, Marie found this was true. Despite her inner turmoil, her self-guilt, she was feeling more confident in dealing with Lucy.

Marie poured them both a glass of wine and began to prepare dinner. It felt good to see him sitting there as she stirred the spices into the mince and took the taco shells from the cupboard. 'We normally have an easy meal on Sundays,' she said. It was a far cry from the Sunday roast of her parents, but it was a custom she and Frank started in the early days of their marriage and it had stuck. Lucy liked it too.

'Can I help?' Drew asked, when she began to shred lettuce and had placed the tomatoes ready to chop.

'No, just sit there and talk to me,' Marie replied, unconsciously repeating Drew's remarks of the previous week. Had it only been a week ago? On one front it seemed she'd known him forever, on another there was still so much to know.

'Tell me what's worrying you.' Drew put his glass down and leant his elbows on the table. 'You've been tense ever since we got back. Is it something I did or said?'

'Nothing to do with you.' Marie laid down her knife, surprised Drew was so perceptive. She'd come to expect it from Frank, but Drew was still such an unknown quantity.

'Is it too terrible to share?'

'Not terrible at all, but…' How could Marie explain she didn't feel she knew Drew well enough to share her family's confidences. She looked across at him, at his eyes full of compassion, and weakened. 'It was seeing Pia on her own with the baby – a single mother. It reminded Lucy of her own situation and she asked where Tor's dad was. Then, coming back in the car…' Marie relived the conversation in her mind, '…Lucy started to ask about her dad again.'

'Her dad?'

'I didn't mention it before but lately she's been trying to find him. I suppose it's natural now her mum's gone, for her to want to contact her other parent. But…'

'He's not someone you want her to be in touch with?'

'I'm afraid she'd be disappointed. I think she's been building him up in her mind as some sort of hero. It was a shock to her to discover some men don't want to be a dad, that they run a mile from the responsibility.

Dee was a wonderful single mother. I don't want anything to tarnish that.'

'I'm sure nothing would. But, would it really be so bad for Lucy to meet him? He is her dad, after all. Maybe he's changed. A person can change a lot in fifteen years.'

'Fourteen,' Marie corrected, picking up her knife again and chopping the tomatoes as if the poor tomato were the man who'd broken her sister's heart. Marie had always had her doubts about Robbie Drake. He was too charming for his own good. But Dee was head-over-heels in love and wouldn't hear a word against him.

'She's been trying to trace him without success?'

'Yep. She won't manage it. He's gone for good.'

'What makes you so sure?'

'I…' Marie wasn't really sure, but she hoped Lucy wouldn't find him. Robbie was a troublemaker. Marie was sure there'd be unpleasant repercussions if he were to reappear in their lives. 'Dinner's almost ready,' she said instead of replying. 'I'll fetch the girls.'

'I'll do it, while you set the table.' Drew rose and disappeared, following the sound of music Marie only now became aware of.

She wasn't sure why a sudden feeling of dread engulfed her.

Drew came back with the girls chattering away as usual.

'Yum, tacos!' Jess exclaimed. 'We never have them at home.'

'They're not hard to make,' Lucy said. 'I often helped Mum do it.' She fell silent as images of her absent mother seemed to fill the room.

During the meal, Marie was conscious of an underlying sense of excitement in the two girls, so it was no surprise when, as they were finishing, she saw Jess nudge Lucy.

'Aunt Marie,' Lucy began in a wheedling voice, 'there's going to be a disco at the PCYC next Friday. Can I go?'

'And me?' Jess asked Drew.

Marie and Drew looked at each other, both remembering what happened last time the two went out together for an evening.

'It's all above board. There won't be any drugs or alcohol there,' Lucy said, seeing their obvious reluctance.

'That's true,' Drew said. 'I know these Police Citizens Youth Club events are well run. But…'

'Please, Dad. Ryan Kerr will be there too.'

'I seem to remember he was the one who encouraged you to go to that party, then stayed home himself.'

Jess shifted uncomfortably. 'Yes, but…'

'What do you say, Marie? Shall we give these two rascals another chance?' he asked with amusement.

Marie pretended to consider before replying, 'I suppose we could, but only if one of us drops them off and picks them up again.'

Both girls looked stunned.

'But…' Lucy began.

'Sounds like a plan,' Drew said. 'That's the condition. Take it or leave it.'

'Okay,' Jess said reluctantly. 'But what will everyone think – seeing us treated like little kids?'

'If you'd rather stay home?'

'It'll be all right.' Lucy elbowed her friend.

'Right then. I guess we should be going. Thanks for a lovely meal, Marie. It's been a real pleasure.'

'Not at all. There wasn't a lot to do.'

They made their way to the door, the girls whispering to each other. On the doorstep, Drew and Marie stood, unsure how to end the evening. Finally, Drew gave Marie a brief peck on the cheek, then stood back, his glasses glinting in the light from the outdoor lamp. 'If the girls are going to be busy on Friday, why don't we enjoy a dinner neither of us have to cook?' he asked.

'You mean…. like a date?' He couldn't mean that.

'Exactly like a date. What do you say?'

Marie didn't know what to say. This was the last thing she expected. A date with Drew Hamilton. Dinner with no teenagers around to interrupt.

'Yes, I'd like that.' The words flew out of her mouth of their own volition.

'I'll call you,' he said, leaving Marie gazing after him in amazement.

Twenty-eight

The week passed too slowly for Drew, with fewer dramas than usual. Since the fated party, the police had been on school grounds interviewing senior students. Their interrogations had proved fruitless, but at least there had been no further reports of plumes of marijuana smoke rising from behind the sports sheds.

At breakfast on Friday morning, Jess was more animated than usual. She was actually humming to herself as she poured out her favourite cereal and splashed it with milk. Drew smiled to himself, thrilled to see the change which had taken place in Jess in the past few weeks. Maybe Granite Springs would prove to be a blessing for both of them after all. He still couldn't quite believe he was attracted to another woman – after all his vows to the contrary. But Marie Cunningham wasn't like any other woman he'd ever met. And he wasn't sure she was completely over her ex – she and Frank seemed to still be pretty close.

'You won't need to drive me and Lucy tonight, Dad. Ryan's offered to take us.' Jess beamed at a message on her phone.

Stifling the urge to remind her he'd banned her phone from the meal table, Drew took a deep breath. 'That's not what we arranged,' he said, with as much calm as he could muster.

'I know what you and Lucy's aunt said, but this will be better.' Jess's smile disappeared, and the old pouting expression threatened to reappear.

'It was Ryan last time who...' Drew saw the expression on his daughter's face and changed his tack. 'Okay, let me think about it. I'll give you an answer later today.'

'I've already told him we'll go. I'll look stupid if I have to change it.'

Drew sighed. *Why did everything have to be so hard?* 'I'll give you my answer later,' he repeated, deciding to check with Nick. Ryan appeared to be a responsible guy, but Drew would feel more confident if he checked with his dad. And there was Marie to consider. How would she feel about the change of plans?

He and Jess left at the same time, Drew to drive to school and Jess to cycle. As he drove off, he could see Jess going slowly past their neighbour's house. She stopped as Ryan appeared on his bike, and they cycled on together.

Arriving before school began, Drew picked up his phone to call Nick. He wanted to talk with him before he called Marie. He'd already spoken with her earlier in the week to make arrangements for their date. He was to drive over with Jess to pick up her and Lucy, then they'd drop off the teenagers and go on to Pavarotti's for dinner. He was looking forward to seeing her again – without danger of interruptions from their respective children. Hopefully this new wrinkle wouldn't put a spanner in the works.

'Drew, what can I do for you?' Nick asked.

Drew cleared his throat. This was awkward. How did you ask a friend if his son could be trusted? 'It's about this disco tonight. Jess says Ryan's offered to drive her and Lucy…'

Nick laughed before Drew could finish speaking. 'That's not quite accurate. I'll be doing the driving. Ryan doesn't have his license yet. He's still on his L plates, so to his disgust, he's still reliant on his old dad – or his sister if she's feeling generous. But she has her own social life to keep her busy on a Friday night.'

'Oh!' Drew felt a wave of relief flow through him. 'That's all right, then. The way Jess put it…'

'That'll be Ryan trying to impress. He's good at that. I expect he's hoping I'll let him drive, but I'll be there with them. I think half the girls in Jess's year think he's something special given the number of calls and texts he receives. I don't pay much attention as I don't think he's really into girls yet. But he does seem to like Jess and Lucy. I tell you, I'm not looking forward to the next few years. It's hard enough dealing with Sam. Send Jess round when she's ready.'

'I was intending to pick up Lucy, too. Marie and I…'

'No worries. I suppose Ryan included Lucy in his invitation? A wise move, worthy of his dad.' Nick chuckled, making Drew realise young Ryan was being shrewd in his attitude to the girls. Though would they see it that way?

The next call was an easier one, the thrill when he heard Marie's voice putting a shine on his day. Like Nick, she laughed when she heard about Ryan's offer to drive them to the disco. 'He's going to be a real heartbreaker if he isn't already,' she said. 'I probably don't need to let Lucy know. I expect she and Jess have already been in touch and they'll see each other soon.'

'Our arrangement still stands. I'll pick you up at seven. I'm looking forward to it.'

'Me, too.'

*

A strong aroma of garlic and herbs met Drew and Marie as they entered Pavarotti's that night. They'd both laughed to see Jess and Lucy's faces when Ryan arrived accompanied by his dad. 'No chance of any hanky-panky there,' he said, as they drove off with Ryan at the wheel and the girls sitting in the back seat.

'This is nice. I haven't been out like this since… I can't remember when.'

The warmth in Marie's eyes made Drew's stomach flutter. He wanted to reach over, to place his hand on hers, but it was too soon. He wasn't sure how she'd react. 'Would you prefer red or white?' he asked instead.

'Red, please. I love the *Ciao Bella Sangiovese* they serve here, unless…'

'*Ciao Bella Sangiovese* it is. I suppose you know the menu off by heart, too? What do you recommend?'

Marie nodded, looking amused. 'You haven't been here before?'

'Afraid not. I have to confess I've been leading a pretty sheltered life up till now. But that's all going to change. It already has.' Drew fixed Marie with what he hoped was a meaningful gaze only to see her avert her eyes. *Damn, had he said too much?*

'I'm going to have the seafood linguini, but for you I'd recommend the Gnocchi Pavarotti. It's their speciality. Frank always orders it.'

Drew gave her a quick glance, but there was no hint of guile. It was clearly natural for her to speak of Frank in the present. She said he was her ex, but he was obviously still very much a part of her life – not only her working life. 'Sounds good.'

A waiter appeared with menus which Drew waved away and ordered the wine and the dishes Marie nominated. He loved gnocchi. There was no reason to refuse her recommendation, just because it was a favourite of Frank's. Drew liked what he'd seen of the guy, so why did he have this burning sensation in his chest every time Marie mentioned his name?

'You were right. This is delicious.' Drew forked up the last of his gnocchi. 'It's one of the best I've ever tasted.'

'Only one of them?'

'Okay, you got me. The best. More wine?' Drew picked up the bottle which was still half-full. 'I'm driving so you'll have to help me out.' Without waiting for a reply, he topped up both their glasses.

The rest of the evening passed pleasantly as Drew and Marie shared information about themselves and gradually both lowered their defences.

'Do you have time for coffee?' Marie asked, as Drew pulled up outside her house. 'They did say the disco wouldn't finish till ten thirty.'

The invitation was a surprise, but one Drew was delighted to accept. The evening had gone well, better than he could have anticipated. Coffee with Marie, in her house, would be a bonus.

It was good to be in Marie's home again. The house smelt of her – a delicate scent of something floral with a hint of lemon and just a touch of something more exotic. Then there were the cooking smells. It was so obvious Marie's kitchen was the heart of the house. The entire place was filled with the aroma of the last batch of whatever she'd made for the café.

'Brownies,' she said, seeing him stop and sniff the air. 'I made a batch earlier. Would you like one with your coffee?' She grinned when Drew nodded eagerly.

Seated at the kitchen table with coffee and the best brownie he'd ever tasted, Drew wondered how he could get to know this woman better. Although they'd spent the evening together, he felt she remained pretty much a closed book to him. He wanted to know the part Frank played in her life, if they were still… But there were some things he couldn't ask – or could he?

'You and Frank… you seem close.' Drew took another bite of his brownie, the chocolatey concoction melting in his mouth making him want to drool in delight. These were seriously good.

'We…' Marie fidgeted, clutching nervously at the tea she was drinking in preference to coffee. 'It's complicated.'

Drew waited.

Marie sipped her drink. 'We're friends, good friends. You don't suddenly turn that off because you decide not to live together.'

But Irene and he had. Did that make them odd? Or was it the relationship Marie and Frank still appeared to have that was unusual?

'And there's the café…'

The café. That dammed café. Drew couldn't be jealous of a café, could he? No, he was being ridiculous. Marie was right. She and Frank were two of the lucky ones who'd managed to survive a breakup and remain friends.

'I have to admit,' Marie continued, 'I was considering making a change and then Dee…' Her voice dropped to a whisper. She put down her mug and spread her hands. 'Frank was so good. I couldn't have coped without him. And,' she raised her head, 'Lucy needs the stability of the familiar. The café with Frank and me is what she knows in Granite Springs. She's lost so much. I couldn't take away that security from her.'

'I'm sorry. But she seems to be adjusting.' Just as Jess was.

'Jess, too,' Marie said, echoing Drew's thoughts. 'Tonight's a prime example.'

'It's been good for me, too, to get to know you a little better.' Drew finished his coffee and stretched his arms above his head. 'I guess it's time for me to go. I want to be home when Jess gets there.'

He followed Marie to the door. Once there, they stood close together. For a moment Drew hesitated then he moved closer. 'Marie…' He put a finger under her chin, tipped her head up and was lowering his lips to hers when… he was almost blinded by a sweep of headlights in the driveway.

Twenty-nine

'Aunt Marie! Were you and Jess's dad going to kiss? Gross!' Lucy's face was screwed into such an expression of distaste, Marie had to pinch the inside of her arm to prevent herself from laughing.

'If we were, would that be so wrong?'

'He's the school principal! And what would Uncle Frank think?'

The mention of Frank's name brought Marie down to earth. Frank had been behaving oddly recently. Drew had asked about him, too. Marie was aware she'd become secretive with her ex, something she'd never been before. They'd always shared everything – their joys and their sorrows – and that hadn't changed when Frank moved out. Now Marie was beginning to think it should have. She should have become more independent.

But she'd appreciated Frank's support when Dee died, needed it, even. In fact, Marie didn't know how she'd have made it through those first few weeks without him there as her sounding board and to provide a much needed helping hand. But now it might be time to loosen those ties.

'It's nothing to do with your Uncle Frank,' Marie said, the memory of Drew's breath on her cheek giving her a warm glow. 'How was the disco?'

'It was lit.' Lucy's eyes glowed with delight. 'I danced all night and the music was fire.'

It was a different language for Marie, but she supposed her own teenage words had sounded foreign to *her* parents. 'I'm glad, sweetie. I had a nice time, too.'

'Huh.' Lucy gave her a brief hug and stomped off.

Marie heard the bedroom door slam shut and sighed. Back in the kitchen she dropped the empty mugs into the dishwasher. It had been a lovely evening. She felt closer to Drew than before. It was a pity Nick drove up when he did. She was sure Drew was about to kiss her and… And what? Frank was the only man Marie had kissed since she was eighteen, though these days it was more of a quick peck and the odd cuddle. But Frank was familiar, comfortable. What would it be like to feel the lips of a stranger – Drew's lips? Thinking about it sent tremors up and down her spine.

*

After the excitement of Friday evening, the next day felt flat, even Frank's attempts at humour in The Bean Sprout failed to elicit more than a brief smile from Marie. She only came alive when Lucy burst in accompanied by Jess, the two girls intent on talking Frank into giving them weekend jobs.

'What do you think, Marie? Should I hire these two scallywags?'

Marie pretended to give his question serious consideration before replying, 'Maybe we need to give them a trial before we decide.'

'Good idea. Lucy, how about you and your friend come back this afternoon at closing time. You can help us wipe down the tables and clean the floor. If you can do that properly, then maybe we can find something for you on a regular basis.'

'Will we get paid?'

Frank chuckled. 'Paid? Well, for today, you might be able to help finish off any leftover cakes. If we come to a more permanent arrangement, we can talk money. What do you say?'

Lucy and Jess looked at each other and some unspoken message seemed to pass between them. 'Okay, Uncle Frank. We'll see you later.'

'Was that really such a good idea?' Marie wanted to know when they sauntered out. 'It means… We always said we didn't need more staff.'

'Lucy's family,' Frank said. 'This'll be hers one day.' He waved a hand around to encompass the café. 'Best she gets an idea how we work as soon as she can. And it'll do her good to discover what it's like to have to follow a routine.'

'Yes, but…' Marie bit her lip. She wasn't sure why, but the idea Lucy would fall heir to The Bean Sprout didn't sit well with her. There was nothing wrong with the notion, but it assumed she and Lucy would continue to be part of Frank's life – and he part of theirs – until both Marie and Frank could no longer work there. It was a sobering thought, and one which she needed to think through.

Any further thoughts on the subject were dismissed by a flurry of customers as the morning sports gatherings finished and families arrived with exhausted and excited children for a pick-me-up of coffee, soft drinks and burgers.

Then the door opened, and Drew walked in. Marie felt her temperature rise and forced herself to focus on the table she was serving, pretending she hadn't been hoping he'd come here this morning.

'Hi Drew. The girls seemed to have had a good time last night,' Frank greeted him.

Marie didn't look in their direction but was conscious of Drew glancing towards where she was helping a young boy decide between a banana smoothie and a flavoured milk. Was Drew going to mention their dinner to Frank? It wasn't really a secret. Nothing in Granite Springs could be kept secret for long. But Marie hadn't mentioned her date with Drew to Frank, thinking he might not approve. As she'd rightly told Lucy, it was none of Frank's business who she spent time with. But Lucy was aware of what Marie knew so well. Frank still regarded Marie – and now Lucy – as family, and as such, felt responsible for them. Till now, it hadn't mattered. Marie had welcomed his concern, but now things had changed, and she was finding it irritating.

Marie listened intently, pleased when Drew gave nothing away.

'They certainly did. And I believe you have two new employees? Jess came home full of how she and Lucy are going to work here. I thought I'd better check it out before they get too wound up.'

So, he hadn't come to see her? Marie felt a flash of disappointment, quickly followed by relief.

'Yeah, we're giving then a trial this afternoon – wiping, sweeping and mopping. Don't worry, we won't be letting them loose on the customers – not yet, anyway.'

'Good luck with that, unless Lucy is more housetrained than Jess.'

'Maybe some of it will rub off at home.'

'Hope so.'

'Have a coffee now you're here?' Frank picked up a cup, just as Marie returned with the order.

'Hello, Drew,' she said, trying to stifle the embarrassment threatening to overwhelm her. What was she embarrassed about? 'I heard what you two were saying and I'm afraid Lucy's probably not much better than Jess in that regard. Though she has the makings of a good cook. I've been giving her lessons in baking and she's become pretty adept at making brownies and banana bread.'

Frank's eyes widened. 'You didn't say.'

'It didn't come up.'

'Right.' Frank's eyes swept round the café, clearly noting that, apart from the table Marie had just served, all of the others were busily eating. 'Marie, why don't you sit down with Drew. I'll bring you both a coffee and maybe you'd like a piece of that vegetable lasagne, Marie. You've been on your feet all morning. I can take a break later.'

'Thanks, Frank. I might go for some of the lasagne, too.' Drew slid into a bench seat.

Marie followed suit, taking her place opposite, after a sideways glance at Frank to determine if he suspected anything. But he appeared as unruffled as usual as he made the coffee and slid two pieces of lasagne into the microwave.

'Thanks for last night. Frank doesn't know?' Drew whispered. He took off his glasses, breathed on them and rubbed them absentmindedly with a cloth. He held them up to check the lenses, then replaced them. 'That's better. You didn't tell him we had dinner together?'

'Why should I?' Marie was becoming irritated the way everyone seemed to think Frank ruled her life. Well, not everyone, she allowed, but Lucy – and now Drew.

'We're not a couple. I told you.'

Frank arrived at the table with coffees and lasagnes, preventing her from saying any more.

'Maybe someone should tell Frank that.' Drew nodded to where Frank was watching them carefully.

'That's just Frank. He likes to keep an eye on everything that's happening in the café. It's nothing to do with you and me.' But, stealing a glance to where Frank was pretending to be busy cleaning the espresso machine, Marie wasn't so sure. He did seem to be taking an unusually keen interest in their table.

'Okay.' Drew seemed convinced. 'Tell me about this new venture of Jess and Lucy's. I was surprised Jess took the initiative to find a part-time job.'

Marie laughed. 'I suspect it may have been Lucy's doing, perhaps even egged on by her uncle. Frank came up with an odd suggestion after they left. He seems to think Lucy will take over the café one day.'

'And you don't? It's a flourishing business, and I recall he told me it's been in the family for generations.'

'That's just it. His family. Not mine, not Lucy's. I don't think it's what Dee would have wanted for her. She had ambitions for Lucy to do something with her life.'

'So, it's good enough for you but not for Lucy?'

Marie felt trapped. How did she explain her present ambivalence about the café; how she'd been considering a change when Dee died and her life turned upside down; how Frank had been there for her; how she had stayed on for Lucy's sake? 'It's complicated,' she said at last, realising she'd said before. But sitting here, talking with Drew, a warm glow flooded over her. There was something about Drew's presence that had a calming effect on her – odd when she remembered their first encounter.

'Tonight?' Drew asked, as he rose to leave.

Marie's stomach fluttered. She hadn't expected this. Maybe she'd been wrong. Maybe Drew *had* come here to see her. She nodded and mouthed, 'Where?'

'I'll text you.' He grinned and left.

'Seems a nice guy,' Frank said, when Marie took their empty plates and mugs over to the servery. 'It's good Lucy has made a friend.'

Marie peered at Frank to determine if there was any hidden agenda in his comments, but he looked as laid-back as usual. Perhaps this idea he might be jealous of Drew was all in her imagination.

'Yes. They seem to be a nice family.'

'No mother?'

'I think Lucy said she's in the US.'

'Another single parent. He must be finding it difficult.'

'I suppose so.'

'Dinner tonight, Marie? It's been ages.'

'Not tonight.' But Marie felt bad about rejecting Frank again. 'Lucy will probably be out with Jess again tonight. Why don't you come around for dinner tomorrow? I'll make an exception and cook a roast.'

'Sounds good. Now, I guess we should close up and prepare for our new helpers to arrive.'

*

The text from Drew arrived as Marie was leaving The Bean Sprout, the ping making her heart leap. This was ridiculous, she told herself. She barely knew the man, but she couldn't stifle the tremor of excitement at the sound, though she managed to wait till she reached home before reading it.

How does a movie night appeal? The local fleapit is showing an oldie but goodie – Butch Cassidy and the Sundance Kid. Want to share a bucket of popcorn?

Marie smiled. She'd heard about that movie, but never seen it. It was way before her time. She quickly texted her agreement. Drew texted back. He'd pick her up at seven.

'Can Jess stay to dinner and have a sleepover?' Lucy asked, wandering into the kitchen where Marie was trying to decide what to cook for dinner. 'What is there to eat?' She opened the fridge door and peered inside.

Marie reached over to close it. 'You can have fruit for now. Didn't Uncle Frank let you have some leftovers from the café?'

'Mmm, but that was ages ago.'

Barely an hour, Marie thought. 'And dinner will be tuna casserole with salad. Is Jess's dad happy for her to have a sleepover?'

'Dunno.' Lucy picked two apples from the fruit bowl.

'She should call him.'

'Okay.' Lucy disappeared, and Marie heard her yell, 'Have you called your dad yet, Jess?'

She sighed, and muttered to herself, 'Teenagers!'

*

The movie was fun. Marie enjoyed sitting close to Drew, their thighs touching, hands entwined, his squeezing hers as the action grew more tense. It was a surprise to come out into the cool evening air, to the familiar Granite Springs Main Street, after watching the two heroes riding across the arid desert. Marie shivered, and Drew threw an arm around her shoulders and pulled her close.

'Straight home or… given our two charges are busy at your place, what about coffee at mine?'

Marie was torn. One part of her wanted to go home to make sure the girls weren't getting up to mischief, the other to accept Drew's invitation. The imploring expression in Drew's eyes won the day. What harm could befall Lucy and Jess while they were at home?

'Coffee sounds good, but only a quick one. I need to get back.'

'Point taken.' But Drew pulled Marie into an embrace that left her in no doubt of his feelings.

She shivered, but not from cold this time. This was what she wanted, wasn't it? Ever since their attempt to kiss – she was sure that's what it had been – had been interrupted, she'd been secretly imagining how it would feel to have Drew's lips on hers.

Back in Drew's kitchen, in the brightness of the downlights, Marie wondered if she'd been mistaken. Drew was all business, filling the coffee maker, preparing two mugs, and finding a packet of Tim Tams in the pantry. Maybe the hug had been an instinctive thing because of the cold.

'Let's take these through to the other room.' The coffee machine had stopped its hissing and gurgling and Drew had poured coffee into two large mugs. He handed Marie the plate of biscuits and led the way into the living room. Putting the mugs down on a low coffee table, he switched on a dim table lamp and pulled Marie down onto the sofa beside him. 'That's better,' he said, reaching an arm around her shoulder. 'I've been wanting to do this all night.'

Thirty

Marie floated through the next few days in a daze. Somehow, she'd managed to make conversation with Frank over dinner on Sunday. It had been easy as Lucy took up most of the discussion, telling him about what she was doing at school and the movies she and Jess had watched the night before. There hadn't been any time for him to ask Marie about what she'd been doing on Saturday night.

Now it was mid-week and it seemed a long time to wait to see Drew again on Sunday. They planned to drop the girls off at a horse-riding trail while they visited a couple of wineries, before all four of them enjoyed a bush picnic. It sounded idyllic and she was looking forward to it. Lucy and Jess were excited, too.

After a busy day at The Bean Sprout, Marie arrived home ready to relax. Lucy was at the library with Jess and wouldn't be home till later, so Marie was looking forward to making a cup of tea and putting her feet up while she had the house to herself.

She settled herself in a favourite armchair, her lemon and ginger tea within arm's reach, and flipped through the day's mail, discarding the inevitable junk mail. She was about to drop them all on the floor when her phone rang. Seeing Frank's face, Marie grimaced for a moment before answering. What did he want? She'd left him at the café less than an hour earlier.

'Hi, Frank, what's up?' she asked wearily, picking up her cup in her free hand and taking a sip of the refreshing drink.

'I've been opening my mail, and there's one for you. Shall I drop it over?'

'Oh!' Marie had just this minute sat down to relax. She'd spent the day with Frank at the café. Did she really want to see him again?

'It's probably just a marketing flier. It can wait till tomorrow to put it in the garbage – or you can do it for me.'

There was a pause, then Frank said, 'I don't think that's what it is, Marie. It looks official.'

'Official?' Marie put down her tea and sat up straight. 'What sort of official mail could I get at the café?'

'I don't know, but the envelope's typewritten and is postmarked Darwin.'

'Darwin? I don't know anyone who lives in Darwin. I've never been there, as you very well know.'

'That's why I think it's a bit odd. Shall I come over?'

Marie sighed. She knew Frank. He may be laid-back, but when he had something on his mind, he didn't let go. 'I suppose.'

'I'll be right over.'

Marie looked at her tea which was beginning to turn cold. She'd need to make a fresh cup, and Frank would expect coffee. She hoisted herself out of her comfortable chair and made her way to the kitchen.

'What's so important about this letter it brought you all the way here?' Marie knew she sounded annoyed. She was. He'd interrupted her precious alone time. She didn't have too many moments of privacy with a teenager in the house. 'Where is the damned thing?'

'Here it is.' Frank handed her a long white envelope addressed to Marie Beattie c/- The Bean Sprout Café. It was from someone who thought she and Frank were still a couple.

She turned it over, but there was no return address, reinforcing her initial reaction it was junk mail.

'Coffee?' Frank was already fixing himself a cup, as usual making himself at home. While it was good he still felt comfortable in the house they'd shared for years, Marie often wished he wouldn't act as if he still lived here.

'No, I'm having tea,' she replied distractedly, as she slit open the envelope and took out an A4 foolscap sheet. Her eyes slid to the foot of the page and widened. 'Oh, no!' She put a hand out to steady herself.

'What's the matter?' Frank was at her side in an instant.

'It's from Robbie Drake!'

'What does he want?' Frank held out a hand for the letter.

But Marie clung on to it and began to read, her eyes moving quickly through the brief note. Then she held it out to Frank and collapsed into a chair. 'He heard about Dee's death and he wants to meet his daughter. How could he, Frank, after all these years? He never contacted Dee when she needed him, never paid a cent of child support, how can he suddenly expect to turn up now and claim to be her dad?'

'He *is* her dad, Marie.'

'In name only,' she countered.

'We have to think what Dee would want,' Frank said in a conciliatory tone.

'I know what she'd want, and it isn't to have that bastard worming his way into Lucy's life and affections now she's gone.'

'Are you sure?'

'Yes!' But Marie suddenly wasn't sure of anything other than the fact she didn't want Lucy to be hurt.

'Where is my favourite niece?'

'She's…' Marie checked the kitchen clock. 'She's at the library with Jess, but she'll be home soon. Frank, she can't find out about this. You keep it. I need to think what to do. Maybe we can just ignore it. Pretend I never received it. After all, Robbie doesn't know I'm still in the café with you.'

'It wouldn't take him too long to find out. You can't just leave it. You'll have to do something, and soon.'

'But not just yet,' she pleaded. 'I need time to get my head around it. I never thought we'd hear from him again. When Dee needed to get in touch, when she was bringing up Lucy on her own, he couldn't be contacted. Why does he have to appear on the scene now?'

'I don't know.'

There was the sound of a door opening and closing, and Frank hastily stuffed the offending letter into his pocket as a bright-eyed Lucy bounded into the room. She was so unlike the Lucy who'd spent weeks depressed and grieving, Marie's determination to keep her from being hurt was reinforced.

'What are you doing here, Uncle Frank? Come to dinner again? Can't keep away?' She winked and whirled out of the room.

Marie winced. Trust Lucy to get the wrong impression, seeing Frank here on a mid-week evening.

'I could...' Frank began.

'No, Frank. I'm tired. Go home. We'll talk about this another time – when I've had time to digest what it means.' But Marie knew what it meant. It meant Robbie Drake was about to turn up in their lives like the bad penny he was, and who could predict what the fallout would be?

Thirty-one

Drew couldn't wait to see Marie again. It had been a long week and only the thought of the Sunday he'd planned had helped him through the various challenges he'd had to face. But now it was Sunday morning, the sun was shining, and Drew's mood lifted as he made coffee for himself and took the pancake mix out of the cupboard. He wanted today to be special for Jess, too, and that meant a special breakfast.

'Hi, Dad!' Jess appeared in her nightie, rubbing the sleep out of her eyes. Her hair now had a buzz cut at the back and sides with a stylish quiff that showed only a hint of the horrendous pink, thanks to a trip to the hairdressers yesterday. Both she and Lucy had decided to take the plunge. He had to admit it suited them, and it would soon grow.

'Wow, pancakes!' Jess poured herself a glass of orange juice and pulled out a chair. 'When do we have to leave?'

'As soon as we've eaten breakfast, and you're showered and dressed. Remember to wear something warm and put on your boots.'

'Yeah, yeah. I know all that. I'm not so sure about the horses – getting on one, I mean, but Lucy says it'll be lit. She used to go with her mum.' She took a gulp of juice. 'It must be hard for her. I mean, my mum isn't here, but I can Facetime her and visit – if I can put up with horrible Jake. But hers is gone forever.'

'Yes, you're lucky. Even if you and your mum don't always get on, she's there for you.' Drew deftly flipped two pancakes onto a plate for Jess and set it down on the table. 'Strawberries and maple syrup in the fridge, and yoghurt if you want it. Can you get a carton out for me?'

Jess lazily moved to do as he asked, then, waving her fork in the air, continued, 'When I met Luce, I thought what we had in common was that our mothers had left us. But mine hasn't, not completely.'

'I'm glad you've realised that. She'd like you to visit her again.' Drew held his breath waiting for Jess's response. Irene had emailed him only the day before, suggesting Jess make another trip to LA in the July holidays.

'No way! Not if it's like last time.' Jess forked up her pancake and slurped the juice.

Drew sighed. He wasn't keen for Jess to go either, especially now she was settling into life in Granite Springs. But, when Irene left, they'd made an agreement – Jess would spend time with her mother in LA in her school holidays. It was just a pity the Easter trip had been such a disaster. He could see Jess's point of view. If Irene wasn't prepared to spend time with her, why was she so adamant Jess make the trip? And what was Jake's view on it?

'Well, there's no need to decide just yet,' he said, bringing his own breakfast over to the table to join his daughter.

*

The car trip was like no other Drew had ever known. Having two teenagers in the back seat was an experience in itself, their constant chatter and giggling plus their choice of music sending him into sensory overload. And Marie's presence beside him in the front added to his heightened senses. It was a relief when he turned into the riding stables.

Both Drew and Marie got out with the girls who were bubbling with excitement, Lucy having infected Jess with her enthusiasm and dispelled her earlier nervousness.

After a chat with the owners who assured Drew they catered for both beginners and experienced riders, and seeing Jess and Lucy led away to don helmets and protective vests, he and Marie got back into the car, promising to pick the pair up again in two hours' time.

'I'm glad that's over.' Drew put a hand on Marie's thigh and squeezed it before waving to Jess and Lucy and driving off. 'I was a bit worried Jess would call off at the last minute. She hasn't had the experience with horses Lucy has.'

'She'll be fine. Dee swore by that riding school and she was very fussy about where she allowed Lucy to go. I hope…' Marie bit her lip.

'You're doing okay,' Drew reassured her. 'I never met your sister, but I'm sure she'd be happy to see how much care you take of Lucy.'

'I hope so. It's hard to know what to do for the best.' She twisted a strand of hair in one finger.

Drew shot a glance at her. There was something bothering Marie and it had nothing to do with leaving the girls to go horse riding. Now wasn't the time, but he determined to find out before the day was over. 'What you need is a good wine-tasting to take your mind off Lucy,' he said.

Marie perked up and gave him a smile. 'You're probably right.'

After an hour sampling the various vintages offered by the boutique winery, Drew and Marie headed to the adjoining café. 'This is lovely.' Marie sipped her herbal tea and nibbled on a piece of carrot cake.

'As good as yours?'

'Almost.' She took another bite. 'It may need a touch more cinnamon.' She looked up to meet Drew's eyes. 'What?'

'I love watching you judge the taste of other people's cooking, the way your lips purse and your eyes close.' He smiled, then became more serious. 'Something was bothering you earlier and I don't think it had anything to do with the girls going riding.'

Marie stared down into her cup. She frowned.

'If you don't want to talk about it… But sometimes talking can help.' He waited.

'You're right.' Marie took another sip of her tea. She sighed. 'I don't know what to do. You may remember I told you Lucy was determined to find her father?'

'Yes. But you also said it was an impossible task, one you hoped she'd give up on. Has there been a development? Has she managed to trace him?'

Marie shook her head. 'Worse than that. I've received a letter from him. Robbie Drake wants to meet the daughter he abandoned fourteen years ago. He…' her voice rose, '…he's heard about Dee's death and has taken it into his head he wants to become a father. I can't believe he could be so…so…' She stopped, clearly unable to find the words.

'How did he know where you live?'

Marie looked up, her eyes filled with anguish. The happy woman of a few minutes ago had disappeared, replaced by this troubled one.

Drew cursed himself for having shattered her mood so abruptly with what he thought was an innocent question.

'He wrote to the café. He knew Frank and I worked there when he and Dee married. I guess he thought it was a safe bet we'd still be there – or someone would know where we were.'

'Does he know Lucy is with you?'

Marie shook her head. 'But it wouldn't be difficult for him to find out – or to guess.'

'And Lucy?'

'I haven't told her. I can't. You don't understand what he was like. He'd ruin her life, just as he ruined Dee's. Dee would never forgive me if…'

'Dee's not here.' Drew's voice was gentle. He tried to lay a hand on Marie's arm, but she shook it off.

'You don't understand,' she repeated. 'Sorry, I need to go to the loo.' She stood up and walked off.

Drew watched her go, walking unsteadily till she disappeared around the corner. 'Well, you could have handled that better,' he murmured, berating himself yet again for raising the subject. The day had been going so well.

'Sorry,' Marie said, when she reappeared, her eyes suspiciously red. 'I shouldn't have taken my annoyance out on you. It's not your fault the bastard has come back to ruin our lives.'

'What do you intend to do?'

'I have no idea. What I want to do is forget all about it, ignore his letter and hope it will go away. But Frank says…'

Frank again.

'Frank says I can't let it go, that I need to reply. But how can I do that? I keep thinking of Dee; of how devastated she was when he left; of how she had to survive all those years as a single mother; of how she had just met someone else when she… Sorry,' she rubbed away a tear. 'I'm not being very good company.'

'What are friends for if you can't share your troubles with them? I hope I'm a friend, more than a friend,' Drew said daringly, and this time she didn't brush away the hand he placed on her arm.

'Thanks, Drew. I don't know what made me break down like that.' She sniffed. 'I'm spoiling your day – our lovely day. I shouldn't have said anything.'

'I'm glad you did. It's not healthy to bottle up those feelings. How long have you known?'

'Since Wednesday. The letter was posted in Darwin. He's not in Granite Springs. It's not as if he's going to walk into…' She paused, turning white. 'He's not, is he? He couldn't come here?'

Drew felt the tension that wracked Marie's body. He wished there was something he could do. For a few moments they sat there in silence, Drew trying to work out what to say that wouldn't upset her. Finally, he took a deep breath and asked, 'When your sister died, when Lucy came to live with you, did you… did you adopt her?'

Marie looked at him wild-eyed. 'Adopt her? She's my sister's daughter. And she didn't *come to live with me*. She was already there. Dee and Lucy were in Granite Springs when Dee died. I don't understand. Where else would Lucy go?'

Drew cleared his throat. He was no lawyer so wasn't sure of his facts. 'Do you… could Lucy's father want to do more than meet her?'

Marie looked at him aghast. Suddenly his meaning sunk in. She began to shake her head furiously. 'No! No! He couldn't. He wouldn't. Not even Robbie Drake could be so devious. But why?'

'Didn't you say something about selling your sister's house in Canberra? Did she leave a will? Were Dee and this Robbie divorced?'

'I don't remember about a will. Frank took care of everything because I was so grief-stricken. But it didn't matter. There was only Lucy.' She fell silent, then, 'You can't mean Robbie is after Dee's money. Oh, that would be just like the bastard. But it belongs to Lucy. He gave up all his rights when he left, didn't he?' The last two words came out in a wail.

'Maybe you need to talk to a lawyer.'

Marie took a shuddering breath. 'Maybe I do.'

She hadn't answered the question about divorce. And Drew didn't want to repeat it. It might make no difference anyway.

'Maybe we should open one of those bottles we stashed away in the boot,' he suggested, in an attempt to lighten the mood, but it fell flat.

'No, and I don't think I could face another winery. Sorry. I feel washed out. I must look a wreck.'

'No worries, and you look lovely, as usual.' But there were shadows beneath her eyes that hadn't been there before. 'I should take you straight home, but I guess we need to go through with the picnic. The girls…'

'Of course.' Marie sat up straighter. 'We can't disappoint them.'

'We were due to pick up the picnic hamper at our next stop. We can still do that, but we'll give the tasting a miss. Are you sure you'll be okay?'

'I'm sure.' Marie nodded.

To Drew's inexperienced eyes, she looked anything but. He cursed himself again for having put ideas into her head.

'Thanks.' She took his hand. 'Those things you said… They hadn't occurred to me. To Frank, either. Unless he was too worried to say and didn't want to upset me. He's good that way. Dear Frank.' Before Drew had time to feel irked, she added, 'But I'm glad you did. You're right. And I probably should get legal advice. Frank and I spoke to a lawyer when… Col Ford's retired now, but his partner's still there. I'll make an appointment.'

There was no opportunity for further discussion after they picked up Jess and Lucy. The pair were full of tales of the horses and their rides.

'So, you enjoyed it, Jess?' Drew asked.

'So much. Can we do it again, Dad?'

'We'll see.'

'Where are we having lunch? I'm starved.'

'I doubt that,' he chuckled, pleased to see her enthusiasm. The Jess of today was a completely different person from the sullen teenager who got off the plane from LA after her Easter holiday. 'We have a hamper of food in the boot and we'll drive into the National Park and find a good spot to eat. They have picnic tables where we can spread out.'

'Did you enjoy your wine-tasting, Aunt Marie?' Lucy was bouncing around in the back seat.

'It was very nice.'

Drew heard the tension in Marie's voice and wished he could do something to ease it.

'Did you buy lots of wine?'

'A few bottles. Jess's dad bought more than I did.'

'I wish…' Lucy began, before Jess shushed her.

'What?'

'Nothing.'

Drew saw Marie turn to glance at the two girls, then turn back just as they entered the parking lot of the National Park. By the time they'd unloaded the picnic hamper along with a rug from the car boot, Lucy's words were forgotten.

Lunch passed without incident, and they were soon on their way home. When they arrived at Marie's house, Drew got out of the car, ostensibly to help carry in Marie's wine. But he had another motive entirely.

As Lucy scampered upstairs to change, Drew put his hands on Marie's shoulders. 'I haven't forgotten what we spoke about. I want you to know I'm here if you need me – to talk, or… Anyway,' he added as he saw her flinch, 'let me know what you decide and if there's anything I can do.'

'Thanks, but I'll be fine.' She gave a tight smile.

'I'll be in touch.' Drew let his hands drop and stood watching as she closed the door, before turning back to the car where Jess was already busy on her iPhone.

What had just happened? Had the rapport he and Marie developed just gone up in smoke? Would she take him up on his offer to be there for her or would she go back to her ex? Would it be Frank she'd turn to in her hour of need?

Thirty-two

'You're here early.' Frank seemed surprised to see Marie in the café. Now Lucy was living with her, she normally didn't arrive till later, doing most of her baking at home and leaving him to set up for the week.

'I wanted to talk to you before we opened.'

'Sounds serious. What's up?'

'Not like this when you're doing something else. I mean really talk.'

Frank turned off the espresso machine. Marie could see his brow furrow. She knew she'd worried him. He was such an open book to her, so familiar, so dear.

They sat down at one of the tables.

'What's eating you? Have you been thinking about Robbie's letter?'

'I haven't been thinking of much else. Did it occur to you to wonder why he might want to make contact after all this time?'

Frank scratched his head. 'I guessed it could have something to do with money. Robbie always had his eye on number one, and it would be no secret Dee owned a townhouse in Canberra. He never paid any maintenance for Lucy, did he?'

'Not a cent. At first, Dee tried – contacted Family and Community Services – but there was nothing they could do. They couldn't trace him. It seemed he'd disappeared, possibly left Australia. That's when she tried to contact his parents – to try to find out where he'd gone. But, as you know, she struck out there, too. So, she decided to go it alone.'

'And now he's back. What are you going to do?'

'I don't know.' Marie pulled on her hair and twisted a strand between her fingers. 'I thought… maybe I should talk to a lawyer. Would Robbie have any legal claim on Lucy?'

'He is her father.'

'I know that. But he hasn't acted like it for fourteen years. Surely…? Maybe I could adopt her or something. Do you think?'

Frank rubbed his chin. 'Adopt? I don't know. Lucy's fifteen. Isn't that a bit old for an adoption? And what does she have to say about it? Things seem okay as they are.'

'That's just it. Everything was fine till this came out of the blue. Now… I need to do something, Frank. I need to know how I stand, where Lucy stands, if…'

'What if she wants to live with him?' Frank put Marie's worst fear into words. 'She's old enough to choose, Marie. And you say she's been trying to find him.'

'Yes, but…' Marie knew she couldn't bear to lose Lucy. She was all she had left of her sister and she loved her dearly.

'Would you like me to come with you… to see the lawyer?'

'Would you?' Marie felt a wave of relief. Frank understood her so well. And he knew the situation. He'd been there when Dee and Robbie met and married, when Robbie left. He was Lucy's uncle. He was family.

In the back of Marie's mind, a little voice reminded her it was Drew who'd made the suggestion she consult a lawyer and perhaps he should be the one she was discussing this with. But, looking across the table at Frank's familiar face, at the lines beside his eyes and mouth she'd watched form over the years, at the hair now turning grey, she knew he would never let her down. Regardless of what he thought, he'd always back her up whatever she decided to do.

Drew was still an unknown quantity. Sure, he sent quivers up her spine, made her want to know him better, want for more each time they met. But she didn't really know him. Maybe it was safer to stick with Frank to help deal with Robbie.

*

'Ready?'

'Not really.' The appointment with Gordon Slater, the solicitor who was Col's partner, was set for two o'clock. By agreement, they'd closed the café early so they could go together. Tuesday tended to be a slow day, and Frank had waved away any suggestion Marie go on her own.

'She's my niece, too,' he said, when Marie tried to say she'd be okay, and she was glad.

Pushing open the large wooden door and entering the office of the law firm felt just like the last time they'd come to this office. That time, she and Frank had been seeking to dissolve their marriage, only to discover they'd never been legally married at all. Marie hoped there wasn't going to be a similar shock this time.

'Hi there, Marie, Frank. Here to see Gordon? He won't be long.'

Marie had known Dot Armitage most of her life. Dot had been the receptionist in this law practice for as long as she could remember. She had left briefly, taken early retirement several years ago, only to return when her replacement, Carol, married Gordon Slater, and now it looked as if she was part of the furniture. She was the soul of discretion – had to be in this job – but Marie could see her wondering what brought her and Frank here today.

'Thanks.' Marie took a seat and reached for Frank's hand. She needed this reassuring contact to stop her worrying.

'He'll see you now.' Dot's words sent the spiralling in the pit of Marie's stomach into freefall. She clasped Frank's hand tighter as they walked into Gordon Slater's office.

'So, I need to know where I stand,' Marie said, after explaining the situation. 'What rights does Robbie Drake have? Can he take Lucy away from me?'

'Firstly, there's no question of an adoption unless the father agrees.' He looked at Marie. 'I'm assuming that may not be the case?' Marie felt her heart plummet. She'd been afraid of this.

'If he was so minded, he could bring a case in the family court. It could get messy. And there's your niece to consider. She's had no contact from her father? At her age, the court would ask her who she wants to live with and take that into account. She's old enough to make her own decisions. She's happy with you?'

Marie's tongue stuck to the roof of her mouth. She couldn't speak.

Frank answered for her. 'Marie – and me – are the only family Dee, her mother, had, the only family she's known. There was no one else for her, nowhere else for her to go when Dee died.'

'Her father's family?'

'Didn't want to know. Dee tried, but… I don't know if they're still alive. They took Robbie's side and refused to disclose his whereabouts.'

'Well, Marie,' Gordon leant his elbows on the desk and steepled his fingers, 'I'm afraid you'll have to prepare yourself to meet the gentleman or perhaps have to suffer through a difficult court case.'

'But…' Marie didn't want to believe him.

'I assume there's no doubt about paternity?'

'No.'

'And your niece? How does she feel about her father suddenly appearing in her life?'

Marie and Frank looked at each other.

'She doesn't know,' Marie said heavily. 'But since her mother died, she's been trying to locate him. I'd hoped…' she bit her lip. 'I'd hoped she wouldn't be able to, that she'd find it too difficult and give up.'

'That's not likely to happen now.' Gordon's voice was kind but firm. 'I suggest you tell her about this letter – sooner rather than later – and set up a meeting.'

Marie had a strange sense of *déjà vu* as she and Frank walked out into the bright sunlight. But unlike last time, today there was nothing to laugh about. 'What am I going to do, Frank?' she asked, almost in tears. 'I know what Robbie's like. He'll raise Lucy's hopes, get her all excited then let her down when he decides again that being a father isn't for him.'

'You don't know that for sure. He may be a reformed character. After all, he's had fourteen years to come to his senses.'

'Fourteen years when he wanted nothing to do with Dee or Lucy. What does he want now, unless it's money? And where's he been all this time? Why has no one been able to get hold of him? And why now?'

'So many questions, and there's only one person who can provide the answers.'

The one person Marie didn't want to meet.

'Lucy will have to meet him too.'

'I know. She's probably going to be thrilled to hear about this. But he's in Darwin,' she said with a glimmer of hope.

'He can be here in less than twelve hours.'

'Damn!' She fell silent. 'Oh, Frank, it's taken Lucy so long to get settled here, to start becoming involved in things, to make friends. I can't bear to think of her being uprooted again. What if...' Marie couldn't articulate her worst fear – fear Lucy would choose Robbie over her.

But Frank understood. 'Lucy's not stupid. She loves you. She knows how much she means to you, how you've been there for her. Do you want me to be there when you tell her?'

Marie would love to have his comforting presence, his support, but knew she needed to stop being so dependent on him. 'Thanks, Frank, but this is something I need to do myself. I'll tell her tonight.'

Frank drew her into a hug. 'Call me if you need me.'

'Thanks.' She seemed to be saying that a lot lately – to Frank, to Drew. 'I should be getting back. See you tomorrow.' As Marie walked off, she could feel Frank's eyes on her. He was worried about her. The thought gave her a warm glow. But she was wary of what she now saw as her continued reliance on him. Their relationship had been over for some time – for years. Why had she allowed him to remain such an important part of her life? And why was she only becoming aware of it now?

Marie knew she didn't have far to look. Her reliance on Frank had only come to her notice since she'd met Drew Hamilton, since she experienced emotions she'd never imagined experiencing again.

*

'I need to talk with you, Luce.'

The pair had just finished dinner, and Lucy was on her way to her room. Marie knew she couldn't put it off any longer.

'Now? I have heaps of homework to do and...'

'Now.' Marie's voice was firmer than she intended.

'What's wrong? What have I done now?' There was a belligerent note in Lucy's voice Marie hadn't heard for some time.

'Nothing. But I have something to tell you. Let's go into the living room.'

Lucy followed Marie in and curled up on the sofa. Marie took a seat opposite and clasped her hands.

'Well? What is it? Is it about Uncle Frank?'

Marie's head jerked back. Frank? What made Lucy think of Frank? 'No, it's not about your uncle Frank. I need to ask you something first. Are you still trying to find your dad?'

Lucy pouted. 'I know you don't want me to find him, but he's my dad and I have a right to get to know him. If that's all you wanted to say…' She began to rise.

Marie held up a hand. 'Please sit down. I just wanted to be sure.' She took a deep breath. 'I received a letter this week. It came to the café. It was from your dad.'

Lucy stared at her, eyes wide, then her mouth turned up in a big grin. She wrapped her arms around herself and squeezed tightly. 'My dad? Really? He wants to meet me?'

'That's what he says.' Marie was still not sure whether or not to believe Robbie. He could just be out for what he could get and see Lucy as a means to an end.

'Where is he? When can I meet him?' Lucy asked excitedly.

'The letter was posted in Darwin, so I presume that's where he lives. I'll reply and let him know you'd like to meet him, but I wanted to check with you first, to make sure you hadn't changed your mind.'

'Changed my mind?' Lucy looked at Marie as if she'd gone out of hers. 'Why would I do that? Oh, this is so great. Wait till I tell Jess. Will he be here for my birthday? Is that why he wrote you now?'

Marie blanched. Lucy's sixteenth birthday was just over four weeks away. She intended to plan something with Drew – perhaps another horse-riding excursion since the girls enjoyed it so much. Knowing Robbie Drake, she doubted very much he'd remember the date of Lucy's birth. 'I don't know, sweetheart. We'll have to wait and see.'

'Can I see the letter?'

'I'm sorry, honey. Your Uncle Frank has it.' That had been a mistake, Marie now realised. She shouldn't have let Frank imagine he was in charge, but she had, and now that had to change. 'I'll get it back from him tomorrow. You can see it then. It says he recently learned about your mum's death and wanted to know what happened to you. He knew Frank and I had the café back when he and your mum got together, when you were born, and…'

'My dad!' Lucy said, her voice filled with awe. 'I don't even know what he looks like. Mum would never show me any photos, not even her wedding photo.' She gave Marie a penetrating look. 'Were you and Uncle Frank at their wedding? Did you take any photos?'

Marie flinched. It was a day she'd prefer to forget, the day her beautiful sister got hooked up with a wastrel. *Handsome is what handsome does*, had been a favourite saying of her and Dee's grandmother, and Robbie Drake fitted it to a tee. He'd certainly been handsome and had bowled Dee over with his charm. What if he was able to do the same with Lucy? 'I'll have a look,' she said weakly.

'Thanks, Aunt Marie!' Lucy beamed, leapt up, hugged an astonished Marie, and raced off, phone in hand, no doubt to call Jess to tell her the good news.

Marie remained seated, bemused. She'd known this would be Lucy's reaction and, while pleased to see her niece so happy, feared for the disappointment she was sure would follow. She thought about Lucy's request for a photo. There was one, perhaps more than one. When she was going through Dee's belongings, Marie had found an old album, one she remembered from the days when Dee had been so much in love. She hadn't opened it, didn't have the courage to look inside. But she hadn't been able to destroy it either. She knew it most likely held photos of the young Dee and Robbie, of happier days before Lucy was born. She got up, stretched and went to the cupboard where she'd hidden it.

Marie had barely found the album and was crouched on the floor in front of the cupboard when her phone rang. She saw Drew's number.

'You told Lucy,' he said.

Marie slumped back on her heels, letting the album drop. She could have hugged him. 'Jess told you?'

'She came downstairs yelling that Lucy was going to meet her long-lost dad. Really?'

'Probably.' Marie sighed. 'Frank and I went to see a lawyer today – I gave my fitness program a miss for once – and he advised me it was the right thing to do.'

She heard a sharp intake of breath.

'You and Frank?'

'He offered, and since he's Lucy's uncle… I couldn't face it on my own.'

'Of course.'

Did Marie imagine a slight distancing? It was only two words but… She continued, 'It seems he – her dad – does have rights, even though he's declined to use them all her life. But if I don't want to be caught up in a nasty court case, I have to play nice. Play nice,' she fumed.

'He's so bad?'

'He was when I knew him. Frank suggested he might have changed, but I can't imagine it.'

'He knew him, too?'

There was that coolness again. Was it the mention of Frank's name? 'Of course. We were… a couple back then. Dee was seven years younger.'

'I hadn't realised.'

Why had he phoned if he was going to be so tongue-tied?

But it wasn't his problem.

'Would you like company? Jess has popped next door again for help with her *maths homework*.' He gave a chuckle.

Marie realised Drew's company was exactly what she needed. 'I'd love that. If it's not too much trouble.'

'No trouble at all. When I heard… I thought… I could imagine… I wanted… Sorry, I'm babbling.'

'I'll put the jug on.'

'No need. I'll bring around a bottle of red. It sounds to me as if you need something stronger than that herbal tea you drink.'

Marie stood up and picked up the album from the floor. Without opening it, she carried it upstairs and knocked on Lucy's door. 'This may answer some of your questions,' she said, handing her the worn book.

'Thanks, Aunt Marie.' Lucy took the album, clasped it to her chest, then turned back to her iPhone.

Back downstairs again, Marie breathed a sigh of relief. She'd done what she promised, what she should have done before. And Drew Hamilton was bringing around a bottle of wine.

She took a quick peek in the mirror, ran a hand over her hair, refreshed her lipstick and went into the kitchen to fetch two wine glasses, her heart lighter than it had been since she and Frank left Gordon Slater's office.

Thirty-three

Was he making a mistake? Drew hesitated as he selected a bottle of cabernet merlot from the wine rack and held it up to check the vintage. It had irked him the way Marie kept bringing Frank's name into the conversation. Frank Beattie was her ex. She didn't even use his name anymore. But it seemed he was still very much part of her life. What did it mean? Did it mean anything? And why was he getting himself tied in knots trying to work it all out?

He raked a hand through his hair. What was the matter with him? He, who'd vowed he wasn't going to let another woman into his life, was allowing thoughts and images of Marie Cunningham to infiltrate his mind at every turn. Even in the heady days of their early passion, Irene hadn't had this effect on him.

Regardless, Drew found himself humming as he drove across town to see Marie. Thinking back on their conversation, it occurred to him why he'd been so annoyed. And it was simple. He was jealous – jealous of Frank Beattie. How pathetic was that? He tried to analyse his feelings. If he was jealous, did it mean he had feelings for Marie himself? What he did know was he wished she'd asked him to accompany her to the lawyer. Wasn't he the one who suggested it, who urged her to take action, to find out where she stood?

But instead she'd gone to good old Frank.

Drew was still trying to work out his emotions when he arrived. Seeing the light above Marie's door sent a flash of what could only be desire through him. 'Drew,' he said to himself, 'you're falling for this woman.'

A smiling, but weary, Marie greeted him at the door. 'Lucy's in her room,' she said, leading him into the kitchen where two glasses were sitting on the benchtop.

Drew held up the wine and gestured to Marie's family room which, unlike the bright kitchen, was lit by the dull glow of a floor lamp.

Marie picked up the glasses and followed him in, taking a seat on the sofa and placing the glasses on the coffee table. Before he had time to open the wine, Marie turned to him, her eyes filled with tears. 'I'm so glad to see you. You can't imagine how…'

Without thinking, Drew placed the bottle on the coffee table, joined Marie on the sofa and pulled her towards him, leaning his chin on her head. He inhaled her unique scent, the scent he remembered. This time he was able to identify the elusive fragrance. It was bergamot. He only recognised it because Jess had a collection of essential oils she'd asked him to sample. The combination Marie was wearing was intoxicating.

'Sorry!' She pushed him away and sat back against the cushions. 'You were right. I do need a drink.'

Drew poured out two glasses, wishing he could have held her properly. But it would be wrong to presume. She was upset, hurting, and he wasn't the sort to take advantage of her situation. But he couldn't stifle the flood of longing he felt when she was in his arms.

'Do you want to talk about it?'

'No. Yes. Maybe. I don't know.'

Drew gently placed an arm around Marie, his fingers only just touching her shoulder. He didn't want to frighten her off.

Marie picked up her wine and took a sip. 'Thanks for coming over. It's been quite a day. I thought… as you said… maybe I could adopt Lucy. But Gordon said not. Despite everything, Robbie's still her father and has rights. He could get a court order. I'd never subject Lucy to such a process.'

'How did she take the news?'

'Oh, she's delighted, of course. She's lost her mum and found her dad. Everything's just fine in her world. She has no idea what sort of disappointment might be in store.'

'So, what happens now?'

'I'll reply to his letter. He didn't include a phone number or an email address which seems a bit odd in this day and age. But I'll find it easier to write. I don't want to hear his voice.' She shivered.

Drew wanted to pull Marie closer again, but she leant forward to pick up her wine.

'Then I suppose he'll fly down from Darwin. As Frank said, he can be here in less than twelve hours.' She shivered again.

This time, Drew didn't hesitate. He took the glass from her hand, tightened his grip on Marie's shoulder and pulled her around to face him, heedless of how she might react. To his surprise, she buried her face in his chest. His heart thumped so loudly he was sure she could hear it. He stroked her hair and uttered what he hoped were soothing murmurs.

'You expect him to come straight away – as soon as he receives your letter?' he asked, when Marie pulled away again, this time remaining in his arms.

'I guess so. I don't know his circumstances. I assume he's working there.'

'What sort of work does he do?'

'I don't know. Back when he and Dee were together, he was with some sort of construction company. But he left that when he left Dee – left without notice, too. She wasn't able to trace him through his employment. Neither it seemed, were Family and Community Services. I always thought Dee should have pursued it more vigorously, but she didn't want to make a fuss. I think the social workers have so many cases, they give up on the difficult ones. He could be doing anything now.'

'What if…?' Drew didn't know whether to ask, but knew it must be in Marie's mind. 'What if he wants Lucy to go to Darwin with him?'

'Oh, Drew! I'm terrified that's what he has in mind. It's been difficult enough for Lucy to adjust to living here in Granite Springs. She's just beginning to settle down. I can't bear the thought of her having to do it all over again in a strange city with a father she doesn't even know.' Her eyes began to fill with tears.

Drew took his thumb and wiped them away, caressing the soft skin on Marie's face. They were so close together he could see the tiny teardrops on her lashes, and it took a mammoth effort of will for him to refrain from kissing her closed eyelids.

But when she opened her eyes and lifted her face to his, he could bear it no longer. When their lips met, it was as if he'd been waiting for this moment all his life.

Thirty-four

Marie couldn't sleep. She tossed and turned. Every time she closed her eyes an image of Drew Hamilton appeared, followed by one of a laughing Robbie Drake.

She must have dozed off at some stage because suddenly it was morning. She opened her eyes to see the sun slanting through the vertical blinds. The kookaburras were cackling their usual morning chorus on the fence outside her window. It was time to get up and face the day.

'Are you going to write to him today?' The excitement in Lucy's voice made Marie wince. A night's sleep hadn't curbed her enthusiasm. 'I spent ages looking through Mum's photos. Dad's really handsome! I can see why she fell for him. Do you think I look like him?' Lucy primped and peered at her reflection in the kitchen window.

'No, you have your mother's eyes and nose and your grandfather's hair. You're all Cunningham, I'm afraid.'

Lucy pouted. But Marie was glad, glad there was nothing in her niece's appearance to remind her of the man who'd abandoned her and Dee.

'So, are you?' Lucy didn't let go easily.

'Yes. But he may not reply immediately,' she warned. 'And he'll probably look a bit different from the photos. They were all taken before you were born. People change.'

'Mum didn't.'

'No, you're right.' Despite everything, Dee had retained her youthful appearance whereas Marie cringed every time she looked in the mirror. Why did her sister have to die? A wave of grief hit her again, as fresh as if it had happened yesterday. Dee! Her little sister! They were supposed to grow old together, to take care of each other in their declining years – share a room in a nursing home. They'd often joked about it. Instead, Marie had been left alone.

She sighed, then remembered the previous evening. Drew. Their kiss. The taste of his mouth on hers. It felt so right when their lips met and clung. Then he moved away, and she thought he was about to apologise. Thankfully he didn't. But his shocked expression was a surprise, almost as much of a surprise as the kiss itself.

They finished the wine and he'd left, neither making reference to the sudden burst of passion, extinguished almost as soon as it flared up. But flared up it had, and Marie had the distinct impression it would happen again. She hoped it would, that it hadn't been some misguided attempt to make her feel better.

But, remembering the taste of him, the press of his lips, the expression in his eyes, Marie knew Drew hadn't been completely unmoved.

'Are you okay, Aunt Marie?'

Marie forced herself back to the present to see Lucy gazing at her curiously. 'Sorry, honey, I was remembering your mum,' she lied. 'What do you imagine she'd think of you seeing your dad?'

Lucy kicked the leg of the table. 'She's not here for me to find out. She never talked about him. It was as if he didn't exist. I used to pretend he was dead, that he'd been killed in a horrible accident saving a child from drowning or from a runaway car; that he was a hero. But it had been so sad Mum could never mention it.'

'Oh, honey, it wasn't like that.'

'I know, but… when the other girls were talking about their dads, it helped to pretend. Anyway, I may not have to pretend any longer,' she grinned. Then she jumped up. 'I need to go, or I'll be late. See you tonight.' She grabbed her backpack and was gone, leaving an emptiness where her cheerful presence had been.

It hadn't taken long for Lucy to become part of Marie's life. It wasn't the life she imagined she'd be living. After she and Frank split up, Marie had been reconciled to spending the rest of her life alone. Lucy was a breath of fresh air. She'd miss her if she was gone. Marie shook her head. It wouldn't come to that. Whatever Robbie Drake wanted, she was sure it wasn't to be saddled with a fifteen year-old – unless he'd completely changed from the man she'd known.

And there was Drew Hamilton to consider. The peck on the cheek when he left was a far cry from the kiss they exchanged earlier, but it was a step forward from their usual farewell. And the firm clasp of his hand as he said, 'I'll call' was a promise of something more.

Marie cleared away the breakfast dishes, and wiped down the table and bench, knowing they were delaying tactics. She couldn't put it off any longer. She'd told Frank she'd be in late so she could compose the letter before starting work. Like telling Lucy last night, it would only get worse the longer she put it off. With a sigh, Marie headed to her study and fired up the computer.

After several attempts, Marie was finally satisfied with her effort and printed it off. Finding an envelope was more difficult but, after searching around she discovered a packet of pre-paid ones. She had no idea when she purchased them but signing her one-page reply, she folded the letter and slid it inside one, after carefully printing the address.

*

'You did it?' Frank looked up when Marie pushed open the door.

The café was half-full, so she only nodded and went into the back to drop off her bag and don the black apron with the café logo on the front. It wasn't till sometime later, during a lull between customers, that there was an opportunity for conversation.

'How did Lucy take it?'

'She was thrilled. I'm worried for her, Frank.'

'She'll be right. She has her head screwed on the right way. Dee did a good job there. And you're doing one, too,' he added, as Marie grimaced.

'We'll see.' She heaved a sigh. 'Anyway, I wrote the letter. I guess it's up to him now.'

'I hope you…'

'Don't worry, I didn't tell him what I thought of his behaviour. I wrote a very polite letter telling him how Dee died, that we still have the café, and that Lucy is living with me. I didn't mention…' she bit her lip, '…that we are no longer together.' Marie wasn't sure why she'd left out that piece of information. Was it because she thought Robbie would be less inclined to make a claim on Lucy if he thought he had a couple to deal with, or because she was ashamed her relationship with Frank hadn't stood the test of time?

'That's none of his business.' Frank didn't appear to have any of Marie's qualms.

'So we wait?'

'I suppose. My guess is he'll be here as soon as he can book a flight. At least, that's what the old Robbie would do – always was an impulsive bastard.'

'I wonder if he's been in Darwin all this time. It's strange no one was ever able to contact him.'

'Bet his parents knew where he was. I always thought it a bit suss the way they refused to have anything to do with Dee and Lucy – their own granddaughter. Maybe he went overseas?'

'That would explain it. And the Drakes could have heard of Dee's death somehow. Anyway, wherever he went, he's back now.'

The café door burst open at that point and a group of chattering women, followed by a couple of businessmen, walked in, keeping Marie and Frank occupied. Then there was the usual lunchtime rush. By mid-afternoon, Marie could hardly keep her eyes open.

'All right?' Frank's brow creased with concern.

'Sorry.' Marie put a hand to her forehead. 'Just tired. I didn't get much sleep last night. It's catching up with me.'

Frank placed his hands on Marie's shoulders and gazed into her eyes. 'You should go home. Put your feet up. Have a good rest before Lucy gets home. I can clear up here.'

'Thanks, Frank.' Marie moved away, not sure why Frank's attentiveness suddenly made her feel uncomfortable. He'd always been there to comfort her, and that hadn't changed when they decided to live separate lives. It hadn't worried her till now. Frank hadn't changed. But she had. Marie knew that ever since Drew Hamilton had come into her life, things hadn't been the same.

Thirty-five

The Parent and Citizens meeting at Granite Springs High was proving to be as boring as Drew expected. He normally managed to avoid contact with the parents en masse but had agreed to be present at this special one to finalise arrangements for the fundraiser.

'We're delighted to have our school principal, Mr Hamilton, with us tonight,' Beverly Williams said, scanning the group. 'He was kind enough to make the initial approach to the university. As a result, we have the promise of a room in the university's new Richard Gill Auditorium for our event.'

There was a burst of applause at which Drew tried to look suitably modest. All he'd done was have a chat with Owen Larsen and get to know him better. It had been a plus to receive the invitation to his place, then to catch up with Marie Cunningham. She was so different from the women sitting in this room, it was a surprise many of them had grown up with her.

He managed to blank out during the rest of the meeting, only coming to with a start when he heard his name again. 'Sorry, could you repeat that?' he asked, embarrassed to be caught daydreaming.

'I was asking if you are taking a table, Mr Hamilton? As principal, it's expected you would. There are tables of eight.' Beverly Williams looked at him expectantly.

A table for eight? Where would he find eight people to fill one? Then Drew remembered Owen Larsen. He'd offered to come, along with Jo and Col Ford. They all knew Nick and Kay. If he invited them, and… maybe Marie – would she agree? – he'd be able to make up the required party of eight. 'Certainly,' he said, with more confidence than he felt. He'd need to contact Owen before he bought tickets elsewhere. And Marie. His heart leapt. This was the perfect excuse he'd been waiting for to contact her again. That kiss had stirred emotions he'd thought dead for ever. Did Marie feel the same way or was she still tied to her ex?

It was a week since he'd seen her, the weekend having been taken up by a school sporting event he hadn't been able to avoid. In the past, Drew would have relished the opportunity to spend the weekend on school activities – that had been one of Irene's common complaints – but since meeting Marie, his priorities had changed. Now he couldn't wait to see her again, to repeat the kiss they'd enjoyed. The memory of the unique fragrance surrounding her; the touch of her soft skin… it was enough to send him into a spin.

The meeting wrapped up soon afterwards, and Drew was free to leave. He was about to get into his car when his phone pinged with a text. Jess!

I'm at Lucy's. Came here after chess. Can U pick me up? Jx

Drew felt his heartbeat quicken. Jess was supposed to be home. He'd told her at breakfast about the P&C meeting and suggested she get a takeaway for dinner. It wasn't the act of a concerned father, but he had a ton of work to get through and didn't want the hassle of driving home only to return to school in the early evening. He'd assumed Jess would be fine on her own. Evidently not. But this was a bonus. Thoughts of Marie had tormented him all week as he tried to work out how and when they could meet again. Now Jess had handed him the opportunity on a plate.

With a song in his heart, Drew turned the car in the opposite direction from home, a warm glow suffusing him at the prospect of seeing Marie.

*

'The girls are upstairs. Shall I…?' Marie greeted him and made a movement towards the foot of the stairs, but Drew placed a hand on her arm.

'Not yet. I've missed you.'

Marie's lips turned up in a delighted smile. 'When you said you were busy at the weekend I wondered if you'd regretted…'

'Never. In fact…' Drew bent his head to touch her lips again, her eager response making him wish they had the house to themselves.

'Not here.' Marie gave a wary glance up the stairs from where they could hear the familiar sound of music.

'Not a lot of homework going on there,' he said, as she led him into the family room.

'Oh, I think there was. The music only started up a short time ago. Jess said you had a meeting at school?'

'P&C for my sins.' Drew raked a hand through his hair. 'I try to avoid those as much as possible, but they wanted my input on a fundraiser that's happening next month.'

'The mock race meeting? Fran mentioned it. Evidently Owen thinks it'll be a hoot.'

'Sounds like Owen. He hasn't bought tickets yet, has he?'

'I doubt it. He gets these hairbrained notions, but it's Fran who does the organising. Why?'

'Good. I've been dragooned into taking a table. I don't really know many people, so I thought Owen and Fran with their friends, the Fords, maybe Nick and Kay and…you?'

'Sounds to me as if you know quite a few. I'd love to come. It might even be fun. I've heard about those nights, but never actually been to one. When is it?'

Drew pulled on one ear. 'July sometime. In the school holidays. I didn't get the exact date. Sorry.'

'No worries. Frank can look after Lucy for the evening. They'll both love that.'

Damned Frank again!

'Do you need to go straight away, or can I offer you something to drink – wine, coffee?'

'A wine wouldn't go astray after the evening I've just had. Where do all those earnest do-gooders come from? Don't they have lives? I know their efforts provide much needed resources for the school, but…' He shook his head.

'Bev Williams and her crew? I was at school with them. They don't have much else to do, so they put their energy into various charities. The high school is only one of those. They do good work, but I know what you mean. They can be a tad forceful.'

'Forceful? That's putting it mildly. Was Beverly always like that?'

'Well, she was a bit bossy at school, so I guess it's just an extension of that. I was never one of her little group.' She chuckled. 'Now, let me get you some wine. White okay?'

Drew nodded and settled himself on the sofa, watching Marie leave. She was the antithesis of those women at the meeting he'd just left with her trim figure and gentle manner – though she could be feisty at times. Drew remembered their first meeting when she'd been like a lioness protecting her cub. But that could only add spice to their relationship.

He hoped they had a relationship or were on the way to developing one. It was so relaxing here. Drew closed his eyes. The sounds from upstairs were muted. The room smelt of that elusive fragrance he'd noticed before. He felt good.

'Here we are.'

Drew's eyes flew open to see Marie with a tray holding two glasses of white wine along with a plate of oatcakes topped with slices of cheese.

'I thought you might be hungry. Jess said you were staying at school and going straight to the meeting. Did you have any dinner?'

Dinner? Drew thought back to the sandwich he'd picked up from the tuck shop at lunchtime, intending to eat later. He remembered opening it, taking one bite, then… It was probably still sitting on his desk growing stale. 'Not really. This looks great. Thanks.'

Marie took a seat beside him on the sofa, the touch of her thigh pressing against his sending a flare of desire through him.

Drew shot a glance at his companion. Did she feel it, too?

Blushing, Marie moved away slightly. 'Cheers,' she said, raising her glass. 'To a successful fundraiser.'

Right now, the fundraiser was furthest from Drew's mind. He was caught up in a bubble of emotion. 'Cheers,' he said, clearing his throat, and taking a gulp of wine to hide what he was thinking. 'Have you had any reply to your letter – the one to Lucy's father?' That should be a safe subject.

'Not yet.' Marie frowned. 'It's been not quite a week, but I thought… I gave him my email address and phone number. I thought I'd have heard by now. Do you think… he's changed his mind?' Her face assumed a hopeful expression.

'How's Lucy taking it?'

'She's been unbearable. It's good in a way – to see her so excited after her outpouring of grief after Dee's death. But I worry for her. What if…'

Seeing her distress, Drew put down his glass and pulled Marie towards him, taking heart when she offered no resistance, though mindful of the two teenagers upstairs who could burst in at any moment. He buried his face in her hair, inhaling her unique scent, his fingers stroking her face gently, feeling her melt into his embrace.

Lifting his head, he put one finger under Marie's chin to lift her face to his, their lips meeting, his tongue seeking hers sending shivers of delight through him as their bodies melded together.

There was the sound of a door slamming in the distance. They jumped apart, Marie patting her now dishevelled hair, and Drew raking his fingers through his before picking up his glass again in a shaky hand.

Jess and Lucy burst in, just as he'd imagined.

'Hi, Dad,' Jess said. 'We're done, now. Can we go home?'

Just like that, Drew's evening was ruined. 'Let me finish my wine first, Jess.'

'Oh, can we have those?' Not waiting for a reply, Lucy picked up the plate of oatcakes which Drew and Marie had barely touched and offered them to Jess.

'Sorry!' Marie mouthed to Drew as the two girls demolished what was to have been his snack.

He shrugged, no longer hungry. He drained his wine and placed the now empty glass on the coffee table. 'Okay, Jess. Let's get you home.'

Outside, Lucy followed Jess to the car, intent on sharing one last piece of gossip. Drew hung back, reluctant to leave. 'I want… we need… I'll figure out a way for us to spend time together when we won't be interrupted. If you…?' His eyes made a silent plea.

Marie smiled warmly. 'I'd like that, but it won't be easy. Maybe if Lucy went to Frank's…'

'I'll figure something out.' Drew had no idea how he'd manage to do it, but he didn't want to be beholden to Frank for time alone with Marie. It didn't seem right, as if Frank was aiding and abetting their relationship. No, he'd have to think of some other way.

'See you soon.' Their fingers entwined, then there was a yell from Jess. 'I have to go.'

Drew heard none of Jess's incessant chatter on the drive home. All he could think of was how it had felt to hold Marie, her warm pliable body close to his and the fragrant scent of her skin and hair. He'd work out something. He had to. They couldn't go on like this.

Thirty-six

This was the moment Marie had been dreading. It was over a week since she posted the letter to Darwin – a week of worrying and waiting for a response. This was what she'd been afraid of – that he would turn up out of the blue.

The man who walked into the café looked like a stranger. He was tall and rangy, but there the similarity to the Robbie Drake Marie had known ended. This man was bald, his face lined, ravaged by years of the strong rays of the sun. His skin had toughened, making him appear almost disfigured.

'Robbie?' she asked, peering into the face trying to see any glimmer of the man Dee married. Life certainly hadn't been kind to him. Only the eyes were the same – piercing blue eyes, the eyes that could charm the birds off the trees; the eyes that had charmed her little sister. Eyes didn't change.

'Not what you expected, eh?' His voice was the same too, but there was a bitterness in his tone.

'I had no expectations. Where have you been hiding all these years?' Marie felt a tightness in her chest, her body tensing and her muscles quivering. She sensed Frank's calm presence behind her and took a deep breath. Frank was right, there was no sense in getting into an argument.

'Why don't we sit down,' Frank said evenly, moving between them and reaching out to shake Robbie's hand. 'There's a lot to talk about.'

A quick glance around the café showed Marie it was empty of customers. It was three o'clock, almost time to close for the day.

'Why don't you put up the closed sign while I get us coffee, Marie? Robbie?' He raised an eyebrow.

'Black thanks.' Robbie took a seat, his right knee jerking up and down involuntarily.

Marie did as she was bid, delaying her return till Frank carried over the three coffees.

She and Frank took their places opposite Robbie.

'I got your letter.' Robbie spat out the words, then took a gulp of the hot coffee.

Marie sipped hers, feeling Frank's hand on her thigh. But if he thought the familiar touch was going to soothe her, to stop her anger, he was wrong. 'How could you?' The words she'd been bottling up for years exploded. 'Where have you been all this time? You left Dee with a young child to bring up and disappeared into thin air. Have you no sense of responsibility?'

'I was sorry to hear of her death.'

'Sorry? Now you're sorry? Where were you when she needed you? You…'

Frank's hand tightened, forcing Marie to fall silent. 'We were surprised to hear from you, Robbie,' he said. 'No one seemed to know where you were, yet you heard about Dee's death. Don't you think we deserve some sort of explanation?'

Marie opened her mouth to speak again, only to see Frank glare at her. She pressed her lips together, grinding her teeth.

Robbie gazed into space and tapped his fingers on the table. 'Mum told me about Dee,' he said after a long pause. 'She's in a nursing home in Canberra. She heard it there.' He paused again, his knee bouncing up and down under the table. 'I just want to meet my daughter. Mum would like to meet her too.'

'No!' The word shot out without her volition.

Frank glared at her again. 'Marie is naturally upset,' he said. 'You do know Dee tried to find you, to contact you – as did Family and Community Services?'

'Yeah, I guessed they might.' He gazed into space again as if deciding how much to say. 'I was out of the country.' Then his voice rose. 'I couldn't take it – the crying, the lack of sleep, the perpetual nappies. It wasn't what I signed up for.'

Marie took a sharp intake of breath. 'She was your wife, your daughter. What did you expect?'

Robbie shrugged and swept a hand over his scalp as if forgetting there was no hair to drag it through. He shook his head. 'I heard about this job going in Papua New Guinea. The company needed a project manager. It was a good move for me – a step up, more responsibility, more money…' His voice dried up at Marie's contemptuous expression. 'I thought I might come back when…' He shook his head again. 'But things didn't pan out the way I planned.'

Marie clasped her cup in both hands to stem her anger and stop them from shaking. She had no desire to hear about Robbie's failure to make good in New Guinea, sure he never had any intention to return.

He continued, 'I got caught up in some riots – wrong place, wrong time – was mugged and robbed. You might say I got what I deserved for being greedy, for abandoning Dee and the kid.' He exhaled heavily. 'Maybe I did. Fate certainly had it in for me. I was taken into hospital, then I developed dysentery and my immune system is shot to hell after bouts of malaria.'

He can't be expecting us to feel sorry for him? It's just like the old Robbie, playing for sympathy. He hasn't changed a jot.

'And you suddenly remembered you have a daughter?' Marie asked, unable to remain silent any longer.

'Not exactly. It was Mum. She hasn't long left. She wants to…' He broke into a fit of coughing. 'Sorry.' He pulled a handkerchief out of his pocket to wipe his mouth. 'I came back to Darwin for medical treatment. Lucy'd be a teenager by now?'

'Fat lot you care!' Marie couldn't help herself. 'She's managed without you for fourteen years. Why should she want to see you now?' She conveniently forgot Lucy was desperate to meet him. But what would she make of this shadow of a man? He was a far cry from the handsome young man in the photographs; from the romantic vision she held of her father.

'Marie!' Frank's warning voice halted her before she could say any more. 'We understand you want to meet Lucy,' he said. 'I'm sure that can be arranged without too much difficulty. You have to understand she was traumatised by her mother's death and she may have developed some…' he cleared his throat, '…unrealistic ideas of who and what her father might be.'

'But she's here in Granite Springs? You said in your letter she was with you.' He gazed expectantly from Marie to Frank and back again.

Marie nodded reluctantly. 'How long are you here – in Granite Springs?'

'A couple of days. I thought if I met Lucy, I could take her to Canberra to meet Mum.'

Marie felt a cold shudder up her spine. *Take Lucy to Canberra? Then what? What if…?*

'I don't know about Canberra,' she said, realising as she did so she'd agreed by default to a meeting in Granite Springs. She bit her lip. But she knew there was no way she could keep his arrival secret from Lucy.

'I'm staying at the Motor Inn on Yeo Street. Maybe we could meet there. They have a restaurant…'

Marie could picture the scene. 'I…'

'I think Marie would like to be there with Lucy. You have to appreciate it'll be quite a shock for her.'

'You mean I'll be a shock, huh?'

Frank pursed his lips.

'When?' The one word was all Marie allowed herself to utter. Now it was going to happen she wanted to get it over with, while wishing Robbie Drake would disappear from their lives and never be seen again.

'Sooner the better,' Robbie said, leaning back in his chair, more relaxed now they'd agreed to what he wanted. 'Who does she look like?' he asked. 'Mother…'

'She looks just like Dee,' Marie replied with a heavy heart. Apart from her hair colour, which she got from her maternal grandfather, Lucy was the image of what Dee had been like at her age.

'And you'll be returning to Darwin?' Frank asked.

'That depends.' Suddenly Robbie's face changed and developed a sly expression. 'I hear Dee has a house in Canberra.'

Where did he hear that? Though it was no secret. The house in Belconnen was still on the market. But that house was Lucy's inheritance. It was nothing to do with Robbie Drake. Were Drew and Frank right in thinking this was all about money? And would the opportunity of returning to Canberra with her new-found dad be one Lucy would grab with both hands?

Thirty-seven

'What did Mum have to say?' Drew looked up from his computer as Jess slouched into his study.

'She was cool. I don't think she wants me there these hols. Jake has a big game somewhere – boring!' She yawned.

'I'm sure that's not true – about wanting you there.' But Drew wasn't sure at all. Since Irene had moved to LA, she seemed to be distancing herself from everything in Australia – including her daughter. He was trying to keep his side of the bargain and had done his best to persuade Jess to make the trip, to no avail. Now it seemed it had all been pointless. Irene didn't care. 'I suppose they may have to travel to Jake's games.'

'Yeah. Anyway, I told her you were taking Lucy and me horse riding again. You are, aren't you? You promised.'

'I did.' And he meant to talk with Marie about it. Instead, they'd been side-tracked – wonderfully so. 'I plan to catch up with Lucy's Aunt Marie later today. I'll set something up with her then.'

'You're seeing a lot of her, Dad.'

Drew glanced at Jess to figure out what she was thinking but, as usual, her face was a closed book. 'Not really.' He tried to appear unconcerned.

'Hmm.' But Jess's interest had wandered.

Drew was worrying unnecessarily. 'What do you plan to do today?'

'Luce and I are catching up at her place. We're going to make brownies. If you're seeing her aunt, can I have a ride?'

'Of course you can.' Drew sighed. He and Marie wouldn't be alone again, but he had to see her. Perhaps they could go for a drive, leave the girls to their baking. Jess and Lucy were becoming good at putting into practice what they'd learned from Marie. He was grateful to her for providing the girls with another interest, one they enjoyed and which couldn't get them into any mischief.

*

'Hi, Drew,' Marie blushed as she greeted him at the door, Jess flying past them to catch up with Lucy who was waiting behind her aunt.

'Marie, good to see you.' He'd dearly like to kiss her but was conscious of two pairs of eyes behind them. He would have to wait till later.

'Coffee?'

'I thought perhaps we could go for a drive? If you think this pair can be trusted on their own.'

Jess pouted, but Lucy only smiled.

'Oh, I think they can. Lucy has everything ready, Jess. We'll expect you to leave some for us to taste when we get back. Okay?'

'Okay. Maybe we can try making some of that banana bread too. There are a couple of very ripe bananas,' Lucy said.

'Sure. The recipe is on my iPad. You should be right.'

'You're turning them into proficient cooks.'

'Hardly, but they're both fast learners. And they're easy recipes. Wait till we get to the complicated stuff.'

Drew laughed. This was a different side of Marie. 'Let's go.'

Once outside, Drew slipped an arm around Marie's waist, feeling her respond by moving closer.

'Later,' she whispered.

'Where are we going?' Marie asked, as they drove off.

'Surprise.' Drew grinned as he steered through the Saturday afternoon traffic and left Granite Springs behind.

Marie seemed content to let him take charge, and they barely spoke as he drove in an unfamiliar direction out of town. He knew where he was headed. Nick had mentioned this neighbouring town to him and told him about the small country pub. 'Like something from another era' had been his exact words, but he also said they served good beer and snacks if one was so inclined. It was a good opportunity to spend private time with Marie in a place where neither would be recognised.

Drew wasn't sure why that seemed important. Maybe it wasn't. But time enough to go public with their relationship at the fundraising dinner which was only a week away. There was something particularly intimate about maintaining their secrecy for a little longer. Even though he was sure Jess had guessed, he wasn't sure about Lucy. Who was he kidding? Those two shared everything.

'Here we are.' Drew pulled into the car park of the only hotel in the one-horse town. He hadn't been aware there were still places like this. They certainly wouldn't run into any of the school parents here.

'This looks interesting. How did you find it?' Marie stretched as she stepped out of the car.

'I didn't. Nick Kerr told me about it. He and Kay come here when they want to get away from things.'

'They'd certainly do that here.' Marie gazed at the old white painted stone building, the characteristic iron lacework on the veranda overlooking the street on one end. 'It looks as if it's been here forever.'

Inside was dimly lit and the few locals were old men who looked askance at the new arrivals before turning back to their beers. Marie and Drew shuffled into an alcove table, before Drew went up to the bar to order, returning carrying two beers and two bags of potato chips.

'Thought these might go down well.' He placed the beers on the table and tore open one of the packets, letting the salt and vinegar chips spill onto the table. 'Beer okay?'

'Sure. It wouldn't seem right to drink anything else in a place like this.' Marie smiled, but Drew sensed there was something worrying her.

'What's up?' He took a long draught of beer, then wiped his lips. 'You've been very quiet.' Drew hoped she wasn't having second thoughts about them. He still hadn't worked out how they could be together.

'It's Lucy's dad. He came into the café a couple of days ago.'

Drew swore silently. The café. Frank again. Why couldn't it have been Drew who was with Marie?

'What happened?' He tried to keep the irritation out of his voice. 'What did he have to say for himself?'

Marie sighed and twirled the glass around in her hands, stroking the moist surface with one finger. 'He spun us a sob story about being caught up in riots in Papua New Guinea, being sick...'

'You believe him?'

'I don't know what to believe. But he's in town and he wants to meet Lucy.'

'When?' Drew could feel his temperature rise. This had happened two days ago. Marie had known for two days – and he was only finding out now.

'Tomorrow. He's coming to the café again. Frank suggested it. I didn't want him in the house and he's staying in a motel. It wouldn't... Lucy's excited, of course, but...'

'You're not.' Drew covered Marie's hand with his and squeezed it.

She gave him a grateful look. 'No.' She paused. 'His mother's in a nursing home in Canberra. He wants to take Lucy to visit her. He mentioned Dee's house, too.' Marie freed her hand and took a sip of beer. 'What if...' Her eyes clouded.

Drew reached across the table to take both of her hands in his. 'You're not alone in this. You have me – and Frank.' Despite wanting to ignore the involvement of her ex, Drew knew it would be futile.

'Frank's been great. He managed to stop me from throwing things at Robbie.' She gave a wry laugh. 'I did get angry for Dee's sake, but he was so plausible. It's just this Canberra thing. What if...'

'If Lucy wants to live with him.'

Marie's eyes began to fill. 'I don't think I could bear it. I never imagined having to parent a teenager, but now I have Lucy, I can't envisage a life without her.'

'Hopefully it won't come to that. How did he seem? You worried he might not have changed?'

'Oh, he's changed – in appearance, anyway. He's lost what good looks he had. But underneath he's still the Robbie Drake who abandoned my sister and her daughter.'

'Is there anything I can do?' Drew dearly wanted to be there to support Marie, but feared Frank had already claimed that role.

'No.' She sighed again. 'It's enough to know you're there, that you care. I think I'm going to need all the care and support I can get. I seem to have lost my positive attitude to life where he's concerned. It's hard enough seeing Lucy full of the joys of life, talking about her newly found dad and how great it is. I'm sure Jess has heard all about it.'

'She hasn't said.' But when did Jess ever confide in him?

'I'm sorry. I'm not very good company today.'

Drew gazed across at Marie's downcast expression. All he wanted to do was take her in his arms and kiss away her unhappiness. 'What you need is a good hug.'

She looked up at him, a sad expression blotting her pretty face. Then she smiled. 'I'd like that, too.'

'Let's get out of here.' Leaving the still half-full glasses of beer and the uneaten packets of chips, he pulled Marie to her feet and led her out to the car.

Drew drove in silence along the country road, till they came to a quiet layby. He stopped the car and took Marie into his arms, gently kissing her hair, eyebrows and eyelids before taking her mouth in his. Her urgent and eager response was all he hoped for.

By the time they drew apart, the sky was beginning to cloud over.

'I guess it's time to go home.' Drew stroked a strand of hair from Marie's face. 'I haven't smooched in a car since I was a teenager.'

'Me neither.' Marie chuckled. 'But I feel much better now. Thanks.'

'Always happy to please.' Drew grinned. 'We should get back and see what those two are up to.' He disentangled himself from Marie, drew a hand through his tousled hair, and turned on the ignition.

Thirty-eight

'Hurry up, Aunt Marie. Do I look all right?' Lucy hopped from one foot to another unable to keep still. She'd been like that all morning, like a firecracker waiting to go off.

'You look lovely as always.'

'Do you think he'll like me? Should I call him Dad?'

Marie winced. But Robbie *was* Lucy's dad, regardless of how negligent he'd been of his responsibility. 'Would you like to?'

'It'll feel odd, but I would. Just think – my dad. Jess can't wait to meet him, too.'

Marie recoiled. Lucy was already speaking and behaving as if Robbie was part of her life. But he lived in Darwin – it was so far away. She conveniently pushed his comments about the house in Canberra to the back of her mind. He couldn't have meant what she thought he did. The house was on the market. The realtor was hoping for a sale before too long. No. It was all in her overactive imagination.

'Ready?' Marie picked up her bag. 'I thought we could walk over.' The walk to the café would give her time to draw breath and to summon up the courage for the meeting ahead.

Marie walked at a steady pace, while Lucy skipped alongside most of the way to the café, where they arrived before Marie was ready to face Robbie.

Frank greeted them at the door.

Marie peered behind him.

'He's not here yet. You look as if you could do with a coffee. I have the machine on.'

'Thanks.' Marie slid into a chair, put her elbows on the table and cupped her chin in her hands.

'Isn't it exciting, Uncle Frank? I can't wait to meet my dad.'

The word sounded strange on Lucy's lips, almost as if she was trying it on for size. Dee would be turning in her grave.

'Here you are.'

Marie looked up gratefully as Frank placed her coffee on the table. 'Sit down, Luce. You'll drive us mad bouncing up and down like that.'

'But… Oh!'

Marie followed Lucy's gaze to see a tall figure standing outside the door.

'Is that him?' Lucy whispered.

'I'll get it.' Frank made his way to the door, and Marie heard the two men greet each other. They walked in together.

Lucy took her first look at the man who was her father, her eyes devouring him.

Marie wondered what she saw. Did she see the rakish young man from the photos, the romantic hero of her dreams? Or could she see him as he was today – a sad reflection of his younger self, a man who'd suffered, who might still be suffering, one who'd taken a wrong turning in life and lived to regret it. Or had he?

'Dad?' she said in wonderment.

'Little Lucy.' But Robbie made no move to embrace her. It was as if he was turned to stone.

What was the matter with the man? Couldn't he see Lucy was dying to have him acknowledge her, wanted some form of affection from the man she'd been longing to meet?

'You've grown,' he said after a long pause.

'I'm fifteen, almost sixteen.' Lucy's voice was proud but held a tinge of uncertainty. 'But you knew that, didn't you?' Her voice began to falter.

'Of course I did.' Robbie sounded more confident. 'And you look just like your mother did when we first met.'

'Coffee, Robbie?' Frank broke in. 'And why don't you both sit down?'

They did, Lucy taking a seat next to Marie and Robbie the one opposite.

Marie didn't know whether to be glad there had been no warm, welcoming embrace, or disappointed for Lucy that there hadn't been.

Robbie accepted the coffee from Frank, seemingly glad to have something to do with his hands. He looked across at Lucy, who was fiddling with the straw in the smoothie Frank had handed her, then smiled with a touch of his old charm. 'Tell me about yourself, Lucy. What things do you like to do?'

Lucy, relaxing now she was the centre of Robbie's attention, immediately broke into a long chat about school, chess, cooking, and horse riding.

'Sounds busy. You do all this in Granite Springs?' Robbie gazed scornfully around the café.

Marie felt a bolt of anger surge up. How dare he disparage the town where she and Dee had grown up. But she'd always thought he looked down on them as country bumpkins, before he whisked Dee off to the city.

'My mother – your grandmother – lives in Canberra,' he said, after another awkward pause. 'She'd like to meet you.'

Lucy's eyes widened. Her mouth opened and closed, then broadened into a smile. 'I have a grandmother? Did you know, Aunt Marie?' She turned towards Marie with an uncertain expression.

'Not till your...' she couldn't say it, '...Robbie told me. She never replied to any of your mum's letters. I didn't know if she was still alive.'

'And she's in Canberra? She's been there all the time?'

Marie could see Lucy trying to grapple with the fact she had a grandmother who lived in the same city as she had for years, but didn't want to contact her or her mother.

'She's not a well woman, and it's her dearest wish to see her granddaughter while she still can.'

Typical Robbie – playing for the sympathy vote. He hadn't changed.

Excitement and curiosity won the day. 'I'd like that. Can I, Aunt Marie?'

'You're old enough to decide for yourself.' Marie pressed her nails into the ball of her thumb to stem her anger and disappointment. She knew Lucy would react this way. This was her new family. The idea of them must seem more appealing than good old Aunt Marie and Uncle Frank who'd been around all her life.

'Then, yes please. When can we go? Where will we stay in Canberra?'

'I thought... there's Dee's house...' Robbie looked at Marie.

'No!' Lucy yelled. 'Sorry, Dad. But it wouldn't feel right… not without Mum there. Anyway, it's up for sale. There could be people going through it. Strangers.' She shuddered. 'Can't we stay in a hotel or somewhere?'

'I suppose…' Robbie stammered, surprised at Lucy's vehement refusal.

'And can Jess come with me?'

'Jess?' Robbie's eyes widened. 'Who's Jess?'

'My friend. I've told her all about you. We do everything together and…'

Robbie looked to Marie for guidance.

'It's true. It might be a good idea, Robbie.' Marie would feel more comfortable, too, if she knew Lucy wasn't going to be alone with him. She didn't anticipate he'd harm her but felt uneasy all the same. And she cringed each time Lucy called him Dad.

'When?' Lucy looked from Robbie to Marie and back again.

Robbie only hesitated for a moment. 'Next weekend? I can pick you – and this Jess – up on Friday and get you back in time for school on Monday. Maybe we could do a few things together.'

'Oh, can we go horse riding? Jess and I went to the trail Mum used to take me to near Canberra and it was lit. We'd love to do it again.'

Robbie blanched. 'Let's see,' he said cagily.

That seemed enough for Lucy who began texting furiously.

'What?' He looked to Marie for guidance again.

'She's a teenager, Robbie. Her phone is an extension of her arm. She'll be letting Jess know what's happening.' Marie felt a tinge of pleasure to be able to impart her superior knowledge of Lucy's habits. But it was short-lived.

'Maybe we can find something more exciting to do than horse riding.' He grinned.

Lucy's eyes widened even further with barely supressed excitement. *Damn the man!*

Robbie started to tell Lucy about his family, about growing up in Canberra, sharing some of his childhood escapades. Marie tried to blank out the conversation, but couldn't help hearing Lucy's cries of delight at some common experiences.

When Robbie finally stood up to leave, she was glad Frank clasped her hand firmly and squeezed it – a sign he understood exactly how she was feeling.

'I'll see you on Friday,' Robbie said at the door of the café. 'Where will I pick you up?' He raised an eyebrow in Marie's direction.

Marie was about to answer when Frank beat her to it. 'You can pick Lucy up here, Jess, too. Okay, Marie?'

'Yes.' Frank had saved her the awkwardness of having Robbie Drake come to her house. She wasn't sure why she felt so strongly about it. It was as if his very presence there would violate it in some way.

It wasn't till Marie was home again, and Lucy in her room that Marie remembered. Friday was the evening of the fundraiser she was attending with Drew. They'd have a child-free weekend.

Thirty-nine

Drew hurried Jess along. He wanted to see this monster for himself, this man who was sending Marie's life into such a whirl. But at least one good thing was coming out of it. With both Jess and Lucy in Canberra till Sunday evening, he and Marie could spend the whole weekend together. She'd be working in the café on Saturday, of course. But that still gave them two nights together and most of Sunday. He couldn't wait.

'Are you sure you have everything?' Drew looked dubiously at the large holdall Jess deemed necessary for her two nights away. How could a teenage girl need so much luggage?

'I think so.' Jess pursed her lips, considering the question. 'Luce said we might go horse riding on Sunday, so I packed my boots. You don't think…?'

'I'm sure you'll be fine.' Drew regretted his question, feeling somewhat irked Lucy's dad was encroaching on what he viewed as his territory. It gave him a tiny inkling of how Marie must be feeling. 'You okay about this trip?' He knew he didn't need to ask. Both Jess and Lucy had been unable to suppress their excitement all week. Jess was eager to meet Lucy's *new* dad.

'But he's not new, really,' she'd explained to a bemused Drew. 'He's always been her dad, but she's only just met him. Isn't that weird?'

'Duh!' she said now, hoisting her bag into the boot of the car without waiting for Drew's help.

In what seemed like no time, they arrived at the café, now closed for business. As soon as they drew up behind what appeared to be a rented car – a full size Hyundai SUV, Lucy bounded out to greet them. 'He's here!' she said in a loud whisper.

Inside the café, Frank and Marie were standing with a tall bald-headed man who looked as if he'd seen better days. Drew remembered Marie's story of how he'd suffered. He could see the man was edgy. He'd seen it before in a teacher on his Melbourne staff who'd suffered from PTSD. Was that what ailed Lucy's father? And, if so, were the girls safe with him? He stilled the little voice in his head trying to warn him. Post-traumatic stress disorder was a sickness, a mental illness. It wasn't a sign the man was a danger to anyone else – even if he had some sort of meltdown.

But Marie looked worried. Drew wanted to take her in his arms and comfort her. But here, in the café she ran with her ex, it would be the wrong thing to do. Instead, he had to stand aside while Frank asked Robbie the pertinent questions about where they were to stay, the name of his mother's nursing home, and what he had planned for the girls on the weekend.

Jess and Lucy stood by impatiently during this conversation then, 'Can we go now?' Lucy looked at Marie who was still frowning.

'You have your phone. Keep it charged and let me know when you arrive and if there's anything…' Her voice trailed off as Frank put a steadying hand on her arm.

Drew clenched his fists. He wanted to be the one to comfort her. What was it with Frank? Marie had said they were just good friends, almost brother and sister. Was this how a brother would act? Maybe it was. He exhaled heavily. His time would come.

When the girls were gone, with much waving and giggles, Frank put an arm around Marie's shoulder. 'She'll be fine. He *is* her dad. It's her choice and we have to respect that.'

'I know.' Marie rubbed her eyes. 'Sorry.' She gave Drew a grateful look. 'Thanks for allowing Jess to go with her. It helps to know she has her friend, that there are two of them.'

Frank glanced at Drew, as if realising for the first time that he was there, too. 'Yeah, mate. Lucy and Jess, quite the pair, eh?'

Drew nodded, not quite knowing what Frank meant.

'What are you doing tonight?' Frank asked Marie, ignoring Drew. 'Maybe we can have dinner together.'

'No, Frank. It's the school fundraiser. Remember I told you about it?'

'Oh, yeah – the mock race meeting. Well, have fun.' There was an odd note in his voice, one Drew didn't much care for.

'I should be going,' he said.

'Me, too. See you tomorrow, Frank.' Marie gave him a peck on the cheek, before following Drew outside.

'Phew. Glad that's over, though I'll be worrying all weekend.'

'Not all weekend, I hope.' Drew placed a hand on her waist. He didn't care if Frank was watching them. Marie might want to keep their liaison secret from her ex, but Drew thought it was high time Frank knew the score. *He* was the man in Marie's life now and he intended to keep it that way.

'No, not all weekend.' Marie gave Drew a flirtatious glance which sent his blood pressure through the roof. 'What did you think of him – Robbie?'

'I think he told you the truth about what he's been through. I've seen something like that before – PTSD.'

'I thought it was only soldiers who suffered from that.' A crease appeared between Marie's eyes 'You don't think...?'

'He's dangerous? No, not to anyone but himself. It can be caused by any terrifying event. From what you told me he'd be a prime candidate.'

'What...?'

'He may experience depression, nightmares; may have difficulty in forming a close relationship with Lucy. Any sort of stressful situation may tend to trigger an episode or a meltdown.'

'Oh!' Marie's hand went to her mouth. 'Poor Lucy. I suppose I should feel sorry for him too, but I can't, not after the way he treated Dee.'

'Can I drive you home, or do you have your car somewhere?' Drew looked around in search of Marie's distinctive bright blue Toyota Rav4.

'I walked, and thanks but no. I need a walk to clear my head. But you can pick me up later.' She beamed.

'Six-thirty.' Drew glanced over his shoulder towards the café then risked drawing Marie towards him for a kiss before releasing her again. He hoped Frank was watching.

'Six-thirty.'

Drew watched her walk off, before slipping into his car to drive home.

*

At six-thirty on the dot, Drew pulled up outside Marie's house. He'd dressed carefully for the evening, the new blue and white shirt and navy sweater giving him confidence it would go well. In anticipation, he'd also changed the bed linen, placed a vase of flowers on the chest of drawers in the bedroom and one of Jess's fragrant candles beside it. Weren't women supposed to like that sort of thing or was he trying too hard?

Drew's breath caught when Marie opened the door. She looked amazing in a white outfit with a black design that set off her dark colouring. 'Wow! You look…' He spread his hands, unable to find the appropriate words. Then he took her in his arms, breathed in her perfume and buried his face in her hair, before tilting her face up for a long kiss. 'Just a foretaste of what's to come,' he murmured.

'Hey! We have to get through the evening first.' But Marie gave him another quick kiss before pulling away. 'Lucy called to say they arrived safely and the hotel's *lit*, so I guess all is well. Did you hear from Jess?'

'A text. But you're right. They seem happy enough. You can stop worrying and enjoy the weekend.'

'You're right.' Marie's eyes twinkled, a sight that had Drew grinning back at her. She grabbed a wrap and her bag, and they set off.

There was little time to chat privately to Marie during the evening. The company was good. The meal delicious. And Drew found the various activities, which all took place between courses, highly amusing. First there was the Calcutta, which turned out to be an auction for the horses which were to run later, then there was the race call by the local race caller who was brilliant, given there were no actual horses real or otherwise. Finally, between dessert and coffee, everyone made their way to a neighbouring room where wooden horses were pulled along on ropes to simulate a race. It was a lot of fun, even Jo's gentle warning to Drew not to hurt Marie failed to spoil it.

Marie pulled her wrap closer when they walked out into the clear evening air. Apart from those attending the event, the campus was deserted at this time of night during semester break.

After farewelling the rest of their party, Drew and Marie stood by the car gazing up at the sky.

'The sky's so clear out here. You don't see the stars so plainly in town.' Marie shivered as a breeze blew up, ruffling her hair and moving Drew to wrap his arms around her waist and pull her back against him.

'It must be like this all the time for those guys who live out of town. Recognise the Southern Cross?' Drew pointed to the distinctive constellation.

Marie tipped her head back. 'That's about the only one I do recognise.'

'I'll have to educate you then. Look!' He pointed again. 'There's Venus and Jupiter...' His finger moved, '...Orion, and the Big Dipper. But perhaps that's enough for now.' The sensation of her body so close to his was making him long for more. 'Home?'

She nodded.

They got into the car. As Drew started it up, Marie put a hand on his arm. 'My place?' she asked with a winning smile.

'You bet,' Drew said thickly. So much for the preparations he'd made at home, but on reflection maybe he'd tried too hard. He should have guessed Marie would feel more comfortable in her own house, in her own bed. The thought of what lay ahead was already making his temperature rise.

Forty

This was it. It seemed so cold blooded, but that's not how she felt. All evening Marie had been conscious of Drew's nearness, her nerves on edge each time their legs touched under the table. She imagined everyone could tell what was on their minds.

Now they were home and she didn't want to get out of the car. Was she making a mistake? The only man she'd ever been with was Frank. What if Drew found her to be a disappointment? What if…?

'Here we are.' Drew turned to face her, his expression so tense Marie almost laughed. What if he felt exactly the same way? 'Want to change your mind? It's not too late.' But the anxious look in his eyes belied his words.

Marie reached out to touch his cheek, enjoying the roughness of his stubble on her fingers. This was Drew, the man who made her knees weak, the man she'd wanted to be with all evening. Too full of emotion to speak, she shook her head, to hear him breathe a sigh of relief.

The door was barely closed behind them when he took her in his arms. 'I've been wanting to do this all evening. I couldn't wait for that damned thing to end.'

'I thought you were enjoying it?'

'I was, but I like this better.' His lips travelled across her eyelids with butterfly kisses, then to her cheeks, the tip of her nose, before settling on her lips. He pushed her against the wall, the hardness of his body against hers sending her into a paroxysm of desire. This is what she wanted. How could she ever have thought it was a mistake?

But... 'Not here,' she managed to murmur between kisses. 'The bedroom.'

To her surprise, Drew deftly slid one arm under her knees, lifted her and, before she knew what was happening, she was lying on her bed, Drew beside her. He was skilfully removing the dress she'd chosen so carefully, and she was helping him out of his clothes, till they both lay naked, kissing, hands exploring.

Drew was a gentle lover, considerate of her needs, practiced in bringing her to heights of passion she'd forgotten existed, if she'd ever known them.

When at last they lay spent and satisfied, he tilted her face to his and smiled. A warm glow suffused Marie as she snuggled into his arms. She'd come home.

*

The loud koo-koo-koo-koo-koo-kaa-kaa of Marie's resident kookaburras wakened her next morning. She stretched out, turned to gaze at the man sleeping beside her, and smiled. Drew Hamilton was a man in a million and he'd chosen her. She curled up beside him, determined to enjoy every minute of their time together this weekend.

It was a pity she had to work till early afternoon, but she couldn't let Frank down. He was so good at allowing her time off. But he might not be so understanding if he knew she wanted to spend time with Drew. Marie wasn't sure why she'd kept her feelings for Drew – their burgeoning relationship – secret from Frank. Perhaps it was because of the sense of underlying antagonism she noticed between them – a sort of rivalry. But that couldn't be right. She and Frank were over, had been for ages. They were good mates. He'd be happy for her, wouldn't he?

Thinking of Frank spoiled her mood. She uncoiled herself, ready to get out of bed, only to feel Drew's arms encircle her.

'Leaving me already? Come here.' He pulled her back towards him. Powerless to resist, she allowed herself to be drawn into his embrace, their bodies once again melding into one as they repeated the intimacy of the night before until both were spent, entwined, holding each other with such incredible warmth between them, a feeling Marie could so easily get used to.

She sighed. 'It's a shame, but I really must get in the shower.' She extricated herself from Drew's arms. 'I have to get to the café or Frank will…' She took one look at the expression on Drew's face and said, 'He's nothing to me now, Drew. I told you – brother and sister.'

'You did.' Drew sat up, propping himself on a bank of pillows. 'But I've seen the way he looks at you. When were you going to tell him about us?'

'There wasn't anything to tell.'

'But there is now. I'm falling for you, Marie. I never thought I'd say those words again. I never thought I'd feel this way again. I hope I'm not alone, that…'

Marie glowed, but didn't know how to respond. It was too soon. They'd only just… 'I care for you, too, Drew. And I will tell Frank. I just have to find the right time.'

'Well, don't take too long.' He pretended to scowl. 'Now come here and give me one last kiss before your shower.'

Marie leant across the bed to kiss him.

'Mmm, you smell so good. When are you going to be free again? I don't think I can wait till tonight.'

'I finish at three. Will you stay here till then, or shall I come to your place?'

'Why don't I pick you up at the café?'

Marie hesitated. That would tell Frank all he needed to know. But he had to find out sometime. There was no sense in delaying the inevitable. He'd probably guessed anyway. 'Okay. Three o'clock at the café. What did you have in mind?'

'Surprise.' He grinned.

'Lovely! I love surprises.'

*

'How was your evening?' Frank asked, as they were setting up for the day.

'Good.' Marie felt herself blush. 'I didn't have time to bake this morning. I'll get started now and have the first batch ready before the morning rush.'

'Okay.' Frank gave her an odd look, but this was nothing new. Marie didn't always bring trays of goodies from home. The kitchen at the café was a great standby and one she used in her cookery classes. She hadn't conducted any recently, not since Dee died. Lucy had taken up the time she previously allocated to the classes and the children's parties. But, she reminded herself, she was tiring of those, wanted to change her life around. Caring for a teenager wasn't the life she imagined leading either. What had she imagined?

'Heard from Lucy?'

'She called when they arrived in Canberra. She sounded happy, excited. You were right. She'll be fine. I hope...'

'Robbie won't hurt her.'

'I know.' Frank had said that already. So why did Marie have this sense of foreboding? It had disappeared when she was with Drew, replaced by the exhilaration of being with him. But now, back to her routine, it surfaced again – a tiny niggle in an otherwise perfect day.

Fortunately, it was a busy Saturday, leaving Marie little time to think and less time to chat with Frank. In one spare moment, she wondered how she could tell him about her and Drew, but it was all too hard. She couldn't do it with a café full of customers. And what would she say? Marie couldn't imagine casually saying, 'By the way Frank, Drew and I...' So, she said nothing.

As three o'clock approached, Marie's mouth felt dry. She was conscious of being clumsier than usual as she cleared the last few tables.

Frank noticed. 'What's up, Marie? You're not still worried about Lucy?'

'No.' She took a seat close to the counter where Frank was cleaning the espresso machine. It was time to tell him – before Drew arrived to pick her up.

'Frank...' Her phone rang. *Damn!* Marie gave it a quick glance, planning to ignore the call, when she saw Lucy's number. She pressed *accept*. 'Luce, what's up? Still having fun?'

'I want to come home.' Lucy's breath caught in what might have been a sob. 'We went to see Dad's mum this afternoon – to the nursing home, and it was horrible. *She* was horrible; she said dreadful things about Mum – and he just stood there and listened. He didn't try to argue with her, to say Mum was a good person.'

'Oh, Luce. She's an old woman. Maybe she didn't know what she was saying. And she's your dad's mother. He may not have wanted to contradict her.' *That was just like Robbie, to side with his mother over Dee and Lucy.* 'But the visit's over now. What else has your dad planned for you and Jess?' Marie tried to make her voice sound upbeat.

'It's not just that.' There was the sound of another voice which Marie thought must be Jess. 'Dad's… he's strange. Not all the time, but he gets these moods. He goes all quiet and grumpy. It scares us. And last night – we have adjoining rooms in the hotel – we could hear him in the night. He was thrashing around and yelling out as if he was in pain. It woke us up. I was glad Jess was there. We hugged each other till we got back to sleep.'

'Oh!' Marie's eyes went to Frank who'd stopped what he was doing. 'Well, if you really want to…'

Marie was interrupted by the café door swinging open.

Drew walked in.

'Lucy,' she mouthed, pointing to the phone. She was about to continue speaking when she looked across the café to see the two men facing each other like two stags at bay. It would have been funny if it wasn't so serious. Marie had no time to be worried about either Frank or Drew's finer feelings. Right now, Lucy was her primary concern.

'Sorry, Luce. I was interrupted. If you and Jess are sure. Jess's dad is here now. We'll drive over at once.' She raised one eyebrow in Drew's direction.

He nodded.

'I'll text you when we get close. What'll you tell Robbie?'

'Can you tell him?'

Marie sighed. 'I suppose. You and Jess take care till we get there. Love you.'

'Love you too.'

Marie hung up and turned to Drew. 'They want to come home. I said…'

'I heard. No problem.'

Marie was relieved he accepted the need to pick the girls up without any question. Frank wasn't so easy to placate.

'What's Robbie done now? I should be the one going with you, Marie. I can finish up here, and…'

Drew stepped forward. 'I understand your concern, Frank. But my daughter's there too. I can take Marie.'

Was it something in the way Drew said her name, or the way he looked at her that made Frank recoil as if he'd been struck?

'So, that's the way of it. Well, pardon me for interfering. Just make sure Lucy's okay.' Frank went back to cleaning the machine, this time with more vigour than was necessary.

'Frank…' Marie began, but Frank refused to meet her eyes.

'We should be going.' Drew opened the door.

With one last glance at Frank, Marie walked towards Drew. 'I'll let you know how Lucy is,' she said, before the door swung closed behind them.

In the car, Marie found her hand gripped by Drew's.

'Tell me.' His eyes were fixed on the road, his other hand on the steering wheel, his lips taut.

Marie recounted what Lucy had told her. 'I think it's what you said, but the girls are scared. I'm sorry it's spoiled our weekend but…' Marie's own disappointment warred with her concern for Lucy, but there was no contest. Lucy's wellbeing had to come first.

'There'll be other weekends, other times. What's important now is Lucy and Jess. We can't leave them in a situation where they don't feel safe.'

'Thanks.' Marie squeezed the hand holding hers before Drew took it back to focus on his driving.

'I don't think Frank was pleased. You didn't tell him, did you?'

Marie shook her head and bit her lip. She'd been all set to tell Frank when Lucy rang, then everything went topsy-turvy.

'Well I guess he's worked it out by now, unless he's a lot dimmer than I gave him credit for.'

'I know. I didn't want him to find out like this. I thought I could break it to him gently, explain how I felt. I was about to when Lucy rang, then you arrived and…'

'Don't worry,' he said, seeing Marie's rueful expression. 'Frank'll get over it, and I'm sure Lucy and Jess are fine. They're teenagers, remember, and liable to exaggerate. You said Lucy romanticised her dad before. Now, she's seeing a slice of real life – and it can be scary.'

The trip seemed to take longer than usual, perhaps because Marie was constantly checking her watch and her phone. There were no calls or texts from Lucy, so Marie could only assume all was well.

It was a relief when, towards six o'clock, they reached the outskirts of the city. It was already dark, the streetlights making the place look as if it was lit up for a carnival after the pitch black of the road they'd driven along. There was a flurry of something white in the air, glistening in the glow from the lights.

'Is that snow?' Marie asked, peering out. 'It doesn't usually snow in Canberra.'

'Only after a long dry period, I believe. And it has been particularly cold. But it's only a sprinkle. It won't lie. Look, the road's only slightly damp.'

Marie shivered, nonetheless. 'I hope Lucy brought enough warm clothes.'

Drew chuckled. 'If she's anything like Jess, she brought enough for a week at least. You said the hotel was on Northbourne Avenue?'

'Yes, it should be about… There it is!' Marie pointed to an imposing white building on their left. They drove into the circular driveway and parked.

'How do you want to do this?' Drew locked the car and took Marie by the arm.

Now she was here, she wasn't sure how to approach Robbie. If he had no idea he'd upset the girls, it could be awkward.

'Let's play it by ear,' she said, more confidently than she felt, Drew's presence giving her some courage.

They walked inside, Marie gripping Drew's hand tightly. She was plucking up the nerve to ask for Robbie's room number when she felt Drew give her hand a squeeze and, looking towards the elevator, saw Robbie emerge followed by Lucy and Jess. They were carrying their bags. She glanced up at Drew, her eyes wide. 'What's going on?' she whispered.

'Aunt Marie!' Lucy dropped her bag and ran towards her, Jess following more slowly.

'What are you doing here, Dad?' Jess looked from Drew to Marie, her eyes narrowing as she drew her own conclusion.

Robbie walked up, his shoulders bowed, his eyes vacant. 'How did you get here so quickly? I only told Lucy…' He turned to stare at Lucy who was blushing and gazing down at her feet.

'What's happened?' Drew took charge, Marie unable to find words.

'It's Mother. She's taken bad. I think seeing Lucy earlier may have been too much for her. I need to go to her. I asked Lucy to contact you – but that was only half an hour ago. How did you get here so soon?'

'We were in the neighbourhood,' Drew said quickly to avoid any complicated explanation. 'Lucky.'

Robbie gave him a quick glance as if to judge if he was lying, but Drew's benign expression seemed to satisfy him. 'Lucky,' he repeated. 'Sorry I have to cut our weekend short, Lucy. I had lots planned. We'll have to do it another time – yeah?'

Lucy nodded, her eyes still downcast.

'Right.' Robbie seemed satisfied but made no attempt to hug her or show any other form of affection. 'I can be off now your aunt is here with…'

'Drew Hamilton. I'm Jess's dad.'

'I remember. You were at the café.' He strode over to the reception desk, then walked out, leaving Marie and Drew gazing after him in astonishment.

'Thanks for coming, Aunt Marie.' Lucy hugged her aunt. 'It was so weird. *He* was so weird. He's not like I expected.'

Marie returned the hug, burying her face in Lucy's hair, filled with gratitude. She wasn't a religious person, but silently gave thanks to whatever force had opened Lucy's eyes. 'Let's go home now, sweetheart.' She glanced to where Jess was hugging her dad too.

The girls were unusually quiet on the drive back to Granite Springs, and Drew and Marie chose to remain silent too. It had all gone better than expected. But the prospect of Robbie getting in touch again hung over them like a dark cloud.

Forty-one

As the sign for Granite Springs appeared in the headlights, Drew decided to break the silence. 'You guys must be hungry. How about we all go out to dinner?'

'Where?' Jess asked.

'Where would you like to eat?' Drew racked his brains. He'd only sampled two restaurants in town. 'How about The Riverside or Pavarotti's?'

There was a groan from the back seat.

'Okay, you choose.'

'Can we go to somewhere different? Ryan told me about this Thai place his family like.'

'Marie?' Drew knew Marie would be familiar with most of the local eateries.

'Do you mean The Thai Kitchen on River Road? The food's good there, though it's a long time since I've been.'

'That's the one. Can we, Dad?'

'I don't see why not. You okay with that, Lucy, Marie?'

They both nodded.

'The Thai Kitchen it is.' Drew headed in the direction of the river to where the little restaurant was situated.

'It's another family business,' Marie said. 'The family came here several years ago. It took them some time for people to accept it – they were accustomed to Chinese food when they wanted to eat Asian. But it's very popular now.'

'We used to eat Thai in Melbourne before Irene…' Drew let his voice trail off. This wasn't the time to mention his ex-wife.

Inside the restaurant, the four were led through the crowded room to a corner table and handed menus. As Jess and Lucy discussed what to order, Drew's knees met Marie's under the table sending a wave of desire through him. This wasn't what he'd planned for their Saturday night together.

Marie gave him an apologetic look. Drew hoped she was as disappointed as he was. Instead of sitting here with Jess and Lucy they should have been having dinner alone, anticipating another night like the last one, a night when…

'We've decided, Dad.' Jess's voice interrupted his thoughts. 'We'd like spring rolls followed by red curry with chicken. What about you?'

Drew picked up his menu again. He really didn't care what he ate. He glanced over towards Marie.

'The spring rolls are a good choice, as are the chicken curry puffs and the deep-fried fish balls. I'd suggest a variety to share.' She glanced at the others for agreement. 'Then I always enjoy the prawn green curry or the beef with cashew nuts.'

'Sounds good.' Drew was happy to accept Marie's choice. He knew whatever he ate would stick in his throat. When would he and Marie have such an opportunity to be together again?

'It'll be all right,' Marie said, in a low voice only he could hear. She placed a hand on his thigh. 'We can tell the girls…' Her voice faded into nothing.

What could they tell them? That he and Marie were sleeping together; that they'd used their absence in Canberra to consummate their relationship; that they were…what?

Marie's phone rang. She checked the screen. 'Frank.' She gave Drew another apologetic glance.

Drew listened as she took the call.

'Yes.'

'We got there safely.'

'No, Robbie wasn't annoyed.'

'It worked out well.'

'We're back now.'

'There's no need.'

'We're having dinner.'

'Yes, all of us.'

'See you on Monday.'

'Me too.'

It was odd to listen to the one-sided conversation, to imagine what the other party was saying – what Frank was saying. And what was the 'me too' about? Drew tried to remain calm while clenching his hands.

'Uncle Frank wants to speak with you, Luce.' Marie handed the phone to Lucy. 'He's concerned about her. It's only natural,' she said to Drew, with a disarming smile.

He relaxed. Frank was Lucy's uncle, something he tended to forget.

The food was good, better than the Thai food Drew remembered eating in Melbourne, not so spicy or were the spices here different? The girls enjoyed their meals too, Jess asking, 'Can we come here again?'

As they piled into the car afterwards, Drew hesitated. 'Shall I drop you and Lucy off first?' he asked Marie, though he knew he had no other option. He couldn't take them both back to his house, could he? Drew thought of the fresh bed linen, the flowers, the candle, the bottle of champagne cooling in the fridge.

'Can Lucy come for a sleepover?' Jess asked.

Drew felt Marie make a move, then she was still again. Did she feel the same way he did?

'Oh, please, Aunt Marie,' Lucy pleaded.

'Why don't you both come back? We can have a glass of something,' he said to Marie. He couldn't bear to think of her going back to an empty house. Though that wasn't his only reason.

'I don't…'

'Please?' Drew could see Marie weigh this up and begin to weaken.

'Well, maybe just one glass.'

He felt his heart leap. One glass could lead to two, could lead to… who knew where.

Drew felt more comfortable once they were back in his house. In the kitchen, the girls fossicked in the pantry, while Marie made hot chocolate for them. Drew fetched two champagne flutes and released the cork on the champagne, the ensuing pop and froth of wine making Jess and Lucy snigger.

'We'll take our drinks upstairs,' Jess said, giving Drew a goodnight kiss.

Lucy did the same with Marie. 'See you tomorrow, Aunt Marie. Don't come around too early.' She followed Jess to her bedroom.

Drew picked up the flutes of champagne in one hand and, carrying the bottle in the other, led Marie into the living room and closed the door. 'We won't see or hear from them again tonight,' he said confidently, seeing Marie's cautious glance towards the door.

'Are you sure?'

'I'm sure.'

Seemingly reassured, she allowed herself to be settled on the sofa, glass in hand, Drew's arm around her shoulders.

'Not exactly how I imagined this evening, but let's celebrate being together.' He clinked his glass to hers, and leant back, warmth infusing him. He was here. Marie was here. The girls might be upstairs, but the knowledge of their presence didn't intrude on their closeness. Drew had avoided the main light in favour of a dim floor lamp, its glow lending an intimate atmosphere to the room.

The pair cuddled for a bit, drank more champagne, then Marie unwound herself from Drew's arms and checked her watch. 'I should…'

'Stay!' Drew felt her tremble.

'But… the girls…'

'You can be gone before they're awake.'

'Well…' Marie hesitated.

Drew tipped her face up to his, letting his lips do the pleading for him.

'Okay, but…'

He put one finger on her lips to silence her. He couldn't let her leave, not now.

They took the now empty bottle and wine flutes through to the kitchen then, stifling their laughter, tiptoed quietly upstairs till they reached Drew's bedroom, where they closed the door behind them before falling on the bed giggling like the two teenagers in their care.

While Marie was in the ensuite, Drew lit the candle. It had a citrus fragrance similar to the one Marie always wore. He wanted everything to be just right.

And it was.

Despite the two teenagers in the neighbouring room, Drew and Marie were able to rediscover the passion of the previous evening. As their bodies entwined once more, her soft skin against his, Drew knew without any doubt this was the woman he wanted to spend the rest of his life with.

227

Forty-two

Next morning, Marie was standing in the open doorway of the kitchen preparing to leave when Jess and Lucy appeared at the other door, eyes bleary with sleep.

Jess nudged Lucy. 'See, I told you.'

'Marie just came to pick Lucy up.' Drew tried to conceal the two used coffee cups on the draining board.

Marie cringed, wishing the floor would open and swallow her up. She was wearing the outfit she'd worn the day before. It must be obvious she hadn't been home. What were Lucy and Jess doing awake so early?

She could see from the disbelieving expression in Jess's eyes, Drew's explanation wouldn't wash.

He must have seen it, too. 'Okay, Marie stayed here overnight.'

Marie flinched, but Jess only said, 'I knew it!'

Lucy expressed more surprise. 'But... I thought... Does Uncle Frank know?'

'I think he may have guessed. But can I ask you not to say anything. I want to tell him in my own time.' Marie was shaking. This wasn't how she wanted it to happen. She should have known; should never have stayed. But the memory of the night she'd spent in Drew's bed, the depth of emotion they'd experienced – she couldn't dismiss that as a mistake.

Seeming to sense Marie's contradictory emotions, Drew placed a gentle arm around her shoulder. 'We adults have feelings too, you know.

Jess, you've accepted your mother loves Jake. Now I have someone, too.' He gazed fondly down at Marie.

Encouraged by his words, Marie took Lucy's hand. 'Luce, I know you love your Uncle Frank. I do, too. But it's a different sort of love. That's why we don't live together anymore. Now I've met Jess's dad and we…' she drew in a breath, '…we're finding we like each other – a lot. Just like your mum and Tony.'

'Well I think it's weird. I wanted you and Uncle Frank to get back together.' Lucy turned and ran out of the room, Jess following her and calling out her name.

'That's done it! I didn't expect this reaction. I thought she'd be pleased for me.' Close to tears, Marie turned her face into Drew's comforting chest and sniffed.

'Well, the cat's out of the bag now. No more subterfuge. And Lucy'll get used to it. I hope you're not going to let a display of teenage angst spoil what we have together. It's something special.'

'No, but… Lucy's all I've got. I'm all she's got. I can't… I'm sorry, Drew. I need space to think this through. I should go home now. I can pick up Lucy later.'

Marie headed to the door again, wishing she'd been quicker to leave before. But it wouldn't have made any difference. Lucy had to find out sometime. If she and Drew were to have any sort of future together, their relationship couldn't stay secret.

Once outside, Marie dashed away the tears which threatened to blind her. She'd forgotten her car was sitting in the garage at home. She'd walked to The Bean Sprout that morning, knowing Drew was going to pick her up.

Granite Springs streets were almost empty of traffic at this time on a Sunday morning, its inhabitants either attending church services or at home having breakfast with their families, but she managed to hail a taxi.

To her surprise, as they entered Main Street, Marie suddenly felt hungry. She and Drew hadn't eaten anything, the coffee Drew brought to her in bed was the only thing that had passed her lips since last night's champagne.

Making a sudden decision, she asked the driver to make a detour and drop her at the small bakery she knew would be open on a Sunday morning to serve the chocolate and almond croissants for which it was famous. Her mouth watered at the thought of the flaky pastry melting in her mouth. She needed something sweet to take away the taste of Lucy's rejection, and wasn't in the mood for something she'd baked herself.

Walking out of the shop carrying the paper bag of the almond delicacy filled with frangipane and topped with almonds, Marie felt a little better. But she knew she had a lot of thinking to do. If Lucy couldn't accept Drew as part of their lives, then Marie couldn't either.

Back home, she brewed some lemon and ginger tea and sat outside in the weak winter sunlight. As she drank her tea and ate her croissant, the flakes of pastry falling on her lap, Marie contemplated how her life had changed. Before Dee's untimely passing, Marie had a good life. Sure, she'd felt unsettled and might even have considered leaving Granite Springs and moving closer to Dee and Lucy, but on the whole, things were good. She and Frank had developed a working – and workable – relationship, one others claimed to admire.

But now she was guardian to a teenager – one who sought to rewrite Marie's life to fit her own requirements. And she was falling in love.

Marie had never put her feelings for Drew into words before, not even to herself. But she was in no doubt how she felt. And she believed he felt the same way. The only obstacle was – Lucy.

Picking up her plate and mug, Marie headed back inside, determined to find something to keep her busy while she sorted herself out. Her eyes settled on the overcrowded bookshelves in the living room, books all higgledy-piggledy. It occurred to her it would be a good idea to take on the task of ordering them alphabetically, something she always intended to do, but never made time for. It would keep her busy while allowing her to think things through.

Marie started with great gusto but hadn't taken into account the pleasure of being reunited with some of her favourite reads. She found herself unable to avoid dipping into a few, all thoughts of Lucy and Drew temporarily forgotten. She was lost in an old favourite, Di Morrisey's *Heart of the Dreaming*, when she was startled by the doorbell. Dropping the book, she leapt up, all her anxiety returning. Who could be at the door on a Sunday morning?

While part of Marie hoped it might be Drew, she wasn't ready to see him. Not yet, not till she had more time. She walked slowly to the door, rehearsing what she'd say. Then she saw the shadow on the other side of the tinted glass. She breathed a sigh of relief as Fran's familiar outline took shape.

'Fran, what are you doing here?' Marie was surprised to see her friend in town alone on a Sunday morning.

'Owen had a few things to catch up on at the campus, and Pia has taken Tor to visit a friend, so I thought I'd pop in to see how you were doing. It's not a bad time, is it?' She peered past Marie as if expecting to see someone hovering in the hallway.

'Perfect time. I've been trying to reorganise my books and getting lost in reading them.' Marie chuckled, but she couldn't fool her old friend.

'Sounds as if you have something on your mind. Want to talk about it?'

'Maybe. Come in and I'll make us some tea.'

'I won't say no.' Fran gave Marie a hug before following her into the kitchen and taking a seat. She leant her elbows on the table and gave Marie a stern look. 'What's up? It's okay. You can tell me. Is Drew Hamilton not treating you properly?'

'How did…? Oh!' Marie realised she'd given herself away. 'It's not just him, not him at all, really. Drew's been good, more than good.' She turned away to hide her blushes as she filled the electric jug. 'Lucy found out.' She switched it on and turned back to face Fran.

'Lucy found out what?' Fran had a wicked gleam in her eyes.

'It's complicated.' The jug boiled, and Marie put liquorice spice teabags into two mugs and filled them with water before joining Fran at the table. 'I may have some brownies left…' She made to rise again, but her friend stopped her with a hand on her arm.

'Not for me. What's so complicated? You like the man. He obviously likes you. He couldn't take his eyes off you on Friday night at the fundraiser. I'd be willing to bet you ended up in bed. Am I right?'

Marie blushed again. She picked up her mug to take a sip, but the tea was still too hot. She put it down again. Talking about her feelings didn't come easily to her. But Fran was a good friend, and Marie had helped her through her own sticky situation, been one of the few people Fran had confided in when she first came to Granite Springs.

'Well, yes, we did.' She took a gulp of tea, wincing as the hot liquid burnt all the way down. 'But that's not it. I told you Lucy was spending the weekend with her dad.'

Fran nodded, clasping her own mug in both hands.

'It didn't work out, so Drew and I drove over to Canberra to pick the girls up.' She took a deep breath. 'Jess wanted Lucy to sleepover and…'

'Let me guess – you did too?'

Was she so transparent?

'It was the obvious thing to do. But, of course, with teenagers. You were sprung.' Fran chuckled.

'It's no laughing matter. I was about to leave this morning, when…'

'You were sneaking out before anyone knew? It gets better and better.'

Marie wished she hadn't said anything, but she couldn't stop now. 'When did you become so… so…?'

'It must be Owen's influence. Go on.'

'There's not much more to tell. Lucy and Jess walked in. It was obvious I'd spent the night. Lucy was horrified. She thought Frank and I might get back together. She ran off. I came home to get my thinking straight. There's no way Drew and I can have a future, not without Lucy's approval.' Marie picked up her tea again, pleased she'd made a decision.

'Listen to yourself. What does Lucy have to do with it? She's fifteen.'

'She'll be sixteen soon.'

'So? Fifteen, sixteen. What difference does it make? She's a teenager. Her moods change by the day. You can't let her define *your* life. You and Drew – it was…?' She raised one eyebrow suggestively.

Marie nodded, gazing down into her mug, remembering just how it was.

'Well, then. There's nothing complicated about it. Lucy'll come round, I'm sure. I don't have any personal experience of teenagers, but I can see how Kay and Nick's two are, and some of the stories Owen has about when Pia was that age – they would make your hair curl.'

'But Lucy. She's just lost her mum, and her dad's a disappointment to her. I can't let her down, too.'

'So you'll let yourself and Drew down instead?'

Marie hadn't thought of it in those terms.

'It's not...' But she knew Fran was right. Had she been going to throw away her chance of happiness for a whim of Lucy's? Because perhaps that's what it was. 'I'll give it some more thought.'

'See you do. Life's too short to throw away a good man – and Drew's a good man. Lucy and Jess get along so well. It'd make them almost sisters.' Fran buried her nose in her mug.

'Fran! It's not... He hasn't...' But Marie knew what was on Drew's mind. What had been on her mind. What they had might be in its early stages but there was the potential for something lasting. If only...

'I can't stay. I said I'd pick Owen up for lunch. Do you want to join us?'

'Thanks, but not today.' While Marie enjoyed Fran's company, she didn't want her and Owen picking her life apart and offering advice. She had enough to think about now. 'Drew will be bringing Lucy back. I want to be here.'

'Well, remember what I said. It's your life. Lucy will make her own, and she won't thank you for interfering in hers.'

Marie knew her friend was right, but it didn't make things any easier. She owed it to Dee to... to what? She knew Dee would offer exactly the same advice as Fran. She was always encouraging Marie to find someone. Why, just before she died, she was asking Marie about her non-existent love life, even if she considered getting back with Frank.

That was never going to happen. Marie wondered what had put the idea into Lucy's head. Or was it such a bad idea? Her mind was going round in circles.

Putting all thought of men out of her mind, Marie returned to the pile of books which were now spread out on the living room floor. For the next hour or so, she managed to concentrate on the task and put her collection in order. Sitting back on her heels, she surveyed the newly arranged shelves – a job well done. She stood up, stretching the muscles which had stiffened as she sat on the floor. Marie hadn't noticed time pass. It was well past lunchtime and she was feeling peckish. There was still no sign of Lucy, then she remembered she'd promised to pick her up. Damn! Was she ready to face Drew again?

Going into the kitchen, Marie fixed a cheese sandwich and brewed some camomile tea, hoping its calming influence might help her come to terms with the prospect of going back there and facing Drew – and Lucy.

The tea worked its magic and, after the shower and change of clothes she hadn't made time for earlier, Marie was ready. But, before she could set off, there was the sound of chatter outside the front door, and the doorbell rang again.

Forty-three

Drew was wondering if this was such a good idea even as he rang the doorbell. Behind him, Jess and Lucy were vying with each other to take the best selfie, Lucy seemingly having forgotten her earlier anger with Marie. Nervously, he adjusted his glasses and patted his hair.

'Drew!'

'Hi, Marie, I brought Lucy back. I know you said you'd pick her up, but I thought…' What had he thought? He'd wanted to see her again and didn't want to wait. 'Lucy was ready to come home,' he finished weakly.

'Come in.' Marie stood aside to allow them to enter.

Drew walked in slowly, unsure of his welcome, while the two girls rushed past heading upstairs to Lucy's bedroom.

Marie sighed. 'Thanks. Tea? Coffee? I've just been having some – a late lunch.' She seemed nervous.

Once in the now familiar kitchen, Drew took a close look at Marie. On the surface, she looked good, dressed in a pair of jeans with a royal blue sweater, a scarf in various shades of blue thrown elegantly around her neck. But there was a crease between her eyes as she pushed the hair out of her face. She wasn't her usual self.

'Coffee please.' He took a seat. 'Marie…' Drew paused and cleared his throat. There was no blueprint for a situation like this. 'I hope you're not going to let Lucy's comments affect us – what we have… what's between us.'

Marie busied herself with the coffee machine. He thought she was going to ignore his comment. Then she turned with a sudden movement. 'What is there between us? Two nights of passion? That doesn't… We barely know each other, Drew. I've been part of Lucy's life since she was born.'

So has Frank, Drew thought, berating himself for even thinking of her ex at this time. But was that what Marie was thinking?

'So, you've decided?' he asked heavily. Was this relationship going to end even before it began?

'Not quite. Fran dropped around and she… she offered some interesting advice.' Marie handed Drew his coffee but didn't join him at the table. She remained standing.

Drew felt a glimmer of hope. Was Fran on his side?

Marie's next words dowsed his hope. 'But I still don't know. I do like you, Drew – a lot. I never expected to find someone who… But there's Lucy. I have to consider her.'

Drew couldn't argue with that, but where did it leave him, leave their relationship?

'You have to understand,' she continued. 'I see Lucy as a sacred trust from Dee. It's not something I can easily turn my back on.'

'I'd never ask you to do that. I…' *In for a penny, in for a pound*. Drew took a deep breath. 'If you decide we can make a go of it, I'd raise Lucy like my own. She and Jess are already great buddies. They'd be like sisters.'

'That's what Fran said.'

Drew's heart leapt. *Fran said that? How did Marie react?*

'But I'm still not sure. I need to speak with her, to make sure. She's suffered enough, more than enough. And…' she exhaled loudly, '… Robbie's still in the picture. He'll be back, and we'll have to deal with whatever it is he wants to do next.'

Drew picked up his coffee and took a gulp, aware there was going to be no easy resolution. 'Do you want me to be there when he comes back?'

'No, I don't think so. Frank knows the situation. If I can't handle Robbie myself, I can ask him.'

Bloody Frank again! But Drew remained calm. 'Well, just remember. I'll be here if you need me – for anything, anything at all.' He drained his coffee and rose to hug her. She stood motionless in his arms, a different woman from the one who'd moaned with pleasure the night before.

'I'm sorry, Drew. There's just so much…'

'I'm ready to go now, Dad. Have you and Lucy's aunt finished whatever you had to say?' Jess appeared in the doorway, accompanied by a sombre Lucy whose eyes were red.

Maybe it was for the best. Jess was quite a handful on her own. Did he really want to be saddled with two of them? The answer was a resounding *yes*, if Marie was part of the deal.

*

Marie closed the door behind Drew and Jess. What had she done? She'd listened to Fran, listened to Drew, but refused to listen to her own emotions. Lucy had to come first. And there was no way of knowing what Robbie Drake had in store for them. It was convenient his mother had taken a turn for the worse at the same time as Lucy and Jess had been spooked. But he might still want to demand access.

Picking up the dirty coffee mugs, Marie carried them to the dishwasher. Was this the last time she and Drew would enjoy coffee together? She quickly disabused herself of the notion. He wasn't suddenly going to disappear from her life, even if she wanted him to – which she didn't. She'd miss his gentle humour, his… No, she wouldn't think about it. Lucy and Jess were still friends. She and Drew were bound to meet through them, as they had done initially. But there would be no more nights of passion.

'Aunt Marie?'

Marie looked up as Lucy slipped into the room, took a seat at the table, and propped her chin on her fist.

'Yes?'

'I need to talk to you.'

Marie's heart dropped. What now? Did Lucy want some sort of explanation, an undertaking she and Drew were no longer… whatever they had been? She clasped her hands together tightly.

Lucy rubbed her eyes which were still red. Had she been crying all this time? What had Marie done to her?

'I'm sorry.' Lucy folded her arms on the table and dropped her chin to her chest, avoiding Marie's eyes.

'It's all right, sweetheart. You know I'd never do anything to hurt you. If you don't want me to become involved with Jess's dad, then…'

'No! I said I'm sorry. Jess told me it was a dumb thing to say to you. She said I should be pleased you'd found someone at your age, and her dad is a good person. She even said if…' Lucy threw Marie a glance out of the corner of her eye, '…if you did get together, we'd be as good as sisters. I didn't think of it like that. I've always wanted a sister,' she said dreamily.

Marie sat down with a thud. What was it about everyone? Just as she'd made the decision that there was no future in a relationship with Drew Hamilton, everyone was intent on marrying them off – Fran, Drew himself, even his daughter.

'So, you wouldn't mind if Drew and I…?'

'Well, it would be a bit weird. He's Jess's dad – and the school principal. But he's okay. I'd prefer it if you and Uncle Frank got back together. That's why I said what I did. Mum thought you might. She said…'

Marie didn't want to know. The idea her sister had been discussing her future with Lucy was too much to contemplate. Why couldn't people mind their own business?

'Sorry,' Lucy repeated. 'Maybe I shouldn't have said. But…' she said wistfully, '…it would be good to be a family with a mum and a dad – just like everyone else. I thought… I thought Dad would… But he wasn't how I expected.' She shivered.

Marie drew her into her arms and hugged her tightly, her chin resting on Lucy's head. 'I'm sorry it didn't work out with your dad. But we're okay just the way we are, aren't we?' She felt Lucy's head nod and loosened her hold.

'What's going to happen – with my dad?' Lucy looked up at her, eyes wide.

'I don't know, honey. But he can't do anything without your agreement. You're old enough to make up your own mind where you want to live and who with.' Marie spoke more confidently than she felt, hoping Lucy wouldn't have to face a court to determine her future.

'But I will see him again? He's still my dad.'

Marie sighed and bit her lip. She couldn't change the facts. And Lucy seemed to swing hot and cold with regard to Robbie. 'I expect so, but not tonight. Why don't you have a nice hot bath, and I'll organise dinner? Then we can find something mindless to watch on television. You've had quite a weekend.'

When Lucy disappeared, Marie poured herself a much-needed glass of wine and curled up in her favourite armchair. She'd thought everything was cut and dried, that it would be just her and Lucy. But her niece's apology changed things. Maybe there was a future for her with Drew. The thought filled her with both happiness and uncertainty. But there were still a few hurdles to clear before she could make any decision about her future.

Forty-four

It was almost a week since what Marie thought of as the Canberra weekend, and there had been no word from Robbie. She hadn't heard from Drew either, but knew it was up to her to contact him and she was strangely reluctant to do so. It was as if, by delaying matters, she could remain in control, pretend the whole thing had never happened. But it had, and lying in her lonely bed each night, Marie relived those two nights with Drew.

'Have you heard from Dad?' An anxious Lucy asked at breakfast on Thursday morning.

'Not yet.'

'D'you think he's gone back to Darwin already?' she asked hopefully. 'It's not that I don't want to see him, but… he was seriously weird.'

While Marie was pleased to hear Lucy's reluctance to see Robbie again, she knew he'd not give up so easily. 'I doubt it, Luce. But what you saw as weirdness may be a sickness. If all he told Uncle Frank and me is true, he's been through a lot. That can take a toll on a person, change them.' Marie remembered Drew's take on the situation. 'He may be suffering from what's called PTSD. It's an illness, a mental illness.'

Lucy wrinkled her nose. 'Isn't that what soldiers get? He wasn't in the army, was he?'

'No, but it can happen to anyone who's experienced a traumatic event.'

Lucy seemed to digest this for a few moments. Then she said, 'But his mother's not suffering from it. And she said some horrible things. I know you said she's an old woman,' she said, as Marie started to speak, 'but it was awful. I never want to see her again.' She shuddered and pushed away her unfinished bowl of cereal.

'I don't expect you will.' From what Robbie told her, Marie assumed his mother was close to death. 'But you do need to see your dad.' *Even if it's the last thing I want for you.*

Marie loaded her car with the goodies she baked the night before and saw Lucy off to school before heading to the café. Having Lucy around had forced her to change her routine. Now she started work later than before, to enable her to eat breakfast with Lucy and provide her with a routine. She had just arrived at The Bean Sprout when her phone rang.

Fishing it out of her bag, Marie saw Robbie's number on the screen. *Talk of the devil!* Her heart sank.

'Hi, Robbie.' Marie tried to keep her voice calm when all she wanted to do was smash the phone.

'Marie. Sorry I haven't been in touch.' His voice was as smooth and charming as ever, and if she didn't know how much he'd changed physically, Marie could have believed she was talking to the handsome young man who stole – and broke – her sister's heart.

'What do you want?'

'No need to sound so aggressive.'

His silvery tones made her want to puke, but for Lucy's sake she knew she had to be polite.

'Mum passed away on Monday. We've just had the funeral. It was a small affair. I didn't think you or Lucy would want to attend.'

'I'm sorry for your loss,' she said automatically. How could he even imagine Lucy would want to be there after the way his mother had spoken to her? Marie suspected her derogatory comments were ones originally made by Robbie himself, and his mother was merely repeating them.

'Thanks. But that's not why I rang. I have to return to Darwin soon and I want to see Lucy again before I go.'

Marie was silent. She'd expected this, as she told Lucy only a short time earlier. But it still gave her a sinking feeling in her stomach.

'Marie! Are you still there?'

'Yes, Robbie. I heard you. You want to see Lucy again,' she said wearily.

'Saturday. Can I come to the café on Saturday?'

Marie thought quickly. Lucy would be there with Jess. After spending a few weeks helping clean, Frank had relented and let the girls loose on the customers. They were proving to have a knack for making people feel welcome and were popular – especially with the younger male customers who thought they were fair game. But they could give as good as they got, and now The Bean Sprout was becoming the place for Granite Springs' younger set to hang out on a Saturday afternoon. There had been a lot of disappointed youngsters last weekend when Lucy and Jess were in Canberra.

But she had no reason to refuse. 'That'll be fine. As you know we close at three, so perhaps three-thirty?'

'Good. See you then. Let Lucy know, will you?'

Marie agreed and finished the call. Her morning was ruined.

There were only a few early morning customers when Marie carried her boxes of brownies, muffins, banana bread and chocolate chip cookies into the café.

'Need a hand?' Frank came out to greet her.

Marie shook her head, but her expression must have given away her mood.

'Something wrong?'

'Robbie.' She didn't need to say any more.

'He called?'

'Just now.'

'And?'

'He wants to see Lucy again, of course.'

'Of course. We expected that.'

'His mother has died.'

'You expected that, too. When…?'

'Saturday. I said after we close. He's going back to Darwin.'

'A hopeful sign.'

'As long as he doesn't expect to take Lucy with him.'

'Oh, Marie!' Frank took the last box of baked goods from Marie, laid it down on a table then, heedless of the customers, took her in his arms. 'Don't fret. We've been through all that. He can't force Lucy to go with him. Even a court case can't do that. Our Lucy will make up her own mind and she's happy here with you.'

The comfort of Frank's arms around her was too much for Marie. The tears she'd been stifling began to flow, their saltiness trickling into her mouth. 'Sorry, Frank.' She pushed herself away from him and rubbed her eyes. 'You're right. I know.' She gave a quick glance around, but no one seemed to be watching. 'I'd better get cleaned up.'

After washing her face and hands and reapplying her makeup, Marie gazed at herself in the small mirror in the back room of the café. How could she have let herself go like that? It disturbed her she could allow Robbie Drake to have such an effect on her. But it disturbed her even more that she'd been glad of the comfort of Frank's arms.

*

Saturday came around all too soon. Lucy was nervous and not her usual self, and even Jess seemed to sense the tension in the air.

'D'you want me to stay, Luce?' Jess asked, as she was preparing to leave, the café closed for the day.

Lucy gave Marie a scared look. 'Aunt Marie?'

'I don't think it would be a good idea, Jess, but it's a kind thought. Lucy will have me and her Uncle Frank here. She won't be on her own. She can call you later.'

"Bye, then.' Jess gave her friend a hug and disappeared through the door.

'All set?' Marie asked Lucy, her own stomach doing backflips.

Lucy nodded. 'But what if… what if he wants me to go to Darwin with him?'

Marie looked towards Frank for support.

'It'll be okay, sweetheart.' Frank hugged Lucy. 'You're old enough to know where you want to live and who with. If you want to live with…' he hesitated, '…your dad, Marie and I would be sad, very sad, but we'd respect your choice. You know we love you – very much.' His voice was close to breaking.

Marie always knew Frank was a softie, but to see his emotions – his love for Lucy – displayed so openly brought a tear to her eyes. He was a good man. It was such a pity he never had the chance to be a father.

Lucy was close to tears too. 'I thought it was what I wanted – to have a dad, my own dad. But…' her bottom lip trembled, '…he was… he wasn't…'

'Oh, honey!' Marie gave Lucy a hug too. 'Life doesn't always turn out the way we expect it to, the way we want it.' She thought of her own life. When she was Lucy's age, she'd already met Frank and imagined how their life would be – married, a family, the café. Well, some of that had come to pass, but look where she was now. 'Why don't you go and wash your pretty face before he arrives?'

Lucy sniffed and went off to freshen up.

Marie and Frank looked at each other. Marie gestured towards him with open hands. 'It's tough for her. She was so excited about meeting Robbie. This is what I was afraid of.'

Frank threw an arm around Marie's shoulder. 'You can do this. We can do this. We've been through worse.'

Marie gave him a grateful smile, wiped her eyes and straightened her back. 'You're right. It's only Robbie Drake.'

At that moment there was a tap on the café door, and they saw Robbie's tall figure through the glass.

'I'll let him in.' Frank made his way to the door and ushered in a somewhat subdued Robbie.

'Where's Lucy?' He gazed around the room.

'I'm here.' The little voice came from the doorway at the back of the café where Lucy stood, shuffling her feet and scraping a hand through her still short hair.

'Can we sit?' Robbie appeared uncomfortable.

'Sure. Coffee?' Frank had deliberately left the espresso machine on. Now he moved towards it.

'Not for me.' Robbie surprised them, shaking his head and taking a seat at the nearest table.

Marie and Frank looked at each other again, before joining him. Frank sat next to him and Marie opposite. She beckoned Lucy to join them.

When they were all seated, Robbie began to speak. 'First, I want to apologise to you, Lucy. It was never my intention to hurt you in any way.' He slid a shaking hand across his head. 'Your aunt may have told you my mother passed away earlier this week. We laid her to rest on Thursday. The things she said to you… they were probably my fault. She was never a kind woman, but she loved me and believed everything I told her. I may have been economical with the truth when I spoke of Dee, of your mother.'

Marie snorted.

Robbie continued, 'Be that as it may. She was my mother and I loved her. But she shouldn't have repeated those things to you.'

Marie felt Lucy tremble and put an arm around her waist, giving it a squeeze.

'I'm sorry too, that you and your friend saw me like… I had a bad episode when you were in Canberra… It's aggravated by stress, and I guess I was stressed – being with you, hoping you'd like me.'

Lucy gave a small gasp.

Robbie's knee began to bounce under the table, the way it had the first time he was there. 'I thought I'd mastered it with the drugs, but… I had a nightmare there again, too. I guess you heard me – the walls were pretty thin. I thought…' he gazed up at the ceiling, '…I thought I could give you a home, a proper home, with me, in Darwin – or even in Canberra, close to my mother. Your mum's house is still there.'

Marie felt Lucy give a start of surprise and a burst of anger flashed through her. She held her breath.

'But I've come to see sense. You remind me so much of your mother, you look so like her. It was like going back in time, remembering how it was when we first met. I was a different person then, though I was pretty selfish too. They were good times.' He closed his eyes as if remembering. 'I wanted Dee all to myself. Then you came along.' He opened his eyes again to stare at Lucy. 'I wasn't prepared to be a father, I couldn't hack it, so I ran. I can't remember what I told my parents, but whatever it was, it was to excuse my behaviour. I knew I had to disappear, so I did. When I heard your mum had died, I thought perhaps I could make up for what I did back then. But it's not going to work, is it?' His eyes focused on Lucy with a silent plea.

She shook her head vehemently and clutched Marie's hand.

Robbie gave a heavy sigh. 'I thought not. But I'm glad we've met. You know you have a dad. I'll let you have my contact details and… if you feel inclined, perhaps you could email me sometimes. And if… if you ever want to come to Darwin…'

There was a long pause when no one spoke, then Frank rose. 'Well, if that's it?'

Robbie looked at them and shuffled to his feet. 'Thanks Marie, Frank.' He looked towards Lucy who was still seated. "Bye, Lucy. I hope we can meet again.'

Lucy turned to Marie as he walked to the door and Frank locked it behind him. 'Is it really over? Is that it? He's not going to come back and demand to see me, want me to spend time with him?'

'It seems not.' Marie was as surprised as Lucy at the turn of events. She'd expected… she didn't know exactly what she'd expected, but not that Robbie Drake would be so apologetic, so… so damned sensible.

'Can we go home now?'

'Let's. We'll be off, Frank.'

'Give me an hour and I'll join you. I'm sure you won't feel much like cooking tonight. Why don't I bring around some dinner?'

All Marie wanted to do was be home with Lucy, but looking at Frank's pleading expression, remembering how supportive he'd been to both her and Lucy, she couldn't disappoint him. 'Okay,' she found herself saying. 'See you soon.'

Forty-five

'Did Lucy's dad come to the café?'

Drew had been unable to settle to anything all day, after Jess told him about Robbie's proposed visit. He tried to imagine how Marie must be feeling. He wanted to be with her, even picked up the phone to call, then stopped himself before pressing her number. He remembered their last conversation, her ambivalence, his decision to leave it up to her.

But he'd hoped to hear from her before now. Had he been right to be worried about Frank? Had Robbie Drake made demands, and was Frank comforting her? Drew's hands curled into fists at the thought of Marie and Frank together. But there was nothing he could do.

He'd finally settled into his study and was making an attempt to get some work done in preparation for the start of term next week, when Jess returned.

'Not when I left. She didn't want me to stay. She was really nervous, Dad. I could tell. She was so quiet all day. You don't think…?' Jess kicked the leg of the desk and, for once, Drew chose not to reprimand her. He knew she was worried for her friend.

'I know you want to help, but maybe the best thing you can do for her right now, is to let her handle it. She has her aunt with her – and her uncle.' How he hated that Frank would be the one to support Marie and Lucy through this meeting. 'How about we do something special?'

'What?' Jess feigned interest. 'I want to be here when Lucy gets in touch. She said she'd let me know what happened.'

Drew racked his brains but didn't come up with anything. He shrugged.

Jess continued to mooch around, picking up and discarding first a book, then a folder of schoolwork. She was as unsettled as Drew.

Drew tried to get back to what he'd been doing before Jess had walked in, but her restlessness made it impossible. What he needed was a way to get rid of his excess energy. 'I know,' he said, shutting down his computer, 'Come for a run with me?'

Jess looked at Drew as if he was mad. 'A run? Dad!'

'It's a good way of getting rid of what's worrying you. I find it helps me.' *It helps me cope with the emotions I can't handle.*

'Okay.' Jess sounded reluctant, but she disappeared, to reappear a few minutes later wearing a tracksuit and runners. 'I'm ready.'

'Right.' Drew pulled on a hoodie and changed into his Converse Star runners. 'We can use the school oval. That's where I usually exercise.'

'You do? I never knew.'

'You don't know everything about your old dad,' Drew chuckled. 'I've been doing it several times a week, it helps blow away the cobwebs and gets things in perspective,' he said, unconsciously echoing Marie.

The school buildings and grounds were deserted this Saturday afternoon, unlike what they'd be come Monday morning when they'd be once again teeming with students.

'It's nice here.' Jess got out of the car, her eyes ranging across the courtyard and parking lot. 'Granite Springs isn't so bad. Though don't expect me to come here with you like this in term time. I'd never live it down. It's bad enough everyone knows you're my dad.'

Drew chuckled. 'So it wasn't such a bad move, after all? You've got over wanting to go back to Melbourne?'

'I guess. It was never going to happen, was it? I suppose I knew that, but at first I missed everyone so much.'

'Not anymore?'

'Not as much. But I'd still like to go back for a visit.'

'We can arrange that.' Drew was pleased Jess had changed her tune where Granite Springs was concerned, knowing the about-face had a lot to do with Lucy – and perhaps Ryan Kerr. 'Maybe after you get back from LA in the Christmas holidays.'

'Do I have to go?' Jess scowled.

Drew immediately knew he'd made a mistake. They'd been getting on so well. 'We can talk about that another time.'

By now they'd reached the oval, and both began a series of warm-up exercises before moving effortlessly together around the track.

After a couple of circuits, Drew was wondering if it was time to call a halt, when Jess's phone pinged with a text.

'Lucy,' she said, stopping to check the message.

Drew waited patiently, running on the spot, seeing Jess texting madly, then close the phone with a disappointed expression. 'Well?'

'It's over. Sounds as if her dad apologised. He's gone back to Darwin. She sounds good. I wanted to go over to see her, but she says she wants to spend the evening with her Aunt Marie and Uncle Frank.' Jess bit her lip. 'Can we go home now, Dad?'

'Sure.' Drew's heart plummeted at the news Frank was there with Marie and Lucy. 'Why don't we pick up a pizza on the way?'

'Okay.'

As he and Jess demolished two large pizzas, his with a beer and hers a Coke, Drew wondered what Marie was doing. No doubt she'd be relieved the meeting with Robbie Drake was over, and it was good news he was returning to Darwin. But for how long? Jess hadn't volunteered any further information. Maybe there was none. But where did it leave Marie – and him?

Drew had meant it when he hinted they could make a go of it. Maybe he should have been more specific – mentioned marriage because that's what he was referring to. But surely she'd work that out. Marie wasn't stupid, far from it. She was one of the most astute women he'd ever met. She left Irene for dead – and beside her, even the indomitable Alison Griffith failed to compare. Strange how his deputy's subtle advances were suddenly of no consequence and served only to amuse him.

But thinking about Marie wasn't going to resolve anything. He needed to take action. Then, if she didn't want him, he'd have to accept it and move on.

Forty-six

Marie wondered if agreeing to Frank coming around to dinner was a mistake. Perhaps she should have given in to her initial reaction, told him she wanted to be alone with Lucy. But he'd been so good about everything ever since Dee's death. She sighed and pushed back a stray curl. It was just another family dinner.

Family dinner? Where had that come from? Frank was the one who still referred to their infrequent meals together as *family dinners.* In Marie's mind they'd stopped being a family when Frank moved out. But at least it meant she didn't have to cook.

Standing in the shower, as the warm water gushed over her, Marie felt she was washing away more than the cares of her day. She was washing Robbie Drake out of their lives. She knew she had a decision to make, a decision about Drew. His hints had been subtle, but she knew exactly what he meant.

But there was time enough for that, time for her to be sure it was what she wanted, that it was right for her, right for Lucy. Her niece had experienced enough upheaval this year already. They both needed time to themselves; time to recover; time to reassess their lives and their future.

By the time she heard Frank's key in the door, Marie was in a better frame of mind. She was wearing a pair of sleek black pants with a cream angora sweater and feeling good. But the sound of the key reminded her she meant to ask for it back. It was time Frank stopped treating this house as his second home. She had no idea why she'd permitted it to go on for so long.

Marie hurried through to the kitchen where Frank was already opening the containers of food he'd brought from the restaurant, the enticing aroma of lasagne and a spicy vegetable stir fry filling the kitchen.

'This looks yum,' Marie could hear Lucy saying.

'Marie, you're looking great!' Frank turned from what he was doing to meet Marie's eyes with more warmth than she expected.

Maybe she should have worn something less attractive. This was Frank. Why did she feel uncomfortable?

'Thanks, Frank. You didn't need to do this.' She reached into the fridge to remove a bottle of chardonnay, then to the cupboard for two glasses.

'Can I have some – just a tiny drop?' Lucy asked, hopping excitedly from one foot to the other. 'We're celebrating, aren't we?'

'Are we?' Marie asked wearily.

But Frank evidently thought so. He grinned. 'I don't see why not. But only a drop.' He took the bottle from Marie and poured a small measure into one glass.

Disapproving, but unwilling to spoil Lucy's mood, Marie fetched another glass and all three took their seats around the table.

'This is great, Uncle Frank. Do you always eat the café leftovers?' Lucy asked.

Frank chuckled. 'Your Aunt Marie and I used to practically live on them. Remember, Marie?'

Marie did. In the early years they were together, when they were trying out different menus, figuring out what worked and what didn't, endeavouring to broaden the conservative choices Frank's father had offered, they'd often been forced to eat their mistakes. They were good years. But they were over, and she saw no need to rehash them now for Lucy's benefit.

But it was good of him to bring food tonight, and Lucy was in her element. She and Frank did get along so well, Marie thought, watching them exchange tall tales and laugh at each other's jokes.

Yawning, Lucy rose when the meal was over. 'I'm off to bed. Do you mind if I don't help clear up?'

'No, sweetheart. You've had a big day. Uncle Frank and I can manage. I won't be far behind you.' Marie could feel her eyes gritty with tiredness and hoped Frank would leave soon.

The dishwasher was full of clean dishes and, as she bent to empty it, Frank put his hands on Marie's waist and drew her upright and around to face him. He leant towards her, their faces almost touching.

The plate she was holding slipped from her fingers and fell to the floor, smashing into pieces.

'Marie…' he cleared his throat, '…I'd like us to get back together.'

Marie stared at Frank, too astonished to speak. Back together? What on earth was he talking about? Did he mean…?

He did.

'As a family. Now that you have charge of Lucy, and Robbie's out of the picture. We both love her. She loves us. She needs to be part of a proper family. We can be a real family, Marie. Lucy can be our daughter – the daughter we never had.' He looked at her so pleadingly, Marie felt her eyes moisten. Frank was a dear, she did love him, but not that way, not anymore. But how could she tell him?

'Oh, Frank. I don't think…'

Anything else she was going to say was stifled by his lips seeking hers. For a moment, Marie responded to the familiarity of his kiss. It would be so easy to give in, to accept what he was offering. Then common sense reasserted itself. They were the wrong lips. Frank was the wrong person. She had a flash of understanding, knowing it was Drew she wanted to be with, Drew's lips she wanted on hers. What on earth had she been thinking when she thought she needed time? Frank was right about one thing. Lucy needed to feel part of a proper family, to have a father figure – one she could respect. But Frank wasn't the answer.

She pushed him away and put a hand up to her now dishevelled hair. 'I'm sorry, Frank. I can't…'

'Not even for Lucy?' he asked, sadly.

'No. I have needs too, and what we had, while it was wonderful, it isn't there any longer. We decided.'

Frank gave her a long look, a look which pierced her to the core. 'I suppose it's that Drew Hamilton? I thought there was something happening there, but I hoped…' He thrust a hand through his hair. 'What does he have that I don't?'

'Oh, Frank! It's not that simple. I never meant it to happen. I was happy the way we were. I never imagined I'd feel this way again.' Marie suddenly recalled Dee's comments, Fran's comments – about Frank still having feelings for her. She'd discounted them as being foolish. But what if they'd been right? What if Frank had always had feelings for her, if he'd only gone along with their separation in the hope of them reuniting?

'I'm sorry,' she repeated, a lump in her throat. 'I do love you, but not in that way, not anymore.'

'I see.' Frank's downcast eyes made Marie want to hug him, to tell him she was wrong, that they could form a family.

But she knew it wouldn't be fair – not to him, not to her, not to Drew, who she now realised she loved more than she'd imagined. How could she have been so stupid not to have seen it before now?

And he'd been so patient. What was it he said – that he'd be there if she needed him? Now Marie knew she did.

Forty-seven

Next morning, Marie woke with a sense of purpose. As the church bells pealed out in the distance, she had the feeling her life was about to change – as long as Drew hadn't changed his mind. She showered and dressed, choosing a casual look with a pair of jeans and a roll-necked white sweater paired with a black puffer vest, teamed with soft black leather ankle boots.

'You're looking very spiffy,' Lucy commented, when she came through to breakfast. 'Doing something special? Did Uncle Frank…?' Lucy winked.

Had Frank said something to Lucy about his plans? Surely not.

'He was looking pretty intense last night. I wondered… I guess not,' Lucy added, as she saw Marie's expression.

'I've been thinking over what you said. I thought I might pop over to see Jess's dad this morning.' Marie held her breath waiting for Lucy's reply.

'Can I have a lift to the library? I said I'd meet Jess there.'

'Sure.' Marie heaved a sigh of relief. It would be much easier to say what she wanted to say to Drew, if Jess wasn't home. 'Scrambled eggs?'

'Sounds good.' Lucy started texting on her iPhone, leading Marie to wonder what would happen if the young girl had to do without it for even an hour.

Marie broke the eggs into a bowl, added water and herbs plus a few chopped mushrooms, and set a couple of slices of bread into the toaster, before making the coffee she knew she'd need to get her through the morning, and pouring a glass of orange juice for Lucy.

They didn't talk much over breakfast. Marie was trying to work out what she was going to say to Drew, while Lucy was busy on her phone. For once, Marie didn't remind her of the no phones at the table rule, too engrossed in her own thoughts to worry.

Her phone pinged.

Frank!

Marie picked it up, a quiver in her stomach. Was he going to be difficult?

I understand, but I had to try. All the best. I'll always be here for you and Lucy. Frank x

'Who's texting you on a Sunday morning?' Lucy wanted to know.

'Your Uncle Frank.'

'Is he okay?'

'Yes.' But was he? Marie knew Frank always had her best interests at heart. That's why they got on so well, why they'd managed to remain friends. Could their friendship continue if she and Drew got together? She'd be sorry to lose it, to lose contact with Frank, with The Bean Sprout. Both had been part of her life for so long. She'd never imagined that would change. But she'd never imagined meeting anyone like Drew Hamilton.

'Time to go.' The dishes were rinsed and in the dishwasher, Marie had renewed her makeup and combed her hair for the tenth time. Her stomach was in knots. She stood at the open door waiting for Lucy.

'Don't know why you're in such a flap,' Lucy grumbled. 'You've met Jess's dad heaps of times. What's so special about today?'

'Did you really mean it – what you said about Jess's dad and me? About not minding?'

'Duh! Is that what this is all about? What did Uncle Frank say last night? Did you two argue?'

'No, Luce. Your Uncle Frank and I never argue.' As she spoke, Marie reflected how true that was, and how odd. Was it that they always thought the same way about everything, or that neither felt strongly enough to make an argument worthwhile? She believed it was the latter. The slight disagreements they'd had over the years never amounted to anything and were always easily resolved. Even when they decided to part, it was an amicable arrangement. It had worked for them but, looking back, had there been a lack of passion? Had their relationship always been based more on friendship than the overwhelming emotion she experienced in Drew's arms?

'So – you and Jess's dad? Does Jess know? She said you two were *at it*.'

Marie blanched at the crude term, but she supposed it was accurate. She and Drew were indeed *at it*, or had been. She drew in a breath. 'There's nothing to know. I just need to talk with him.'

'Huh.' Lucy went back to her phone, then a thought seemed to occur to her. 'If you get together, where will we live – and will you still work in the café?'

Marie sighed, wishing she'd never brought up the subject. 'I have no idea, Luce, and it's not up for debate right now. As I said, Drew and I need to talk.' She tightened her lips and said no more till they reached the library, where Jess was seated on the wall outside. She rose as the car pulled up.

'Guess what?' Marie heard Lucy say as she drove off.

Marie's heart started to pound as she drew closer to the row of homes by the old quarry. She felt faint and almost turned back. But it was too late. She was here. She stepped out of the car and was making her way to the door when it flew open. Startled, she missed her footing and almost fell.

Drew hurried to help her regain her balance. 'What are you doing here?' Although he was right next to her, his voice sounded very far away.

'I'm sorry, if you have to go out, I…'

'I was coming to see you.'

Their faces were so close, Marie could see the tiny lines around his eyes and mouth. For a moment his words didn't register, then she looked at him in amazement. What had he said? 'Why?'

'I think perhaps we'd better go inside if we don't want the entire neighbourhood to hear our conversation.' Drew's voice was amused.

Marie allowed herself to be led inside and lowered onto the sofa – the same sofa where he'd kissed her so thoroughly before… She swallowed, a lump forming in her throat, the words she'd been practicing all the way there drying up.

'I think you need something to drink. Coffee, tea or something stronger?'

'Water, please,' Marie managed to utter.

While Drew went to fetch it, she straightened herself up and took a deep breath. This was ridiculous. She'd come here to tell him… to take him up on… to find out if he'd meant what he said. Instead she was behaving like some simpering damsel from a regency romance.

'Water.' Drew handed her a glass and took a seat opposite. 'Now, why are you here?'

'Why were you coming to see me?'

'Oh, no. I asked first.'

Damn the man! He was enjoying this.

Marie took a gulp of water and, feeling calmer, began to pick at an invisible thread on her jeans. 'You've probably already heard what happened with Robbie?' She glanced across at Drew.

He nodded.

'It was such a relief. You can't imagine.' *Maybe he could.* 'Well,' she hurried on, 'Frank offered to bring around dinner – to celebrate. It would have been churlish to refuse. Then he…' Marie looked down at her feet, then up again to meet Drew's eyes, '…he suggested we get back together… as a family… for Lucy's sake.'

She saw Drew's lips tighten.

'So that's what you've come to tell me? That you and Frank are getting back together? Why should I care?'

'No!'

'No?'

'Not at all. It made me realise that…' Marie looked at Drew again, suspecting he was laughing at her. 'Why were you coming to see me?' she asked again, her curiosity piqued. It seemed she was the one doing all the explaining, when he had some to do, too.

'I guess I had much the same idea as Frank. It seems to me Lucy wants a father and I've already told you how I feel.'

'You haven't, not exactly.' Marie held her breath. Although Drew had implied he had feelings for her, he hadn't actually said the words she now longed to hear.

'Then, perhaps it's time I did.'

In one swift movement, he was by her side, taking her face in his hands and sending waves of desire through her. 'Marie Cunningham, you are the loveliest and most irritating woman I've ever met. Thinking of you keeps me awake at night. When I do fall asleep, images of you invade my dreams. If you don't agree to spend the rest of your life with me, I don't know how I'll survive. I love you, you stupid woman.'

While Marie didn't appreciate being called stupid, Drew's declaration of love sugar-coated the word. And, before she could reply, his lips met hers, his tongue reaching for hers and she was overtaken by a craving she knew only he could satisfy.

When they came up for air, Marie drew in her breath and said, 'That's what I came to tell you. I love you, too. And, yes, I have been stupid; stupid not to realise it sooner; stupid to think I needed time; stupid to imagine I could live without you.'

They sealed their love with another deep kiss and were still in each other's arms some hours later when the door burst open and they found themselves the focus of two pairs of teenage eyes.

'I guess this means we'll be sisters now,' Jess said, as the two teenagers stood, legs apart, arms folded, gazing at Marie and Drew who were trying to hurriedly rearrange their rumpled clothing which only resulted in both of them erupting in laughter.

Two teenage eye-rolls ensued.

'Are you sure you can put up with two of them?' Drew asked Marie ruefully, when the girls had disappeared, and they were alone again.

'It's not the life I imagined,' she said with a grin, 'but I can't wait to try.'

'Me too,' he said and pulled her towards him. 'Now, where were we before we were so rudely interrupted?'

THE END

Look out for the next in the Granite Springs series, a Christmas novella. *A Granite Springs Christmas* is Magda's story.

A return to Granite Springs. A family Christmas. A time for love and joy…or is it?

A year after a devastating bushfire destroyed *Magda Duncan's* home, she returns to Granite Springs determined to resume her life and organise a wonderful family Christmas. But the elation of her homecoming quickly turns to disappointment as she discovers not everyone is in tune with her plans.

George Turnbull was Magda's late husband's best friend. A bachelor, he has always carried a torch for Magda and remained close to her and her sons. When he finally musters the courage to reveal his true feelings, a life changing surprise from his past threatens to ruin any chance at happiness.

Emotions are high as Christmas Day approaches. Will this be the most wonderful Christmas ever? Or will the hopes and fears of the past come home to haunt them?

A poignant story of a Christmas friends of *Granite Springs* will never forget.

From the Author

Dear Reader,

First, I'd like to thank you for choosing to read *The Life She Imagines*. It was almost called The Bean Sprout Café which has featured in all of the series so far.

Having spent seven years teaching university and living in an Australian country town, and don an acreage, I've enjoyed writing a series with a rural setting and drawing on my experience of living in the country – with goats – and teaching in university. This is the fifth book in the series set in the fictional country town of Granite Springs and I'm thrilled by the response of you, my readers, to this series, how you tell me my characters are real people you'd love to have as friends. I feel they're my friends too, and they've become a part of my life. I hope you've enjoyed meeting Marie and Drew.

If you'd like to stay up to date with my new releases and special offers you can sign up to my reader's group.

You can sign up here   https://mailchi.mp/f5cbde96a5e6/ maggiechristensensreadersgroup

I'll never share your email address, and you can unsubscribe at any time. You can also contact me via Facebook Twitter or by email. I love hearing from my readers and will always reply.

Thanks again.

MaggieC

Acknowledgements

As always, this book could not have been written without the help and advice of a number of people.

Firstly, my husband Jim for listening to my plotlines without complaint, for his patience and insights as I discuss my characters and storyline with him, for his patience and help with difficult passages and advice on my male dialogue, and for being there when I need him.

John Hudspith, editor extraordinaire for his ideas, suggestions, encouragement and attention to detail.

Jane Dixon-Smith for her patience and for working her magic on my beautiful cover and interior.

My thanks also to early readers of this book –Helen, Maggie and Louise, for their helpful comments and advice. Also to Annie of *Annie's books at Peregian* for her ongoing support, to Heather for her invaluable assistance in verifying the medical details around Dee's aneurism, and to Pete for his equally valuable help in confirming the descriptions of PTSD.

And to all of my readers. Your support and comments make it all worthwhile. I'm thrilled you enjoy my more mature characters and find the situations they find themselves in resonate with you.

About the Author

After a career in education, Maggie Christensen began writing contemporary women's fiction portraying mature women facing life-changing situations. Her travels inspire her writing, be it her frequent visits to family in Scotland, in Oregon, USA or her home on Queensland's beautiful Sunshine Coast. Maggie writes of mature heroines coming to terms with changes in their lives and the heroes worthy of them. Her writing has been described by one reviewer as *like a nice warm cup of tea. It is warm, nourishing, comforting and embracing.*

From her native Glasgow, Scotland, Maggie was lured by the call 'Come and teach in the sun' to Australia, where she worked as a primary school teacher, university lecturer and in educational management. Now living with her husband of over thirty years on Queensland's Sunshine Coast, she loves walking on the deserted beach in the early mornings and having coffee by the river on weekends. Her days are spent surrounded by books, either reading or writing them – her idea of heaven!

She continues her love of books as a volunteer with her local library where she selects and delivers books to the housebound.

Maggie can be found on Facebook, Twitter, Goodreads, Instagram or on her website.

www.facebook.com/maggiechristensenauthor
www.twitter.com/MaggieChriste33
www.goodreads.com/author/show/8120020.Maggie_Christensen
www.instagram.com/maggiechriste33/
www.maggiechristensenauthor.com/